Publisher:

Inspiring Publishers
P.O. Box 159 Calwell ACT 2905, Australia.
Email: nikkimoyesauthor@gmail.com

National Library of Australia Cataloguing-in-Publication entry

Author: Moyes, Nikki

Title: **If I Wake**/*Nikki Moyes*.

ISBN: 9781520720968 (paperback)

Target Audience: For young adults.

Subjects: Imaginary companions—Fiction.

Victims of bullying—Fiction.

Bullying in schools—Fiction.

Dewey Number: A823.4

If I Wake

I hover unnoticed as the doctor places his hand on Ms Phillips' stooped shoulder and suggests she talk to her daughter. He assures her the girl lying motionless on the narrow hospital bed can hear every word she says. She nods and he glances at his watch, already making his way to the door.

Ms Phillips holds her daughter's limp hand carefully so not to dislodge the tubes trailing from the pale skin. Sitting alone by the bed, the awkward brown chair squeaks when she adjusts her position. Sometimes she talks about the weather, or the broken coffee machine in the hallway. Other times she just begs.

"Please wake up. Can you hear me, Lucy? If you wake, I promise we'll do something special for your seventeenth birthday. I know it's still a couple of months away, but we'll invite all your friends and have a cake. Squeeze my hand if you're there."

The girl's hand doesn't move. Her mother weeps and crumbles another damp tissue in her fist, before returning to absently scrunching the clean white sheets in her free hand.

She rarely leaves the sterile hospital. She should be out working. There are bills to be paid. The landlord will only be understanding for so long. I want to remind her she has other responsibilities, but I'm distracted by Will calling my name.

I cannot loiter in this curtained space either. I don't belong here. I've never really belonged anywhere, but Will needs me and the beeping machines in this room are irritating. I leave her alone with her inconsolable grief.

A shudder racks my body as I drift back into the room. Cheap cologne overpowers the disinfectant odour, tickling my nose and making me want to sneeze. Frank is in the room alone. His face wrinkles into a sneer at the still girl, an expression he reserves for when no one watches. My stomach clenches. I want to leave, but my limbs won't move.

Frank places his hand on the machine by the bed as if the action can stop the beeping. The display continues to reflect the slow pulsing of the girl's heartbeat. I'm torn between screaming to get another adult in here and staying quiet so he doesn't sense me in the room. I stay silent.

I am invisible.

I'm not actually invisible, but I may as well be. People look past me like they do the homeless man in his grubby clothes resting in a closed shop doorway. If they don't make eye contact, he doesn't exist. This is me; if I don't move or make a sound, I don't exist.

Last time Frank was in the room, he suggested if there is no change in condition over the next few days, perhaps the life support should be switched off. This only made Ms Phillips cling to his Ralph Lauren shirt and sob.

"How did this happen?" she asked. Frank didn't know, not the whole story anyway.

I am the only one who does.

Now, alone in the room, he leans over the bed and whispers in the ear of the lifeless girl.

"Your mother doesn't love you. No one wants you." As he leans away, he traces his finger slowly across her cheek. Nausea rises inside me as I choke back a scream. I recoil from the scene and am out of the room faster than I can blink.

Jennypha and Tayla visit later that week. The girls hesitate in the doorway until Tayla's mum nudges them forward. Ms Phillips pushes dishevelled strands of hair from her face and frowns at the girls from school.

"Come to finish the job?" she asks in a broken voice.

"It was an accident." Mrs McKenzie places a protective arm around Jennypha's shoulders and gives her a reassuring squeeze.

Jennypha bites her lower lip and torments a hair tie between her fingers. Tayla loiters in the background as she has always done, twirling a lock of her auburn hair.

"How dare you think you can come in here like you care about my daughter? You think Jennypha can get away with this because her father is a lawyer?"

"The girls have come to apologise for their part in this. I never said…"

"Shush!" A nurse arrives to see what the commotion is about. Negative emotions aren't allowed in the room. Ms Phillips storms out in tears. She is always crying these days. I don't cry. I have no tears left.

The girls shuffle forward and Jennypha rakes her thick, wavy hair into a harsh ponytail. The scent of boronias waft through the room from the bunch of flowers Tayla holds. There's a house in my street with boronias.

"Do you have a vase?" Mrs McKenzie asks the nurse. The woman hurries off to find something suitable. When she returns, she places the bunch gently in a lonely vase of water by the bed.

"Don't they smell nice," she says.

"They're Lucy's favourite," Tayla states.

The nurse leaves and Mrs McKenzie follows tactfully, leaving the girls alone in the room. Jennypha stands by the bed and recites her apology. By the end of the speech she has tears rolling down her cheeks. Tayla reaches out to hold her best friend's hand.

They never considered the possibility of events turning out this way. Every taunt, every shove, every exclusion; Jennypha may be charged with manslaughter if the machine is turned off.

I want to tell Jennypha it's too late to apologise, but I cannot speak. I never could tell her what I really thought; she'd never listen even if I did. I wish someone had stood up for the girl in the hospital bed when she couldn't find her voice. I wish I'd had the strength to do it myself.

The other two girls in their group don't show their faces at the hospital. They hide away pretending Jennypha was the only one involved. I used to hate them, but now I am just empty. Hate requires emotions I no longer possess.

A counsellor mentions organ donation. There must be plenty of needy people out there who would benefit if this one girl dies. It would be nice to know they were being put to better use, that this life hadn't been a complete waste.

Here is my secret. What happened was not completely Jennypha's fault; my own actions were partly to blame. Unlike Jennypha, I had been considering where events were leading for some time.

Don't get me wrong, Jennypha is responsible. I wanted her and her friends to pay for their continued abuse. I did this to stop the endless emotional pain. It was meant to be final, not this half way place.

Will calls me again, reminding me I have a task to do. My being here is not important. The girl in the coma slipped away from life months ago. All I care about is my friend, Will. I need to protect him in a way no one has ever been able to do for me.

I've never met Will in my real life. He lives in my dreams. When I was young I was sure he was real, but life has beaten that belief out of me. He's probably only a figment of my imagination, someone I conjured to give my life meaning.

He feels real to me though. Every moment I've lived with him feels more genuine than my actual life. Perhaps if someone like that existed in my reality, if they had just reached out to me, I wouldn't be stuck in this hospital.

I am Lucy.

My body lies in a coma on the hospital bed being watched over by Mum. My mind has left the room and I'm in Will's world one final time. Sometimes I'm called back into the hospital room, although I don't know why. It's never happened before, but then this is the first time I've ever tried to kill myself.

Occasionally I wonder what would happen, if I wake.

Birthday

It was the night of my eleventh birthday when I first met Will, although in that time, he was known as Wu. I don't have a time machine, nor do I leave my room. I simply fall asleep and don't wake until I die in Will's world. So how can I explain my physical presence in a place I've never seen, in a time before I've even been born?

Wu believed he summoned me, but that doesn't explain the other times. The doctors' tests come back negative. The psychiatrist implies I'm dreaming. The school counsellor asks if I need to access free tutoring sessions, and Mum says I'm making it up for attention, but she could just be repeating what Frank thinks.

Is it all in my head? If it's a dream, why can't I transport myself to Will whenever I need him? Sometimes I think back over that day for clues how it happened, but I come up blank.

I wanted a big eleventh birthday party like other people have. Throughout the year I heard the girls at

9

school talking about how many presents they collected at their parties and I had visions of the gifts I might receive. One from every person who comes, wrapped in colourful paper and tied with pretty bows. People would want to talk to me because I was the birthday girl.

Mum said I could invite all my classmates. We sat up late each night for a week with scissors, glue and pencils to create the handmade invitations. Some people buy them from the shop, but Mum said these were more special. I admired the way they looked with our drawings of cake and presents on the front and each one addressed individually.

I'd never been invited to other parties, but I imagined what it would be like. Mum promised to bake me a cake. The day after we finished our works of art, I walked importantly through the classroom as I handed each person their special invitation.

Rachael decided she wouldn't come. She had beautiful long blonde hair that swung when she walked. I wasn't pretty like her, so I couldn't be her friend. I knew, because she told me so. My hair was dark brown, which contrasted with my greyish-green eyes Grandma called 'witchy'. I didn't want to look like a witch. People liked girls who looked like princesses.

Rachael told me she didn't want to catch any germs from my house. Her friend, Sarah, said she would think about it if I gave her my tartan hair ribbon. Grandpa gave it to me and it was the only pretty thing I owned, but I wanted Sarah to be my friend. I gave it to her.

The next day, Sarah told me her mum wouldn't let her come to my house. I asked for my ribbon back, but she kept forgetting to bring it to school. Eventually I stopped asking for it. Mum yelled at me when I told her I lost it. She said I was irresponsible and how was she meant to trust me alone in the house while she was at work, if I couldn't even look after a ribbon.

Jennypha started a rumour that there would be no party food. She told everyone we would be serving brussel sprouts. I didn't expect this to stop Tayla from coming, but she told me she was going to be at Jennypha's house that day. I knew she was lying to me as she twirled a strand of hair around her finger. Jennypha always went to Tayla's house, not the other way around. I shrugged and pretended I didn't care. They would be sorry they missed it when everyone was talking about my birthday.

I expected some of the boys would come. They liked free food and there was going to be cake. Saturday arrived and I was still hopeful for a great day. A few people were undecided and I knew they would show up. Tayla might have changed her mind and would bring Jennypha with her. Sarah might have found my ribbon and come by to return it.

I put on my best green dress and Mum put the flower clip in my hair that was her present to me. I looked at myself in the mirror and when I smiled I almost looked pretty, despite my 'witchy' eyes.

I helped Mum blow up a couple of balloons to tie to the front fence so everyone knew it was my birthday. We even had a couple of bags of chips, chocolate and two whole bottles of soft drink for my guests.

I watched by the front window as the party drew near. I checked the clock on the wall, shifting from leg to leg as the start time came and went. No one appeared.

I worried people hadn't been able to find the house. Mum assured me they would see the balloons. She suggested I eat something while I waited, but I refused to touch the food until my guests arrived, even though my tummy began to rumble. I wanted them to see all the good treats we had out for the party.

By the afternoon I came to the conclusion there was something wrong with me. I would never have the latest toy to show off at school. I wasn't pretty like Rachael. No one wanted to be my friend. I was an invisible nobody.

Mum came out of the kitchen singing 'Happy Birthday' and carrying a pink frosted cupcake with a single candle. She'd promised to cook me a real cake like the girls at school had. I was glad no one was there to see. I was eleven years old, not one.

"My life sucks. I wish I'd never been born," I yelled.

She has tears in her eyes, but I couldn't take the words back. My birthday had been ruined. I stormed off to my room where I curled up on my bed and cried.

A while later, Mum knocked on the door. I pulled my pillow over my head, muffling her words as she told me she had to go to work. Our neighbour would look in on me later. I lay still, refusing to respond. I knew the routine. It wasn't that I didn't like Mrs B from next door; I just didn't like being treated like a child.

When Mum left, I came out from under my pillow and peeked out of the window. Two of the balloons on the fence had popped and hung sadly by their strings. I crawled back into bed, drifting into a restless sleep before Mrs B arrived.

Family

East Africa 40,000 BC

The cold, hard surface dragged me from a restless sleep. A stick dug into my side. I was sure it hadn't been in my bed when I went to sleep. I reached out to touch the walls of my bedroom, my hands flailing around in the empty space. My stomach dropped. The walls weren't there. A cool wind ruffled my loose hair.

I snapped my eyes open. My bedroom ceiling, with its off-white flaky paint, had vanished. My whole bedroom was missing, including my bed. I furrowed my brow; Mum would not be impressed I'd lost something I was lying on.

I stared up at a night sky, waiting for my room to return. It didn't. Millions of twinkling stars continued to create a glowing world high above me. I searched for the stars Grandpa taught me before he passed away; Orion's Belt, the Southern Cross and the Two Pointers, but there were so many, I couldn't find the familiar ones.

I bit my lower lip. What if my wish of not being born had come true and I was where people go when they no longer existed? They didn't teach us about dying at school. I shivered.

I felt like I was still alive.

I'd once overheard a classmate tell a story about his cousin who sleep walked. I considered this, but I wasn't sure how far I would have had to walk to see that many stars. I guessed it would be far enough to give me blisters, but my feet were fine. Still, it was a possibility.

I sat up. I was perched on a wide rocky ledge, the stone absorbing the chill from the night air. Cliffs rose up behind me and beyond lay the dark and shadowy, shrubby landscape below, not a street light in sight. I rubbed the goose bumps on my arms as the cold seeped through the animal skins I wore. They smelled funny. I didn't remember changing out of my party dress.

I pinched my arm and it hurt, so I figured I'd been magically transported somewhere, like in a library book. One girl in my class went to Fiji with her family and everyone wanted to be her friend when she got back. Maybe this adventure would be interesting enough to get me a friend at school.

A star shot across my line of vision, magically missing a collision with all its neighbours. Its beauty was mesmerising. Grandpa once told me if I wished on a falling star it would come true.

"I wish I had a friend," I whispered as I followed it with my eyes.

The star fell from sight. Below its path, a small bonfire caught my attention. The hypnotic leaping flames had me creeping cautiously towards it, careful not to trip on the uneven rock. I rubbed my arms again imagining the fire's warmth.

A boy danced around the flames, singing and throwing something into the fire. He looked not much older than me, twelve years old at the most. He brushed his dark, matted hair from his face as the light flickered over his tanned skin. He danced as though he was the only person in the whole world.

I stood transfixed until my leg fell asleep and I had to move. I made a slight sound as I did so, startling the boy. He moved swiftly, putting the fire between us while he studied me. He wore animal skins like I was, but moved with the grace of a wild creature. I tried to look friendly.

"Hello," I said. He grinned, showing off white teeth.

"You came!" he exclaimed.

No one had ever been excited to see me before. Perhaps he thought I was someone else. The boy stalked towards me. I stood still as he approached, so not to scare him away.

"Oh Spirit, I am Wu." He tilted his head to one side as he assessed me. "I expected you to be bigger."

I sighed. He did think I was someone else.

"How did I get here?" I asked anyway.

"I summoned you." Wu grinned like he'd created the wheel. It was a better explanation than anything I had come up with, but I didn't know anything about being a spirit. I was just plain Lucy.

Wu reached out and touched my hair. It was smooth because I washed it for my party, even if it was boring brown and not beautiful silky blonde like Rachael's. Wu ran his hands through my hair. I didn't move as he studied me.

"How do you make your eyes that colour, Spirit?" He stared into them like he had never seen anything so amazing. Maybe my eyes weren't as bad as Grandma said.

"I don't know. My name is Lucy."

Wu tried to say my name, but the sounds were unfamiliar to him. He settled on calling me 'Lu'. I liked it. I'd never had a nickname before. Only people with friends had special nicknames. Now we were Wu and Lu, I finally had a friend. That made me smile, which made Wu smile. That was what happy felt like.

Wu collected a burning stick from the fire and kicked out the rest of his bonfire. He grabbed my hand in his free one and led me along a narrow rocky trail towards his home. I'd never been asked to anyone's house before. My stomach churned with excitement.

I would have walked past the cave if not with Wu. The entrance was narrow with stones piled up as a doorway. I slowed as we approached. Wu tugged on my hand pulling me forward. He let go to shift a large rock aside and wriggled through the gap. I bit my thumb nail. My feet hurt from walking barefoot and I was tired. Something rustled in the darkness. I glanced over my shoulder at the unidentifiable sounds of the strange world and darted after Wu. He rolled the rock back into place behind us, muffling the noises.

Wu's flame torch provided a flickering view of the musty cave. A few people lay snoring on the floor, but a woman approached us to scold Wu. He should know better than to go out in the dark on his own, even with fire. She stopped when she saw me. Wu held the flame up so Mother could see my eyes. She gasped in surprise. The flickering light reflected off her brown eyes like Wu's.

"She's a spirit," Wu announced.

I shifted from aching foot to foot, waiting for her to tell me to leave, but instead she studied me intently. Wu lifted a lock of my hair for his mother to touch. She rubbed it gently between her calloused fingers.

"What tribe do you belong to?" she asked.

"I don't have one," I admitted.

"It's dark outside. She'll have to stay here with us," Wu said.

His mother gave a slight nod of her head and Wu tugged me away before she could change her mind. She continued to watch me closely, as did several other sets of eyes in the cave.

Wu led me to a pile of grasses and animal skins on the floor that was his space. He pulled me down to the cave floor and I curled up next to my strange new friend. He wrapped us both in a thick animal skin and I lay still trying to stay awake, so I could hold onto the feeling of his warm body against mine.

I stared at the darkness until I was unsure if my eyes were open or closed, and listened to the sounds of the family shifting in their sleep. I eventually drifted off in the strange surroundings, listening to Wu's even breathing.

I lay perfectly still, keeping my eyes firmly closed as I tried to hold on to the calmness of my dream. All the details from the brilliant starry sky, to Wu's messy hair and friendly smile came back to me. I could still smell the musky odour of the cave and the animal skins. Once I was sure I wouldn't forget the dream, I allowed myself to think about what the day would bring.

Yesterday was Saturday, leaving only one day before I had to go back to school and confront the laughing faces of my classmates who knew no one came to my party. I squeezed my eyes shut further to prevent tears from escaping. I considered how to make myself look sick enough by the evening that Mum might let me stay home on Monday.

The thought of the next day made my stomach clench or it could have been my belly rumbling. I hadn't eaten anything since breakfast the previous day. Mum would have arrived back late from work and would still be sleeping. I'd have to make my own breakfast. Eventually hunger and a full bladder drove me to open my damp eyes to face the day.

Wu crouched next to me in the dim light. I sat up abruptly, narrowly avoiding hitting my head on the sloping cave wall. The animal skin blanket slid off me. The rocks blocking the entrance had been moved, letting a small amount of daylight into the gloomy cave. Several people remained inside with us, but most had left.

"I'm still here!" I reached out to touch Wu's face, he was solid, real. I erupted into laughter. "I'm still here!"

"I worried you might leave, so I hung onto you all night." Wu wrapped his arms around me in a hug to demonstrate. I smiled shyly at him.

I wanted to hang onto the moment, but I desperately needed a bathroom. It looked like the plumbers were taking longer to get here than they did the time Mum had a burst water pipe.

Besides the bedding on the floor and the space where Wu's mum sat weaving grasses together and watching us, there appeared to be a rubbish pile swept into one corner, but nothing to help me with my situation.

Wu glanced at my crossed legs and pained expression and motioned for me to follow him outside. He led me a short distance down a well-worn track from the cave where a few scattered shrubs grew. Beyond us, grassy plains stretch into the distance. He pointed to the bushes and stood there, worried I would vanish if he took his eyes off me. I made him turn around before I squatted.

Wu reluctantly let the women of his clan show me how food was gathered, while he hovered nearby.

"It is women's work," they said, laughing at him good naturedly as they handed me a woven basket to carry. "Lu will not disappear while we look after her." He stayed anyway.

The men came back from hunting with a small antelope-like creature. They strutted around with their chests puffed out as they prepared the animal for the cooking pit. Wu said I brought luck.

The whole family gathered around the bonfire as evening fell. Sparks escaped from the fire and danced up into the sky like glowing fairies. My mouth watered from the smell of roasting meat.

Wu's mother found me hovering at the edges of the light while the food was divided. She took my arm and led me into the circle.

"Lu is family," she said. Her words made me want to smile and cry at the same time. I dashed my tears away so she didn't think I was sad. Wu appeared by my side with two portions of food. He smiled as he handed one to me. We sat on the ground surrounded by family as we ate.

It took many nights before I stopped expecting to wake up in my bedroom at home. Wu slept next to me every night to make sure I stayed. I refused to shut my eyes unless he had his arm around me. Sometimes I thought of Mum and wondered if she missed me.

At some point I stopped thinking I was dreaming and started believing Wu actually called me here. After a while I forgot I had another life in a different time. There was nothing before the moment I first laid eyes on Wu.

Although he was only twelve, Wu hunted with the older men. I asked to go with him, but he said it was too dangerous. Many men died while hunting. I pestered him until he agreed to show me how to throw his spear.

The spear was made from a straight branch with a stone tip tied on using animal sinew. Wu made it himself. He showed me how to hold it near the back end with the stone tip pointing slightly up. He pointed out a shrubby target and threw it. The spear landed upright in the centre of the bush. He retrieved it and offered me a turn.

I held it as Wu had and placed my feet apart. I stuck my free arm in the air, aimed and threw. The spear bounced over the ground, frustratingly closer to me than the target. I glared at it. Wu laughed.

"You have as much skill as a man trying to weave a woman's basket." He retrieved the spear and offered it again. My second attempt was equally as terrible. I stomped my foot.

"The Elders say we should not compare ourselves to others, otherwise we may become vain and bitter. Always there will be greater and lesser persons than ourselves," Wu said.

Lucy would continue to be a failure, but Lu wanted to prove herself. Lu wanted to be good at things Wu was good at. If I couldn't compare myself to him, I would find my own way to do it better.

Some days the family went for a long walk to a lake. The water was clear and icy cold, but it was an opportunity to wash. I took out the braid I adopted to stop my hair becoming matted like Wu's. I shook it out in the water and did my best to wash it without shampoo. Wu watched me. A girl tried to copy my actions, but her hair was knotted and Wu didn't notice.

I was re-braiding my hair when Wu's seven year old sister, Lee gave a gurgled yell. She'd ventured too deep and lost her footing. A man waded over, but he couldn't reach her. The family had always stayed in the shallows unable to swim.

I leapt forward into freestyle stroke. Lee had stopped moving by the time I was in range. I grabbed her hair and tried to keep her head out of the water as I swam back to shore. The men took her from me as I reached the shallows.

They laid her on dry land as everyone crowded around touching her still body. Wu's mother wept uncontrollably, wailing about going to the spirits in the sky. I pushed my way into their centre and rolled Lee onto her side, as I'd read on the signs at the school swimming pool in a dream I had about another life. Nothing came from her mouth.

I rolled her back, measured the centre point where I had to put my hands and started pumping her chest. I said 'come on, come on,' because that always seems to help on the television show about the lifeguards. I kept pressing until my arms felt like they were no longer attached to my body.

Lee choked as water spewed from her mouth. I pushed her onto her side as the water drained from her lungs. She was choking, gasping for breath, but alive. My hands shook and I needed to pee.

Wu grabbed me into a hug. He had never seen someone brought back from the dead. The euphoria of the situation stayed with me for a long time as the family celebrated Lee's second chance at life. I'd saved a life. I was finally someone special.

I was surrounded by people wanting good luck, after I saved Lee. I asked the women for help finding a flexible stick. It took a while to explain as they wanted to give me a stiff one that was good for spears and hitting things, but eventually we found what I wanted.

Lee watched every move I made and helped where she could. She found me a single edged stone for a knife, sinew from whatever it was we ate the previous week, and a couple of miniature spears the young boys played with before they were strong enough to throw the proper one.

I picked up feathers as we gathered food and Lee showed me a gluey sap from a small tree. I worked hard making my tool. Lee watched me practice and told me when I was good enough to show Wu. I gave it a few more tries just to make sure.

The men came home from the hunt empty handed. They'd found more special stones to be made into tools, but they couldn't get close enough to the creature they were stalking.

Lee announced that Wu and I should have a re-try with the spears. The men gathered around to cheer Wu; a competition would take their minds off the failed hunt.

Wu picked a target, but I made him choose something further away to be challenging for a spear throw. Wu's spear fell just short of the target, but the men cheered him for the effort. He retrieved the spear and offered it to me. I shook my head and held up the little spear with three feathers stuck to the sides near the notch in the end. The men laughed at my spear. It was no match for a man's tool.

Lee passed me the flexible stick. I placed my foot on the wood, bending it to loop the sinew over the grooves I'd made at both ends. I released it slowly and it kept its bow. I slotted the spear's notch against the sinew, balanced the front across my fingers and drew the string back then I aimed and released.

My arrow flew through the air with a force Wu's spear lacked. The direction was a little off, but it looked impressive as it disappeared into the scrubby distance. Everyone stared at me until Lee started cheering. Two of the men ran off to find my arrow. Lee tugged on my hand so she could whisper in my ear.

"You belong to us now and if you ever get lost, I will call you back to us so we can take care of you." She looked at me with big serious eyes. I was saved from knowing how to respond by Wu approaching me.

He took the loss well, more curious about how I made the new tool. I showed Wu and the other hunters my weapon. They talked excitedly about how it could improve their chances of taking down game. I was asked to demonstrate it again.

In return for my weapon, Wu took me to his secret hiding place and showed me how to make cave art. He used various powders mixed with water to record our battle between spear and arrow. We placed our hands below it and he blew paint over them to leave our prints surrounded by speckled paint. I liked the idea that a little piece of me would stay there next to Wu even once we were gone. I had found where I fit in, there with Wu.

Eventually we started out for the home cave. The air was chilly, but Wu's hand was warm in mine. As we walked we swung our hands to the rhythm of our footsteps. We followed worn trails and Wu told me about the changing seasons and how the family reacted to them. He included me in the future.

Wu sensed the movement behind us before I did. He threw us to the ground and twisted out of the way as the lioness pounced. I rolled away from him in the fall. The lioness skidded across the short grass and turned on Wu.

"Wu! Look out!" I screamed.

I sprinted to the nearest tree and scrambled up into the branches. Could lionesses climb? I didn't know. My heart pounded as my slippery hands tried to keep their grip. I was out of breath as though I'd run an entire hunt on my own.

Wu threw his stone-tipped knife, but it glanced off the lioness's hide causing as much irritation as a stinging insect. He had no other weapon and neither did I. He took a slow step backwards keeping his eyes on the beast. My stomach turned.

I didn't want to be there. I wanted to be home, safe and sound in our cave with the family. I forced my white knuckled grip to release, so I could break a bunch of twigs from my tree and throw them at the lioness. They rained down like confetti.

"Hey!" I yelled. It turned in my direction and snarled. "Go fetch help, Wu."

"Lu?" Wu hesitated.

"I'm a spirit remember. I'll be safe." I didn't know if it was true or not, but the words sounded reassuring.

Wu backed away quietly over a rise as the lioness advanced towards my tree. I snarled and made swiping motions with one arm to hold its attention. I slipped and grabbed my branch with both arms as a squeak escaped my lips.

I was unable to break eye contact with the beast to see where Wu was. Just as I thought he must be away free, Wu knocked a rock loose. The lioness spun around and dropped into a crouch. It crept back towards the location Wu had disappeared.

I broke more twigs from my tree and threw them, where they landed uselessly on the ground. I hissed and snarled, but the lioness's attention didn't waiver. If I yelled, Wu would come back and be eaten. With only one thing left for me to do, I released my death grip and leapt out of the tree.

I hit the ground hard and rolled a couple of times, bruising my knee on a sharp rock. The pain sent black streaks across my vision and for a moment I almost passed out. As I sprung to my feet, the knee nearly gave way, but I had achieved my aim. I had the lioness's attention. Adrenaline pumped through my body making me feel both strong and weak at the same time. My hands shook.

I reached down without breaking eye contact with my foe and picked up the rock that injured my knee. I threw it at the lioness, but my arm shook so badly, the missile completely missed its target. The lioness glanced briefly towards it and then back at me.

I wasn't actually a spirit. I was just a scared little girl who wanted her family.

Everything happened quickly. The animal leapt at me, I tried to throw myself out of the way, but tripped over a thick tuft of grass. The lioness landed on my chest. Its paws thrust the air from my lungs as it breathed its rancid breath into my face. No one was around to see me wet myself.

I choked on the scream that would bring Wu back to me. Through the tearing pain that followed, I held onto the image of Wu's face and prayed he made it home safely. I didn't make a sound.

My body was stiff and I struggled to lift my arms. A shooting pain originated from my knee. Judging from the agony I was in, all of my limbs

28

were attached. I didn't hear the lioness or Wu's rescue party.

I forced my eyes open. Above me, everything was white. It wasn't the blue sky, the cloudy sky, the starry night or even the cave ceiling. Was this what death looked like, or was I a spirit like Wu said?

I attempted to snort the unnatural smell out of my nose, but it remained like a dense fog. The beeping in my ears belonged to no creature I knew. Perhaps it wasn't edible. I blinked my eyes to clear the whiteness and struggled to sit.

There was no blood. Someone had cleaned my wounds. I was covered by something not made from animal skins or a recognisable plant. Strange translucent vines grew from the back of my hand. The sight made my skin crawl and I wrapped the other hand around the roots to rip them out. A stranger's pale hand covered mine before I could complete the action.

"She's awake." A man pushed me firmly back down. His neatly trimmed hair distracted me. He must have possessed an impressive stone knife. He shone a tiny sun in both my eyes, which he had captured in his hands. I wanted to ask how he had caught it, but I couldn't focus on words.

"Can you tell me your name?" he asked.

"Lu," I said with a voice that sounded like it hadn't spoken for a long time. He glanced at the woman beside him like I gave the wrong answer.

"How are you feeling?" the woman asked. Her clothing was also thin and not a natural animal colour. Something was not right about this place. I felt – displaced.

"Where am I?" I asked.

"You're in hospital. You've been asleep for ten days," the woman said gently.

Hospital? I struggled to connect the word to a thing. Wu never showed me a hospital.

"Where's Wu?" I asked. The people glanced at each other, but none of them knew who Wu was. He must have escaped the lioness. I was the only one that was eaten and ended up wherever here was.

"Lucy!" The voice sounded vaguely familiar, but it didn't know my name. I was Lu.

A woman rushed forward and wrapped her arms around me like a snake about to consume its meal. It hurt. I thought she might never let me go. She smelt like strange flowers and I sneezed. Eventually she drew back enough to look at me.

I had seen her face before. I went through all the faces of the family, but she was not one of them. She was too pale and her hair was smooth like mine used to be. She didn't have the family's dark eyes. She looked like an older version of the me I saw when I looked in the lake. Then it fell into place.

"Mum?" I said.

I'd lost Wu and my family.

It took a long time to reconnect with my own world. I was disorientated, as though this was the dream. I'd lost part of myself in the past. Mum told me she'd arrived home in the morning after my birthday and hadn't been able to wake me. She'd panicked and took me to the hospital. The doctors could find no reason for me to be asleep, all they could do was conduct tests and wait.

The day I woke up, I developed an alarming rash and bruising around my knee. More blood tests were done. I looked at my injuries when I was alone in the bathroom. I didn't see a rash, I saw slashing claws and teeth from a lioness attack.

Mum wanted me to stay in the hospital, but I told the doctors I wanted to leave and they let me go. The beds were needed for people they knew how to fix. It was hard to walk at first due to my injured knee. The bruising and rash took days to fade.

When I arrived at my old home, Mum watched my every move and followed me through the house offering to make me food or fetch a drink. She collected school work from my teachers, so I didn't have to go back until I was feeling better. She found enough spare money to buy me a stuffed toy lion. She named him Wu, because that was what I called out shortly before I woke up. She said it would bring me luck.

I cried when she gave it to me and Mum tried to take it back, but I didn't let her. I placed him gently on my bed and at night I hugged it as tightly as Wu hugged me on that first night to keep me from disappearing. I tried thinking myself back home as I fell asleep, but I couldn't find my way.

I worried about Wu for a long time. What if he was attacked by another lioness when I wasn't there to save him? Was he happy? Perhaps that was how I first developed an interest in history.

I was looking for Wu.

School

My shoulders slump as I walk into my history class to a young substitute nervously shuffling her notes. She smiles and greets the group of girls in front of me. They give her their best, 'why are you talking to me' look and keep walking. The woman's smile slips from her face. I slide unnoticed into a seat to the far left of the middle row.

The woman's demeanour does not improve as she attempts to call the roll. There are a few students whose parents either have issues with the English language or want to draw attention to their child by giving them a unique name. The first one catches the teacher unexpectedly.

"It's Be-ung-ca," Bianca corrects her harshly. She started insisting on that pronunciation shortly after the new girl arrived at our school. That first name makes the teacher doubt the pronunciation of the next.

"Jenny-P-Ha," she guesses.

"It's pronounced Jennifer," Jennypha states.

There are several giggles. I cringe and sink into my seat. The two girls are friends, along with Tayla. The teacher calls her name correctly. The class goes quiet in anticipation as she reaches the final member of their group.

"La'a?" More giggles from the class.

"Ladasha," La-a explains, as if to a stupid child who should be able to pronounce a simple word. The teacher frowns at the name clearly not expecting the dash to be taken literally. She moves on.

"Lucy?" The teacher sounds hopeful my name is normal.

"Here," I reply. She looks relieved.

"Here's Lucy," the girls chime.

They giggle while I pretend to be interested in something scrawled on my desk. Ms Miller would make them stop, but this woman doesn't know what to do. It's just harmless fun. That's what everyone tells me. 'Why are you so upset, Lucy?'

Sticks and stones can break my bones, but names will never hurt me. It's a stupid rhyme. Names do hurt. The wounds just don't show.

I didn't begin High School this way. Mum got a new job just as I was finishing Primary School. We moved to a nearby town. Mum said it would be a good opportunity to start fresh, as everyone I knew would be attending the closer school.

The first day arrived before Mum's pay check so I didn't have a uniform. I wore a pair of faded jeans and my best shirt. Mum gave me a note to give to my teacher for being out of uniform.

At lunch time, I was approached by a group of girls in my year level. The leader was a blonde by the name of Alicia. Her dad was army and she moved schools some months later, but while she was here, she was the person to be seen with.

A moment of joy at being noticed was replaced by queasiness at the sight of Jennypha and Tayla. I hadn't known they'd changed schools, but of course if Jennypha had, Tayla would too. I was planning my escape when it occurred to me they didn't recognise me.

I'd had an awkwardly short hair cut the year before. I tried to copy one of the celebrities from the teen magazines, blonde-haired Rachael always read, but it made me look like a boy. Thankfully my hair finally grew out over the summer holidays. I guess they didn't expect me to be here anymore than I them.

I actually believed High School would be different. It wouldn't be a repeat of the loneliness and isolation I knew at my old school. I could be anyone I wanted to be. I could be brave and bold like Lu. I'd finally be liked and find a friend. I'd be the kind of person who hangs out with Jennypha and Tayla.

Tayla said my lunch box was cute. I picked it up from a garage sale last year, I didn't tell her though. During the second week someone commented on my shirt. Alicia asked where I bought it. I opened my mouth without thinking. I'm sure it came from a popular store that would meet with their approval, but I couldn't remember the name, I admitted it was second hand. Bianca wrinkled her nose.

"I wondered what that smell was." She waved a hand in front of her face.

They all laughed. For the remainder of the day, the girls held their noses whenever they were near me. I started eating lunch on my own. Sometimes I loitered in the library reading the history books, imagining I was back in the past with Will.

After that day, the girls generally ignored me. I learned not to draw attention to myself. Most people don't even notice if I'm around. That changed when the new girl arrived. Her name was Ladasha, spelt with a hyphen and she was slightly older than the rest of us. She and her family recently moved here from interstate.

La-a's father works "offshore" so they have loads of money, even more than Jennypha's family. He is away a lot, but La-a has heaps of photos of him flying in helicopters to remote places, blu-tacked to her locker. My locker door is blank.

Jennypha gravitated towards La-a, Tayla lost her best friend role to the new girl, and Bianca tried to improve her social position by picking on the unpopular girl. Me.

La-a encouraged Bianca at every opportunity. It became the group's favourite pastime to tease me. Bianca started the phrase, "Here's Lucy". It stuck and I hate it. I miss the days of being ignored.

Today the substitute teacher talks about something in the curriculum. No one tells her we studied the same thing two weeks ago. Ms Miller loves history and often gets carried away, forgetting she is meant to stick to a schedule. Her enthusiasm is infectious.

I zone out, focused on sharpening my blunt pencil. It's so short, I can barely twist it in the sharpener any more. I use it to draw in my notebook, calculating how many weeks until my sixteenth birthday. My heart rate increases thinking about it. A year is a long time to wait for something.

The bell rings for the end of class and the students rush out as though they have somewhere better to be. The expression on the teacher's face is one I am familiar with; the look of holding onto tears until she is alone. I put my head down and pretend I haven't noticed how close she is to losing control. I hope Ms Miller is back by next class.

A good day is one where I get through the whole day without being noticed. I make the next class without incident and slide into my seat. Someone bangs their bag against my arm as they pass, but I pretend it didn't happen and don't turn around to see who it was. It's easier that way.

Our English teacher clears her voice and the class quietens down.

"Can anyone tell me what a synonym is?" Mrs Davis asks. No one responds so she scans the classroom for her first victim, settling on me. I shift uncomfortably in my seat and avoid eye contact. "Lucy?"

"It's a word you use when you can't spell the word you first thought of," I reply.

"Interesting definition, give me an example."

My mind is still on the substitute attempting to read the attendance roll. Her look as I left the room bothers me. I didn't even smile at her. I say the first thing that pops into my head.

"Saying 'dash' instead of 'hyphen'." Someone at the back of the class snickers.

"Like Lahyphena instead of Ladasha," one of the boys calls out. The thump of a book hitting something is followed by an 'oomph'. I force myself not to turn around. The class erupts into laughter.

Something hits my back. I wait nervously for the bell to ring so I can disappear quietly. At one point during the class, the teacher passes my desk and places her hand over my tapping pen before moving on.

La-a catches me between classes, shoving me into the lockers and bruising my shoulder where I hit the lock. She gives a toss of her immaculately straight blonde locks, an action perfected in front of a mirror, and stalks off.

By the end of the day, my school bag has vanished. I hide in the toilets so no one sees me cry, while I wait until everyone has gone home and I can look for my bag undisturbed. I eventually find it in a bin at the far end of the corridor. I brush it off and put my books into it, but I've missed the bus. It's a long walk home.

It takes a week for the bruise on my shoulder to fade, but I learn my lesson from that class. Even if I know an answer, I pretend I don't. I also start locking the strap of my bag in my locker, so it can't go missing again.

Mum works several jobs to keep the money coming in. It always seems unfair to me that she works such long hours for so little, when La-a's father works half the year and is practically rolling in money.

To him that hath, shall be given and from him that hath not, shall be taken even that which he hath. I read that in a book once. I think it's from the Bible. Whoever wrote it understood what it was like to have nothing.

I've learned to fend for myself, once spending all my paper delivery money buying a rusty old rabbit trap at a market. I took it into the bush near our house and caught a feral rabbit. I brought it home and skinned it. It was nearly cooked by the time Mum arrived home. The smell was mouth-watering, but Mum was so upset I never did it again. I think she had visions of me turning into a serial killer. She didn't even let me keep the pelt.

I tried to talk to Mum about it once, my dream being real. She said I had an over-active imagination and I should bring friends over more often instead of being on my own all the time. She made it sound like it was my choice to be alone, like she didn't remember my eleventh birthday.

Our battered old car sits in the driveway when I arrive home from school. It's a rare surprise to find Mum at the house midweek and even stranger to see her in the kitchen preparing dinner.

"There you are, darling." She dries her hands on a tea towel as she leans over to kiss my cheek. "How was your day?"

"Fine," I say lifting the lid of the saucepan on the stove and eyeing the contents suspiciously.

"I brought you home a present." She beams at me as I abandon my investigation of dinner.

I look at her in surprise as she squeezes past me to rummage in her handbag left on the kitchen table. She pulls out a long thin item wrapped in a sheet of newspaper and taped together.

"Open," she says, holding it out.

I pick carefully at the tape, peeling away the paper to find three new pencils lying inside.

"2B or not 2B, that is the pencil, is it not?" She smiles at me.

"Thanks Mum." I throw my arms around her in a brief hug.

"The boss went home early, so I had free range with the stationary cupboard," she whispers conspiratorially to me. "By the way, Maree from work is having a birthday on Friday. Now you have new pencils, do you think you can spare a sheet of sketch paper and draw me a card for her?"

I miss Will the most when I wake, but sometimes life is okay when it's just Mum and me.

We receive our history assignment at the beginning of the week. There's an automatic groan from the class, but Ms Miller has recovered from her cold and we don't have the substitute. I'm quietly intrigued by the project.

40

We have to choose a time in history and imagine we live there. The assignment requires us to describe our surroundings, what we are doing and eating. We are to write a story to tell people about this time, starting with the words "I opened my eyes and saw..."

I'm unusually excited for school the day the assignment is due. Standing outside the classroom being ignored as we wait for our teacher to appear, I feel I've captured my chosen time period perfectly. Two of the boys discuss the credibility of their fictional excuses for not being able to submit their work on time. I keep my head down so no one sees me smile and hug my books to my chest.

La-a shoves me into the wall, recalling me back to my surroundings and removing the expression from my face. Ms Miller arrives and I quickly slip through the door and take my seat.

"Place your assignment on the table in front of you," Ms Miller instructs.

I lay my stapled, hand-written pages carefully upside down in front of me. I glance around, I've written far more than anyone else.

Ms Miller wanders the room glancing at everyone's submission. The two boys discussing excuses outside the classroom are given detentions. When they protest that they have good reasons, she informs them they can tell her all about it during lunch. No one argues with Ms Miller. She heads back to the front of the class and studies us.

"James." She singles out a student from the back of the class. "Come to the front and read out what you have written."

James leaps out of his chair and swaggers to the front of the classroom. The other boys cheer him on. He shakes out his single typed page, rolls his neck, flicks his dark hair off his face and clears his throat. The class is silent, waiting for his story.

"I opened my eyes and saw the super cool paint job on the side of my time machine. A noise made me spin around. It was a tyrannosaurus..." He pauses the story to add a loud roar, "... and he was about to eat me. I grabbed my laser gun and commando rolled out of his way." James includes some actions to highlight the story, narrowly missing the teacher.

"Thank you, James," Ms Miller interrupts as James picks himself off the floor. "I don't think you quite understood the point of the assignment. How about we try someone else?"

La-a raises her hand. Ms Miller waves her up to the front of the class as her friends cheer her on. She repeats James' actions, waiting for the applause before starting her story.

"I opened my eyes and saw a naked cave man standing over me. He was very well hung and I was concerned for my safety, but he was more interested in the road kill behind me." La-a pauses to let the laughter die down.

"I think we need someone who may have actually done some research." Ms Miller brings the story to a halt amid groans from the class.

Ms Miller scans the room, her eyes coming to rest on my pile of pages. I pull them towards me as though that will prevent her from calling my name to read my words to the class.

"Lucy?"

I drag myself out of my seat and study the floor as I walk to the front of the class. No one cheers for me. I look at my handwriting on the first page and take a deep breath. Someone makes a rude noise and the class snickers. The teacher shushes them. I try again.

"I opened my eyes and saw the grey, cloudy sky above me, framed by grape vines to either side of my vision. The vineyard was not like the modern ones with rows stretching on uninterrupted. These were short with various trees interspersed between them. I recognised olives, figs and some type of nut.

"I stood and brushed the dark, fertile soil from my dress. Behind me a mountain loomed as though guarding the countryside. It looked out of place and for some reason I felt nervous. I dragged my eyes away. Laid out before me was a town set inside stone walls. I made my way on foot in that direction as the first drops of rain fell from the sky.

"I was following the dirt road to the town when I tripped over an object lying on the ground. I retrieved the small bronze statue of a woman. She held a ship's rudder in one hand as though directing me to my destination. I held onto her as I continued walking in the rain.

"The muddy road became lined with monuments to the dead. They were impressive stone structures, some displaying the urns holding the ashes of their owners. I recognised Roman numerals on some of the plaques as well as a scattering of symbols like the ones we use in maths classes when we don't know an angle of a triangle. In some places there was graffiti.

"Inside the town's gate, I stepped up onto the raised stone sidewalk to avoid the rain water washing the filth from the streets. The stone buildings encroached on the narrow sidewalk. Many of the walls were painted in bright reds and yellows.

"When I reached an intersection, I paused to see if my bronze goddess would direct me. The mountain towered behind me and the water flowed away from me. There were large stepping stones crossing the street leaving enough room for the wheels of a cart to pass between them.

"The goddess appeared to be looking left so that was the way I headed. I passed two more side streets, but I stayed with my direction. I was looking at my statue, when I slipped on the wet stones..."

Something lands on the page, making me jump. The eraser has the name 'Tayla' inked onto the sides. I glance up to see Bianca and Tayla struggling over Tayla's pink pencil case. Bianca grabs for another item to throw, while Tayla tries to protect the contents.

While I was reading, I was lost in the story. Now I am thrust back into the present where there are no interested classmates. Tears form in my eyes and I give up reading my story. I hurry back to my seat and put my head down so no one can see my face.

"Lucy, we'd like to hear the rest of your story," Ms Miller says.

I shake my hung head and refuse to look up. A single tear falls onto my desk.

"Would anyone like to guess where or when Lucy was in her story?" Ms Miller asks the class.

"Loser land," someone coughs into their hand.

"La-a, you can join the boys in lunchtime detention," Ms Miller replies.

"What did I do?" La-a exclaims.

Ms Miller ignores her and moves on to the next topic.

Kindness

Pompeii 79 AD

My head pounded like a rock band had taken up residence in my skull. My hands tallied the extent of my injuries, finding bruising and my dress missing. My underwear was damp under the blanket covering me.

"I think she's awake." A girl's voice pierced my throbbing skull, drowning out the rain drumming on the roof.

I forced my eyes open to find myself lying on a bed in a shadowy room. Two people leaned over me, but the only one I saw was Will. I didn't know where I was in time, but it didn't matter. Will was there beside me.

He was taller and broader in the shoulders than last time we met. His cave boy dreadlocks had been replaced by a short neat trim, but his face was the same, if not slightly older. The pain and noise faded away until all I could hear was my pounding heart.

"Are you alright?" Will asked. Butterflies fluttered in my stomach as though something amazing might happen if I could hold onto the moment.

"Of course she is not alright, Villius. She hit her head," the girl said. My world spun.

"Do you not have somewhere else to be, Elisia?" Will asked.

"No," she replied.

"Will," I said. The room began to fade away. I reached out to grab his hand so I didn't slip away for good.

Time passed. When I woke again, Will was beside me, still holding my hand. Eventually my nausea passed and I heard voices by the door.

"We don't know where she's come from," said a man.

"She must belong to someone," a woman replied.

"Can we keep her?" Elisia asked. "She can have Aelia's bed."

I focused on Will's face in the dim room, his head cocked to one side listening to the conversation outside.

"Will they let me stay? I don't have anywhere else to go," I whispered. Will squeezed my hand.

When I next opened my eyes, Elisia sat on the edge of the bed swinging her feet. Her face was familiar. I blinked several times before I could convince myself she was Lee whose life I saved in Africa. She was not around the last time I met Will.

47

"You should put her in the shrine with the other Gods." Elisia pointed to my statue once she noticed I was awake.

I sat up slowly and swung my legs to the floor, careful to avoid kicking the girl studying me. The room spun for a few moments before settling in place. Daylight spilled through the doorway, illuminating the shadowy paintings on the walls. They either depicted the feats of Hercules, or I'd hit my head harder than I thought.

"Sure," I told Elisia.

She bounded to her feet and tossed me the tunic lying across the end of the bed, before hovering at the door impatiently. I pulled the cloth over my head and tied it at my shoulders like hers. When I stood, it reached the floor. Elisia's dress ended at her knees.

Outside the room, I blinked in the brightness of the ceilingless courtyard dominating the centre of the house. The day was already warm, although by the angle of light hitting the tiled floor, it was still morning. Elisia tugged on my arm and I followed her through to the front of the house where the timber doors were propped open, letting the breeze blow through.

Inside the entrance, an assortment of gods perched on the ledge surrounding a dish in which to burn offerings. I added my statue to the collection. My stomach rumbled reminding me I hadn't eaten for some time.

"You must be hungry. Villius says I'm always hungry." Elisia skipped back through the atrium towards the back of the house.

"Where is your brother?" I followed behind her.

"He's at the bakery with Father and Aelia's husband." She turned and smiled at me. "He didn't want to leave today in case you woke up."

I came to a standstill as Elisia skipped on unaware of my blushing face. I hurried after her trying to keep the silly grin from my face.

Elisia came to a halt in a peaceful indoor garden of herbs, flowers, and espaliered fruit trees surrounded by pillars, and sat down on the stone bench. The back wall was painted with a stunning display of wild animals. The whole house was decorated in bright art, emphasising their fascination with the gods and myths. I studied it all trying to place myself in a time or place.

A servant arrived with our midday meal which we ate where we were. When we had finished, Elisia introduced me to the family living in the house. As well as Will, or Villius as he was known there, Elisia and their parents, there was an extended family of aunts, uncles, cousins, slaves and ex-slaves. The latter of the group lived in the rooms upstairs.

Come Saturn's day, we walked to the market in the forum as a family. Will, making the most of his time off work, ruffled his sister's hair and teased her about what she might purchase from the vendors. Elisia and Mother paused to admire some fabric, while Will inspected the wares of the grain suppliers. My chest tightened to see him acting like an adult. I didn't want him to leave me behind while I wasn't here.

The girls at the market smiled and exchanged banter with Will. I hung back from the world. Will saw me standing alone in the busy market. He walked over and took my hand.

"Why so shy? I thought we were friends." He grinned at me and suddenly even the sun shone brighter. I walked with him, my hand in his and my heart beat faster. I wished I knew how to stay in this world forever.

A girl begged in the marketplace, invisible to most people. I saw a reflection of myself in her eyes. I couldn't help her. I didn't even know how to help myself when I was alone. Will paused when he noticed her. A smile spread across his face as he released my hand and walked towards her.

"Good morning to you, Livia," Will greeted her. He offered her one of the figs we'd purchased that morning. She took it from him and smiled as though he was an angel come to Earth solely for her.

"The gods bless you, Master Villius," she replied. Will loitered for a few minutes to exchange pleasantries with the girl before we moved on.

"Is she your girlfriend?" I asked when we were out of earshot. I glanced back at the girl eating her fruit.

"No, why would you think that?"

"You were very friendly with her."

Will stopped walking and turned to look at me. I dragged my eyes away from the girl who captured his attention.

"Livia has nothing. Sometimes a smile is all that is needed to change a person's day and it cost me nothing to give."

"I don't think I have any to spare," I said.

"The more happiness you put out into the world, the more will find its way back to you. If I can make one person's day better because of my actions, it's been a good day for everyone," Will said.

We collected the last of our shopping and Will sent the house slaves to take the items home. He took me the long way back so I could see some of his favourite places in the town.

Visible cracks ran through several building walls, some with signs of repair. Will told me of a great ground tremor that occurred a year or two before he was born. It did much damage to their town and some buildings had still not been fully restored.

"Why are you sad, Lucy?" Will paused to ask me. I frowned. The dilapidated buildings seeped a depression that affected me more than I realised. They stood as a warning, reminding me nothing lasted forever. I was only visiting.

"Sometimes I forget how to smile," I said.

Will stepped towards me until I was staring into his deep brown eyes. The butterflies returned to my stomach. His expression was serious as he reached up to my face. He placed his thumbs on either side

51

of my mouth and lifted then he leaned in to whisper in my ear.

"It's quite simple. First you lift the corners of your mouth and then imagine a tiny spider wearing a water droplet as a hat."

I laughed as his breath tickled my ear. He pulled away, but took hold of my hand as we continued walking. My smile remained as I glanced over at him.

There was still a concern about the damaged buildings. I ran through everything I knew about earthquakes and kept an eye out for open spaces that would be safe if another big one occurred. I was satisfied I could protect Will and his family. I saw no other dangers that might threaten my friend.

Elisia insisted Will take the both of us to see a play at the amphitheatre. It was often used for the gladiator and wild animal fighting, but Mother said Elisia was too young to watch such bloody sports. I was glad we were not going to see that. Watching someone fight a lion would only remind me of the day I lost Wu.

I sat between Will and Elisia on the stone benches with a view of the performers, as well as the elite members of this town sitting below us. My thigh brushed Will's as he leaned into me to explain what was happening on the stage. Elisia grabbed my arm in excitement.

I took a deep breath and closed my eyes for a moment to hold the image in my mind. I wanted to remember every detail so I could draw it in the future. For the moment I was completely in the present as I was swept up in the performance and Will's attentiveness.

He took my hand as we walked back to the house. I held Elisia's with my other. They were warm in mine. When Will leaned in to ask me what I thought of the performance, his breath tickled my ear in a way that made my stomach do back flips.

I crawled into the bed I shared with Elisia and lay awake committing the evening to memory. When I finally fell asleep, it was with the image of Will's eyes and story repeating in my mind.

I woke abruptly in the early hours of the morning to the bed shaking. Elisia whimpered in the darkness beside me. I reached out to touch the wall and felt the movement beneath my fingers. Something toppled from a shelf and smashed into the ground.

I threw the blanket off and grabbed Elisia. We ran into the atrium where other members of the family joined us. My eyes searched frantically for Will and found him standing not far from us. I hugged Elisia who grasped me like she was never going to let go. I wanted to leave the house, but that would mean passing under shaking ceilings. I stared up into the starry sky above us and whispered to myself that we were safe here. Nothing could fall on us.

The tremor stopped as suddenly as it began. Will grinned and hugged us when he saw my terrified face and his sister still clinging to me. The adults laughed off the situation and told stories of the massive quake that did so much damage only seventeen years earlier. This one was nothing to worry about.

My heart rate refused to slow and I was sure my time in Will's world was drawing to an end. The adults examined the damage from smashed pottery and glass as well as a large crack in one wall. One of the slaves was tasked with commissioning a decorator to repair the damage in the morning.

The family returned to their rooms. I crawled cautiously into bed, but I couldn't sleep. I tossed and turned several times before getting up again.

I sat on the stone bench by the well under the night sky and studied the house surrounding me. Elisia crept out to join me. She lay down placing her head in my lap. I stroked her hair until she drifted off to sleep. I eventually nodded off where I sat.

By morning, my neck and behind ached from dozing on the bench. The crack in the wall taunted me and the faulty water flow through the pipes to the house added to the discomfort of the day.

Will suggested we take a trip to see the countryside to take my mind off the previous night's dramas. As nothing could fall on you in an earthquake if you were standing out in the open, I agreed to the outing.

A slave packed us a lunch of bread, cheese and fruits while Will hitched two mules to the family's cart and took the driver's seat. I sat in the cart and listened to the wheels rolling over the black cobblestone road as we headed out of the Vesuvius

Gate. My shoulders relaxed as we rolled further from the town.

Will's family had land out this way looked after by tenants, producing a mixture of grains, winemaking grapes, and fruit trees including olives for oil. The chickens and pigs provided fertiliser and meat.

Much of the town's food supplies came from the farms that crept up the sides of the mountain, taking advantage of the rich soil. Vesuvius was only five miles from the town and we left the mules to graze at the base while we hiked on foot.

We followed human and animal tracks leading to the summit. When we stopped for lunch, Will told me how Spartacus and his rebel slaves camped on this mountain nearly one and a half centuries ago. I glanced nervously over my shoulder, but no gladiators appeared.

My legs ached by the time we reached the peak of the mountain. I stopped to catch my breath and looked out over the countryside to our little town below. Several roads led from it to other exotic locations. To the south of the town lay the ocean. I turned around and looked at the top of the mountain Vesuvius.

If anyone was ever to ask me what a panic attack felt like, I would describe that moment to them. The mountain had no peak. What I'd seen as I climbed was the ridge around a crater at the top of Vesuvius.

My knees gave way as I dropped to all fours and peered over the edge. I was light headed. Nothing grew from the floor of the stony grey crater. Steam rose in pockets from the cracked floor. I stared in disbelief. An active volcano was the cause of the earthquakes.

"We need to get down from here," I stammered. I backed away and straightened up unable to drag my eyes away.

"We only just got here," Will said.

"It's not safe." My heart tried to escape my chest. I tugged on his hand.

"I've been up here on many occasions to help round up stray animals. It's perfectly safe."

I shook my head. Fear had stolen my words. I could only hope that if I left, he would follow. I turned and ran down the mountain putting as much distance between me and the volcano as possible.

"Lucia!"

His footsteps pounded behind me. I didn't look back, picking up speed as I tore down the mountain with Will on my heels.

"Slow down! You'll hurt yourself," Will called. I couldn't stop, I was terrified if we stayed there we would die.

Will caught up with me where we left the mules to graze. I bent over double with my hands on my hips, gasping for air and hoping my stomach would not revolt. He reached out and touched my arm. I straightened, glancing behind us. I didn't know if we had minutes or months before the eruption.

"The mountain has stood there for as long as time and the town has sat safely at its base for more generations than I can count," Will said.

I'd made a mistake studying the past to find Will. I should have been looking into his future so I knew how to protect him. Right now, I was sure that volcano was not as passive as Will believed.

The whole journey back to town, I kept looking over my shoulder expecting a Dante's peak style eruption, but Vesuvius remained suspiciously silent. We passed several workers digging up the town's water pipes, the stoppage affecting much of the town.

As we neared the house, we passed the laden cart of a family leaving town. The children in the back clutched each other as the adults stared ahead. Their departure did nothing to calm my own fears.

At the house I suggested we also leave, but Will's parents told me the same thing as Will. There was no danger from the mountain. The town had been there a long time. If we left, who would bake the bread for our customers?

Will went back to work at the bakery the following day. He was needed even more now the water had to be fetched from the town's water pumps.

Mother took Elisia and me to the baths and on the way we passed crowds queuing to fill their containers. A scuffle broke out over a spilled bucket and Mother hurried us away.

At the baths, only the women's section was undamaged and operating. A small tremor occurred while we were there, sending my pulse into overdrive. There were a few nervous giggles from the ladies once it passed, but no one rushed to leave as I wanted to.

"See, the shakes are getting less. They will be gone soon," Mother assured us. I tried to believe her, but in my head I knew it wasn't true. A clock hung over my shoulder, counting down the days until I left this world.

That night I dreamed about an archaeological dig I'd read about in an old Roman town called Pompeii preserved under layers of ash from a nearby volcano. Artists' impressions of the fiery eruption, and photos of tortured plaster casts of residents made from the hollows under the ash, plagued my sleep.

My eyes snapped open in the dark room. The house was still, nothing trembled except for my hands. Elisia breathed evenly beside me. I climbed out of bed and paced the floors outside the room. Something brushed my bare leg, but it was only the household dog pressing against me with his tail between his legs.

Will found me sitting on the stone bench by the garden sometime after dawn. "You're up early," he remarked.

"Is this Pompeii?" I held my hands still in my lap. The dog whimpered.

"The name of the town bothers you? Perhaps a visit to see my sister, Aelia, will improve your mood. Her husband is thinking of visiting family in Nuceria while the decorator repairs the damage to their house."

"That's a great idea. We should all go. I've always wanted to see Nuceria." I'd never heard of Nuceria.

"We were only planning on going to their house before they depart," Will said.

"Oh," I replied. "I'm really not feeling well. I think I should stay here and lie down."

I stood without looking at him and headed back into my room. I lay in the dimness and waited until the family left. For a moment I swore the house vibrated again, but it was only Elisia running back in to check on me. I sent her off with the others. Lying on the bed, I took deep breath to calm my nerves.

It didn't work. I swung my feet to the floor and went looking for the ex-slave in charge of running the house. I found him in the kitchen discussing supplies with the cook. I hovered for a few moments before clearing my throat. The adults turned to face me.

"Can we get you something, Lucia?"

"We need to leave," I said.

"Villius mentioned you wanted to stay. They have only just left; we should be able to catch them up."

"No, we need to leave Pompeii. Today. Before the mountain erupts and we all die."

"Vesuvius has stood there as long as time. It's not going anywhere and neither are we without the master's say so."

"Look at the dog." He whimpered in a corner next to an empty sack. He and I both knew something wasn't right. "The earthquakes, the water has almost stopped at the wells, the gods are sending us signs. We have to leave before it's too late."

"What does a young girl like you know about the gods? The master is not worried." His eyes shifted uncertainly to the poor creature on the floor.

I was only thirteen years old, always overlooked and ignored. Will and Elisia's lives depended on me. I stood as tall as I could and opened my eyes wide. I'd been told many times I had 'witch' eyes when I drew attention to them. I marched over to the empty sack and pulled it from under the poor dog. I turned my back on the adults and stalked to the front of the house.

At the shrine I heaped the gods into my sack. I kept my statue of Fortuna in my hand. I turned to find the housekeeper standing behind me with a look of alarm on his face. I waved my god in his face.

"Fortuna has sent me here to save this family. You will do as I say or we will all die." There was a steely conviction to my voice. I was no longer Lucy. I was an actor playing a part to save my family from danger.

For a moment he did nothing then he turned and called the slaves into action. I went to the kitchen for some grain. I threw a small handful into the sack and prayed to any god that might be listening to keep Will and his family safe.

The earthquake hit as the family returned home. The building shook, much harder than any time

60

before. Items smashed to the floor and more large cracks spread through the walls. We ran into the street to avoid being crushed. When the tremor finally stopped, I was surprised the houses were still standing. I glanced at silent Vesuvius.

"We need to leave right now," I announced. I looked at the ex-slave man. He nodded and left to hitch up the mules.

"The worst is over. The shakes always stop," Mother insisted.

"I'm leaving Pompeii and taking the gods with me. We can return in a day or two, but we need to leave now. I was sent here to keep you safe." I would say whatever I had to if it would save them.

"We will leave in the morning after we've had time to plan," Mother conceded.

"We're already packed," I said. My nerves couldn't handle anymore waiting.

Will's mother fluffed around checking bedrooms and the kitchen making sure I hadn't forgotten anything. Someone tied up the dog to guard the house in our absence. When no one was looking, I released him and shoved him outside. I hoped he could survive.

We finally rolled away from our house. The servants, Will, and his father walked beside the cart as we didn't have much room inside it. We were halfway through the town when I saw Livia hobbling along the sidewalk with the aid of a stick.

"Will, she won't make it out the town," I said.

Will looked to where I'd seen Livia. He strode over to the beggar girl and spoke to her for a few moments. She shook her head and Will pointed to me and then the mountain. Finally, she allowed Will to help her towards us. I left my seat in the cart so she could travel with us. I gave her a smile as she settled in. She returned the gesture.

As soon as she was in, I urged the group to start moving again. I had to hurry to keep pace with the cart. My legs were not as long as the men's. We reached the eastern gate of Pompeii as Vesuvius finally erupted. Ash shot miles into the air above us. Everyone stopped to look.

"Go. Keep moving," I yelled, glancing behind us. In my mind I saw the tortured human shells that would be excavated from under a torrent of ash by archaeologists in the future.

I darted forward and slapped the closest mule on the behind. He bolted and the cart jolted forward at a much faster pace. Livia squealed and gripped the side of the cart. Her walking stick fell to the ground, but no one stopped for it. Will grabbed my hand and I hitched up my skirt with the other. We ran after the cart as fast as my legs would allow.

The ash and pumice rained down on us as we thundered along the road away from our town. The large pieces stung as they hit our skin. If we survived we would have bruises to show for our escape. When we could no longer breathe the contaminated air, we slowed to a walk and covered our mouths with our clothing.

We lost sight of the cart in the thick ash. It required all our concentration to keep to the road. I could no longer see Will, although he never let go of my hand. We called out to the others to keep our group together.

After a few hours, they wanted to stop to rest, but I made them keep going. I wasn't sure how far the lava would travel and we moved slowly. As evening fell, we stumbled across the cart waiting for us. Mother had been leading the mules along the shadowy road.

That night we rested on the side of the road. I curled up between Will and Elisia with our heads under the cart to keep the worst of the ash off us, but I struggled to sleep. The night was punctuated by the coughs of my companions. I was afraid if I slept, I would lose my grip on this world. I held onto Will's hand as he did the first time we met to keep me from disappearing.

We woke early, shook the layer of ash from our bodies and had a quick bite to eat in the gloomy morning before continuing away from Pompeii. Everything was gritty and tasted of ash. I had no idea how many people made it out of the town. There had been no time to warn them even if they were likely to believe me. Much of the ash had settled making it easier to see our way.

The secondary eruption took us all by surprise. In the distance, Vesuvius appeared on fire as it spewed its remaining contents into the atmosphere. We watched as a surge of lava and gas from the mountain consumed our town.

We were out of its deadly range although the ash blackened the sky and made us choke. Will was safe for another lifetime, which meant my role in this life was over. I tried to hang on as long as I could.

In the end, I died from a snake bite. It was sudden and unexpected. I was gone within mere hours. The last thing I remembered was looking up into Will's mournful brown eyes as Elisia and Livia tried to comfort him.

I woke up in a hospital bed in the present with two small red marks on my ankle and a bad cough.

Humiliation

I get my history assignment back with a big red 'A' scrawled across the top, followed by 'excellent research Lucy' and a smiley face. I leave the class with a smile on my face, like the one I shared with Livia.

"You look happy," a boy in front of me announces. Shaun, one of the good-looking boys who sits at the back of my history class, is friends with James.

The smile slips from my face as quickly as it appeared. People don't talk to me unless they have something mean to say. I do what I do best, nothing. He frowns at my silence before trying again.

"Get a good mark in history?" Shaun asks.

"Yeah," I stammer.

"Cool story you were reading the other day," he says. I stare at him until I realise he is expecting a response.

"Thanks," I mutter studying the floor.

"See you around," he says and leaves me standing in the hall blushing. I have no idea what just happened. Maybe he thinks I'm someone else.

I see Shaun again at lunch time. He waves in my direction. I glance over my shoulder, but there is no one behind me. He has walked away before I can convince myself he was waving at me.

I spend the rest of lunch in the library, but no matter how many times I read the same sentence in my history book, I have no idea what it says. I give up and stare into space until the bell rings. There are two more classes to get through before I can go home. Luckily one of them is art.

The teacher hands back everyone's last assignment depicting friendship. Neither Tayla nor I get ours back. I fidget in my seat imagining my drawing has been lost, or the teacher didn't like it and has given it a bad mark.

"I've kept two pictures back to show the standard I expect from this class." She holds up a photograph of two smiling young girls sitting on swings in a playground holding hands. The teacher discusses what she likes from the image before handing it to a beaming Tayla. Several students congratulate her on the work.

Mine is held up next. I have mixed emotions about it. I tried to recreate the image of Wu's and my hands on the cave wall. It worked out well except both hands are mine. No matter how much I imagine the second hand is Wu's, I know it is not. None of the students say anything to me like they

66

did for Tayla. We move on to the next topic; thinking outside the box.

"Someone tell me their favourite flower," the teacher says.

"Rose," Kate, a tall girl who plays on the school basketball team, calls out.

"Boring cliché, be creative. I want you to think of something different. Lucy, what's your favourite flower? If you say rose you can leave my classroom right now," the teacher jokes.

"Boronias," I say.

"Why?"

"I love the smell of them," I reply.

"Where are you standing as you smell them?"

There's a house in my street with a beautifully kept garden. When the boronias are in bloom, I smell them as I pass. Sometimes I stand on the pavement with my eyes closed and breath in the scent. When I grow up, I want to live in a house with boronias in the yard.

"Outside my neighbour's house," I reply.

"Excellent. Hold onto the image the flower represents, not just the flower itself. So if I give you an assignment on an animal, I don't want boring horses, cats or dogs. I want the equivalent of Lucy's boronias in her neighbour's garden."

Tayla watches me. I focus on the class and count the minutes until home time.

When I arrive home, Mum is already there. An eye-watering smell rises from the bowls of chopped onions placed around the room. She looks off-colour as she drinks lemon and honey tea. I wrinkle my nose and raise my eyebrows.

"Onions absorb bacteria from the air. Apparently it worked for the Plague." Mum blows into a tissue.

"How did you catch the Plague?" I ask.

"The flu's been going around at work and I need to get better by tomorrow night." She appears to be blushing, but it's difficult to tell as she is already a funny colour.

"What's special about tomorrow?" I lean on the door-frame and hitch my school bag higher up my shoulder. We haven't made any plans.

"I've been asked on a date."

My mouth drops open to say something, but I have no words. My father walked out on her before I was born and as far as I'm aware, she hasn't dated anyone since. When she doesn't get a response, she continues self-consciously.

"His name's Frank. He comes into work sometimes and we get to talking. Yesterday he asked me out." She is definitely blushing now.

It has only even been the two of us before. The thought of my mum dating makes me feel – lonely, reminding me no one wants my company.

"I've got homework to do." I walk away.

In my room, I sit on the old chair at my second hand desk and pull out my tattered text books. I open the cover of one and then slam it shut again. I shove the books to one side and open my sketchbook. That evening I add another sketch of Will to my book.

I devote the next few weeks to counting the hours until my sixteenth birthday. There will be no party or birthday wishes from friends. There may be a small present from my mum, but what I am looking forward to is seeing Will. A year is a long time to wait for something good to happen in your life.

Writing about Pompeii made me miss him and his family more. Every year drags on longer than the last. As time draws near, my mind is filled with memories of Will's warm brown eyes and cheeky smile that for some reason he regularly directs at me. I spend more time reading, trying to guess where or when he might be living this time. Sometimes uncertainty grips me and I worry he might not be there this year. Would he move on without me?

My thoughts of Will are now interrupted by Shaun. He doesn't have Will's beautiful smile or passion for life, but like Will, he is fit. The girls at school talk about how attractive he is and he's good at sport.

Shaun waves when he sees me and I've even given a little wave in return, although I still check behind me before I do. He knows my name and uses it when he greets me, even when his friends are nearby.

We have a new assignment for history class where we need to work in pairs. Shaun offers to be my partner, as I'm good at history.

Tayla glares at us as Shaun moves to sit next to me, surprising me with her animosity. Although she hangs out with La-a, Jennypha and Bianca, she has never directly been mean to me. She's always just there when the others are.

We spend the remainder of the class with me discussing the project and Shaun watching me and interrupting occasionally. When the bell rings, he suggests we meet at his house later in the week to finish it off. I agree. I've never been invited to someone's house before, except for Will's, but that doesn't count.

As I cross the football field at the end of the day, something slips from the bag of a dark haired girl in front of me. I stoop to pick up the MP3 player and its headphones from the grass.

"Hey! You dropped this," I call out, jogging after her.

She turns her head at the sound of my voice. For a moment I think she must not go to our school. She is dressed completely in black with eye makeup to match. I can't tell what her natural hair colour is, but the satchel bag slung over her shoulder gapes open revealing the same text books I'd have if Mum could afford them.

"Well, that confirms it. It's clearly not worth stealing," she says, taking it from my outstretched hand.

"I wouldn't know. I don't own one," I say.

"Do you not live on this planet? How do you listen to music?"

"Mum has a couple of CDs," I say.

"That is incredibly sad. Thanks anyway, Girl From School." She turns away.

"I'm Lucy," I call after her.

"Emma." She waves one hand in the air and continues on her way. I sigh. I've spoken to two people today that aren't teachers. I guess that makes it a good day.

I arrive home, parking my old push bike in its usual place at the back of the house. As soon as I walk in the back door, I hear laughter. I don't remember the last time Mum laughed. She doesn't laugh with me anymore no matter how hard I try. I walk cautiously towards the sound coming from the living room. I stop in the doorway. Mum sits on the couch with a man. Her legs are over his lap and his hands are under her shirt. Mum jumps, pulling away when she sees me. She clears her throat.

"Lucy, I didn't hear you come in."

I don't say anything. His cologne is overpowering from across the room. I'm not sure how Mum is able to breathe that close to the source. He has a stupid looking moustache and is staring at Mum's chest.

"This is my friend, Frank. Frank, my daughter Lucy," Mum attempts the introduction.

I don't move from the doorway. Frank looks me up and down briefly before returning his attention to Mum. He places his hand on her leg, but she covers it, stopping it moving higher.

"Hello, Lucy," he says, his eyes on Mum.

"I've got homework to do." I don't wait for either of them to respond. I escape to my room and lock the door, but I can't concentrate on study. I stand with my ear pressed against the door waiting to hear him leave so I can have my space back.

I catch up with Shaun after school several days later. When I don't laugh at his joke, he asks what's on my mind. I mention meeting Mum's creepy new boyfriend. Shaun laughs and tells me that must suck.

I wish I could talk to Will right now. He would make me laugh and forget about my troubles. I glance at the time on Shaun's bulky sports watch. I don't have to wait much longer. Tomorrow is my birthday, I just need to keep it together for another night and day.

All the more reason to get this assignment done, I never know how long I will be gone. I don't want to mess up my history mark by not finishing an assignment.

We head up to Shaun's room and he shuts the door behind us. His parents won't be home until later, but he has a younger brother who he says is really annoying. There is only one chair by the computer, so I sit awkwardly on the end of his unmade bed and study the posters of footballers blu-tacked to the walls.

I try to imagine what it would be like to have an actual boyfriend and be sitting with him in an empty house. The room has a funny smell like a dirty sock may be hiding somewhere, mixed in with large amounts of spray-on deodorant, shattering my fantasy. Will is neat and clean.

Shaun starts the computer, where he has already begun with what we discussed in class. I let out the anxious breath I was holding. He is not going to mess up the assignment. We continue where we left off.

I have the text book open across my knees and a reference book beside me while Shaun types. I relax as we fly through the project. A sensation a bit like fitting in begins to creep through me. I'm smart, someone popular wants to be my assignment partner, and when I go back to school, people will see I'm no longer a loser.

Shaun calls a break and goes to the kitchen to get us both Cokes. The room is warm, so I remove my jumper. When Shaun returns, he sits beside me and passes the drink. His thigh touches mine. I take a sip and wonder where I should be looking. There's a calendar picture of semi-nude woman reclined across a car on his wall. I glance away.

"You're pretty smart, you know," he tells me. I blush and stay silent. I have another sip of my drink for lack of any better response.

Shaun takes my half-finished drink and puts it with his on the desk, running his fingers over the keyboard before returning to sit next to me. He reaches up and brushes a strand of hair from my face then he leans in and kisses me.

It's slobbery and his mouth covers the whole of mine like he is trying to swallow my face. It's not at all like the perfect kisses in movies. I imagine I hear a hushed snort of laughter, but I'm distracted by Shaun unclipping my bra through my shirt.

I place my hands awkwardly on the bed behind me, but I'm not sure if pulling away will make me look silly and naïve. This is the first time a boy has shown interest in me and I don't want to mess it up. I want him to like me. I need a friend on my side to get through school. Shaun pulls my bra straps out from my shirt and down my arms.

I put my hand to my chest to hold my bra in place, but he just pushes it aside forcefully and reaches up under my top to claim his prize. He pulls away, whoops and holds it above his head.

Now I definitely can hear laughter. It comes from the computer where Shaun has a webcam. He pushes a button on the keyboard and a new screen appears. I can see La-a, Jennypha, Bianca, and several boys from school, all laughing hysterically.

I've been set up. Shaun never really liked me. He doesn't think I'm smart or worthy of being his friend. He and his mates just wanted to humiliate me. There is a hollowness inside of me.

I try to grab my bra from Shaun, but he is taller than me and holds it above his head. I'm not going to make a further fool of myself by trying to get it back. I grab my school bag off the floor and flee his house. A steady stream of tears flow down my cheeks by the time I reach my bike and start pedalling home. I ride like I am fleeing Pompeii.

I throw my bike down at the back of my house, race up the steps and fumble for my house key. I don't feel safe until I am inside with the door locked behind me. I hide in my room trying to decide how to get out of school the next day. Everyone will be laughing at me. On the other hand, if I don't go tomorrow, the teasing will be worse when I do.

I'm so full of nervous energy I don't eat dinner and can barely sleep. I pace my bedroom floor until my legs tire. I curl up in a ball on my bed clutching Wu the Lion until he becomes damp with tears. Mum gets back late from her shift work and I listen to her getting ready for bed. If I don't go to school in the morning, I will have to tell her what's wrong.

By the time my alarm finally rings in the morning, I actually do feel sick. I wish I had some sleeping pills so I can skip today, jump straight to the moment I can see Will.

I crawl out of bed, get dressed and ride to school. I am determined to ignore the bullies as Mum told me to do in Primary School. It didn't work back then, but I'm older now and I can always hide out in the sick bay if the day gets too hard.

The pointing and laughing starts as soon as I park my bike. I may be becoming paranoid, but even the students I'm sure don't know me, are in on my humiliation. I try to avoid everyone and move from class to class throughout the day as quickly as possible. I can feel people whispering behind me and La-a makes kissing noises as I pass. This is not how I imagined spending my sixteenth birthday.

"Loser," a dark-haired girl states as she passes me in the corridor. I look up to see Emma, the girl who dropped her MP3 player on the oval, wearing the same dark makeup and complete disregard for the school uniform. Tears threaten to spill over the comment. I've never done anything to her.

Emma walks past without looking at me. She maintains her look of contempt, but it's not directed at me. I glance over my shoulder to see La-a creeping up behind me. She pauses at Emma's look. I bolt while she is busy looking insulted.

Emma's dismissal of La-a helps me keep going until I get to sport. I hold on to the thought that not everyone worships my enemy as I walk into the stadium. No one has gone to change into their sports uniform yet. They stand in a loose circle, waiting for me to arrive. I hesitate as I approach them.

I wipe my sweaty palms on my trousers as I assess if it is safe to enter the change rooms. My eyes scan the stadium and come to rest on the basketball hoop. My stolen bra dangles from it. My class erupts into laughter at my horrified expression. I turn and run from the room. I can't stay at school any longer. I have to get away.

I grab my bike and pedal out to a place I have always found calming. It's a steep ride to reach the lookout at the cliffs. Mum and I came here once when we first moved to this town. It was drizzling so we had the place to ourselves. I felt like we were the only two people in the world. We stood in the rain as though it could wash away all our troubles. Afterwards we drove back into town and Mum bought us both hot chocolates.

I rest my bike against the railing a short distance from the car park and climb over the protective barrier. The cliff edge is unstable in places so I tread carefully. A fall from here would be fatal. I sit down on the protruding rock ledge out of sight of the viewing platform above me and look out over the valley below. The breeze ruffles my hair as I breathe in the smell of approaching rain.

A car pulls up, its tyres crunching over the loose gravel of the turning bay, but the people cannot see me. Sitting here I'm completely free from the world that doesn't care about me. I lay back on my rock absorbing the fading warmth from the day, close my eyes and let it rain down on me. The cold reminds me I am alive.

The rain has eased off by the time I start the ride home. I shiver as my wet uniform sticks to my body making pedalling difficult. I try to hold onto the feeling of sitting on the edge of the cliff as I head back into the real world.

A small neatly wrapped present sits on the kitchen table. Next to it is a note wishing me a happy birthday and letting me know Mum will be back late tonight.

"Happy birthday to me," I say the words out loud because no one else is here to say them.

I leave the gift untouched, peel off my wet clothes on my way to the bathroom and run a hot shower. I wash my hair and shave my legs. When I am done, I dry off and dress for bed. I find myself laughing about dressing up to go to bed. The sound echoes in the empty house. It is still early, but I don't care. I don't want to wait any longer. I lie on my bed with my eyes closed, willing sleep to find me. Waiting for Will.

Faith

Britain 1348-9

I wake up in a ditch by the side of a dirt road. It may sound strange, but lying there in a gully in the countryside, I feel safe. I have left my reality and am once again in Will's, I hope. The stress seeps from my body as I relax for the first time in a year. I'm nearly home.

Luckily it hasn't rained recently so I can brush the dirt from my long skirt as I stand. The day is still early, but it feels like it will warm up later. I have two directions I can take along the empty road. As I try to guess which direction will take me towards Will, a plaintive meowing reaches my ears.

I step carefully over the uneven ground until I reach the hessian sack, nudging it gently over until I can find the knotted string to untie and open the bag carefully. The two kittens are small enough for me to retrieve from their prison without fear of being ripped to shreds. I slip the siblings inside my coarsely woven shirt. Their claws scratch me at first, but they relax in the darkness of my clothing.

I continue my journey in the same direction, walking slowly to avoid twisting an ankle in the cart ruts or treading in animal manure on the road. I wrap one arm around my middle so my new friends don't fall out.

I'm studying the scattered farmhouses when I notice a young girl sitting on the ground with her back against a sign post. As I get closer, Will's sister's face becomes clearer. This is only the third time I've met her, the first time as young Lee in Africa, the last being in Pompeii. I stop in front of her.

"Hello," I say.

"I dreamed of you. I came to meet you, but I twisted my ankle." She points to the injury. "I'm Elizabeth."

"Lucy," I say. "Do you need me to carry you?" She is still small for her ten years of age. At her nod, I kneel down so she can climb onto my back. I have to re-arrange the kittens so they don't get squashed, but eventually I can stand with everyone on board.

"Are you a witch?" Elizabeth asks when she catches a glimpse of the animals.

"No, I found them on the side of the road," I reply.

"Just like I found you," she states.

The journey is hard going carrying Elizabeth and the kittens. The buildings become denser as we reach the village. They're made of a variety of materials in varying conditions with thatched roofs. There are no people around that I can immediately see.

My footsteps falter. What if Elizabeth is the only one to meet me in this life? I am fond of the girl, but I don't want to be here if Will is not. I can't wait another whole year to see if I meet him.

"Where is everyone?" I ask.

"It's Sunday. William, Archer, and Mother are at church with the rest of the village. I snuck out when no one was looking so I could find you. God will forgive me because He was the one who sent you to us," she adds.

"Who's Archer?"

"My little brother. William is my older brother," Elizabeth explains.

She points me towards the small church in the centre of the village. I breathe a sigh of relief knowing I will see my friend soon. I let Elizabeth slide back onto her feet and put my arm around her slim body to help her hobble along. We quietly join the back of the congregation while I search the crowd for Will.

He sits next to his mother and a young boy near the middle of the room, focused fully on the priest. The crowd shifts nervously dragging my focus from the back of my friend's head to the words of the priest.

The man standing at the front of the church instructs the congregation to confess their sins and seek forgiveness from God so that they might be spared from the raging pestilence. At first I am unsure what he is talking about, but the more I listen to the frightened whispers in the room, it dawns on me. The Black Death is approaching.

I glance around the room, wondering who will still be alive in a year's time. There is nowhere to run. I don't know how to protect Will and his family from something like this. I have the sudden urge to walk out of the church and back down the road to the point where I arrived. If I can go back to lying in that ditch, I can reclaim the feeling of peace.

There is a feeling of terror among these people, an unpredictability in how they might act. They have heard rumours of the destruction occurring in Europe. Someone notices me, a stranger standing in the rear of the church and there is tension in their movements as they crowd towards me. I search for Will in the moving mass. He meets my eye. For a moment confusion crosses his features as though he recognises my face, but cannot place where we've met.

"What are you doing here?" a burly man demands. Elizabeth hobbles forward.

"She's here to visit my family," she says. The man glances at Will who approaches me and his sister.

"Do you know this girl, William?" Will looks at me uncertainly. There is a familiarity about me that confuses him as we have never met in his lifetime.

"Her name is Lucy," Elizabeth interrupts. "Remember I told you yesterday she was coming."

She stares at her brother as though she can force him to remember.

Surprise crosses Will's face. The crowd halts it surge forward, momentarily pacified by Elizabeth's statement. She takes my hand and leads me outside still leaning on me for support.

"I told William I dreamed of you," she whispers in my ear. Before I can question her, we are joined by Will, his mother, and a boy of around six.

"Who are you and why are you here?" Will's mother asks. For the first time in my dreams I'm concerned I will not be accepted into their family. I'm not sure what I'd do if they rejected me.

"I'm Lucy. I'm here to save William," I say.

"I don't need saving," Will says.

"But I always save you. That's why I'm here," my voice catches.

"God sent her," Elizabeth tells her mother. I don't believe in God. I only believe in Will.

"Where are you from, child?"

I open my mouth and realise I don't know how to tell them I live on an as-yet undiscovered continent on the other side of the world.

"How did you get here?" Will's mother tries a different question when I am unable to answer the first.

"I woke up here," I say. I'm afraid I will start crying. Elizabeth slips her hand into mine.

"Won't your family be missing you?"

"I don't have any family," I say. All I have is a mother who is too busy to wish me a happy birthday in person.

Will's mother considers this as she studies me. One of the kittens sticks its claws out making me wince. Mother frowns when she sees the kittens.

"Cats keep rats away and the rats will bring the plague," I say.

"What do you know about the pestilence?"

"I know it will be bad and you cannot run from it."

"Where are you planning on staying while in our village?"

"I always stay with you," I say. A tear trickles down my face. I dash it away with the back of my hand and stare at the ground.

"An extra hand would be helpful for the harvest," Will says. I look up at him gratefully. It has never taken so long for me to be accepted before. Mother ponders his suggestion for several long moments before giving a slight nod.

I walk with Will's family to their cottage. Elizabeth keeps hold of my hand. She is able to put more weight on her ankle, but still leans on me as though trying to demonstrate my importance in being here.

They live about half a mile from the little church in a cute little cottage situated on several acres of land. I release the two kittens into the house and they cautiously explore their surroundings. They hide if anyone tries to approach them.

Elizabeth shows me to her and Mother's tiny room to settle in. The two boys share a separate room. The next morning is Monday and time to start harvesting the summer crops. What we can't grow has to be bought, so we work hard to gather what we can. I enjoy the challenge. It gives me a purpose.

Will has taken on his deceased father's role with the help of Mother and me. Elizabeth and Archer look after the smaller animals and help where they can. By the time harvest is over, I am sure that I will never be able to move ever again, but when Will directs his smile at me I know I would do it all over again.

Every Sunday we walk to the church and pray to a God I have never known. He rules the lives of the fourteenth century population. The priest uses Him to keep the village from sin, but I am not convinced He likes me. He hasn't made my life an easy one.

"He only gives challenges in your life, He thinks you can handle," Will says when I share my thoughts. I'm afraid He has overestimated me.

Village life is simple, revolving around the various festivals that mark the changing harvest seasons. The only interruption is the approaching pestilence. Traders bring news along with goods for sale. Everyone hangs off their words eager for the latest updates and hopes for salvation.

The plague spreads throughout Europe seemingly carried by water. Millions of people die within days of falling sick. There is no cure. The people of our village believe God is angry and they must confess their sins to be spared. They hope it will not reach England.

My two kittens grow fast and one catches a little field mouse. While we wait for the inevitable, our family tries to continue to live as normal, but some nights, worry prevents sleep from claiming me.

The end of August 1348 brings news of the Black Death reaching our shores. From the traders' talk, it first appears in one of the sea ports. The villagers increase the time spent in church, so many people now attend services on Wednesdays as well.

Some punish themselves to appease God. They walk barefoot, some crawl on their hands and knees, and one lies on his belly on the dirt road while having his back whipped. They don't understand weakening themselves makes them more susceptible to the illness.

I'm relieved Will's family believe in leading a good life over punishing themselves. We still attended church twice a week though, which concerns me. Quarantine is our best tool in preventing death.

Many people travel the country selling items sure to protect us from death. I have never seen quite so much timber claiming to be from Christ's cross. Add this to statues and trinkets and some people are making a lot of money from the despair we are about to face.

Will's mother buys us all a small trinket for protection, but I am more interested in other items. I ask for onions and honey. What I really need are antibiotics, but they haven't been invented yet.

The months pass as the pestilence creeps across the countryside following the waterways. We receive news of the sickness in London. Stories spread of bodies left in the street while family and friends abandon the sick. The villagers are shocked and claim they will not act in such a manner. I know they will though. Avoidance is the only way to ensure survival.

The New Year passes with many of our neighbours packing up and leaving. It won't help them. We cannot run from this. We can only wait for it to come to us and hope to live. We continue the cycle of planting and reaping while we wait. Those who survive will need to eat.

I watch William working when he is not looking. He is fit and strong for a boy of almost seventeen years. I blush when he catches me watching, glancing away and pretending to be focused on whatever job we are toiling over. I smile as I work and for a moment I forget about death.

One evening when we are laughing and washing up after the day's work, Will leans in towards me. His face is so close; I think he is going to kiss me. He reaches out and brushes a stray strand of hair from my face making my heart pound. Elizabeth calls us in for dinner and Will pulls away. The moment is lost as we head inside.

The festivities leading up to Easter leave a lot to be desired. People are terrified of being in each other's company. One of our neighbours receives news of his brother's death in a nearby village. He talks excitedly to anyone who will listen about taking ownership of the little block of land that now belongs to him. We think nothing of it until he returns several days after his departure.

"I didn't expect to see you again," Will calls out to the man when he catches sight of him.

"Another relative has already claimed the land," the man replies, unwilling to meet our eyes. He glances around him as if expecting someone to sneak up on him any minute.

"If you still need help mending that fence, let me know," Will offers. I grab his arm to hold him back.

"The plague has arrived, hasn't it?" I ask the young man. He glances up startled.

"No?" His voice rises making it sound like a question. He lies. He has seen the Black Death and brought it to us.

"You need to go home immediately. Do not approach anyone. Stay there until you know you have not got the sickness," I tell him.

"I don't take orders from a girl," he mutters.

"I suggest you do as Lucy says, until you are sure you haven't come into contact with the pestilence," Will stands his ground. The man glances towards his dwelling.

I loosen my tense grip and Will flexes his arm to get the blood flowing. He will probably have finger prints on his skin when I release him. I wait for the man to shuffle off before dragging Will away.

The first case of the plague appears days after the Easter Sunday celebrations. It is rapidly followed by several more. My cats kill a rat and leave the dead carcass by the back door. I use a shovel to throw it on the fire, holding the tool over the flames for several extra moments. I wash my hands and arms thoroughly.

We stay in our house as much as we can when we are not working in the field, but news of the spreading disease still reaches us. We work even longer hours than usual as it is impossible to hire help. Every night I fall into bed sure I will never be able to move again.

The church bells toll regularly as the priest and sexton try to manage the dead. I avoid the village, not only to reduce the chance of infection, but also not wanting to know the names of those who have already been lost. They are our neighbours; people we have regular contact with. If I don't hear their names, the deaths won't be real to me. This is just a dream.

I cut an onion, leaving it sitting in a bowl in the main room of the cottage in the hopes it will absorb any bad bacteria in the air. I pray my modern understanding of diseases and hygiene can spare our family from the worst to come.

A knock on our cottage door has me peering out the window suspiciously. One of our neighbours, Margret holds the hand of her six year old child. I crack the door open cautiously so she can speak.

"My husband has fallen ill. Please take my girl," the woman begs.

"We can't have her here. She might already have the illness," I say. The child stands forlornly grasping a tattered doll.

"She has no symptoms. If she stays in our house she will surely die," Margret wails.

"Lucy, what is the matter?" Will appears behind me.

"Her husband has the plague," I warn.

"Open the door. The girl must stay here," Will says.

"She could have already contracted the plague," I say, blocking the entrance.

"Lucy, there is no point spending Sundays in church if we ignore those teachings in life. We have to do the right thing by ourselves because doing nothing is much worse." Will turns to Margret. "We will look after your daughter until your husband is better," he says.

"He won't get better," I say under my breath.

"She has a long journey ahead of her. She doesn't need to hear she will lose before she even begins," he replies quietly.

The mother kneels down and embraces her child. She whispers words of encouragement and love into her child's ear before kissing her forehead, standing and wiping her tears away. She gives the girl a gentle shove towards us and then runs back to her house.

"Mama!" the girl cries. The mother pauses at her doorway for a moment before disappearing inside, closing it behind her.

"Let's get you inside, shall we, Maggie?" Will sounds much more positive than I feel as he reaches out to the child. I put my hand on his chest and push him away.

"Go boil some water," I say. "I don't want any of you near her until we know she isn't sick." I pick up the crying child on our doorstep and carry her into the house.

Will stokes the fire in the hearth and sets some water on to boil. I stand Maggie by the fire, making sure Will keeps his distance and strip the child of her clothing. When the water is hot, I wet a cloth letting it cool only enough so it won't burn her fair skin. I scrub her from head to toe in this manner, before tossing her garments and doll in the boiling water.

Will disappeared while I was at my task, returning with Elizabeth carrying one of her old dresses. I take the offering, pulling it over the child's head. The dress is much too big for her, but at least it's not contaminated.

"Maggie and I will stay in the barn for a few days, until we know she is fine." I pick Maggie up again and carry her out to our new temporary home.

"I want my mama," Maggie whispers as I make a temporary bed in the hay. I pull her towards me and cradle her against my chest. If she has the sickness, she has probably already passed it on to me, so I have nothing to fear from comforting her now.

"I know you do, sweetie," I whisper, brushing her hair from her face. "You're safe here."

I stay by her side for the next several days. She is calmer once I return her doll, even if it is a little worse for wear after its boiling. Luckily, neither of us show symptoms of the plague so I make the decision to join the family back in the house.

Will brings news that Maggie's father has passed away and her mother is now ill. Maggie is part of our family now. Young Archer takes it upon himself to show her his house and struts around with a superiority only a child can manage. As much as I'm glad Maggie is healthy and safe, I hope we don't get any more requests like that.

In the end, it is Elizabeth who brings the sickness into our house. I find her sneaking into the house one evening after being unable to find her.

"Where have you been?" I ask.

"I was visiting my friend Anne." She doesn't look at me as she speaks.

"Why?" I place my hands on my hips blocking her entrance into the house.

"I heard she was sick. I needed to see it for myself and say goodbye in case I didn't see her again," Elizabeth tells me.

"You're staying in the barn until I say so." I point in the direction she has to go.

"I never looked in her eyes," she justifies.

"Barn, now!"

Elizabeth marches off with a scowl on her face, but I know it won't last. She smiles nearly as much as Will does and she never gets angry with me. I fetch her some leftover food and an extra blanket and take them to her. When I return, I find Archer sitting with her, so I quarantine him as well.

Will tells me I am being over-cautious, although he follows my instruction about keeping his distance. By the second day, Elizabeth has a temperature. I make her drink hot water mixed with

91

honey and lemon juice as often as she can, but she gets worse. Archer falls sick the following day.

I surround them with cut onions to absorb the bad air and cover my face with cloth if I am near them. I scrub thoroughly whenever I leave the barn and keep my distance from the rest of the family.

Hard boils form under Archer's armpits and Elizabeth's groin, but they resist piercing. I try placing an onion half on Archer's sore, but even the slightest amount of pressure causes him to scream in pain. I trickle honey over them for lack of any modern antibiotic.

William finds me sitting outside the barn on his way to feed the animals. He stops a short distance from me, making my chest tighten with the strain of keeping myself from falling apart. I want to be held and told that everything will be alright.

I don't know what I'm doing. I don't know if I have the ability to save Elizabeth and Archer. I'm not a doctor. I'm not sure if I will even survive high school. I know I can't stay with Will forever as much as I want to.

"Perhaps I should fetch the priest for a remedy," Will says.

"No. Heaven forbid the sort of crazy Middle Ages cure they might try on her." The doctors of this time like cures such as mercury, or leaches that suck blood and weaken the already sick. Will frowns over my words, but by now he is used to the odd things I say at times.

"I need modern medicines to save her," I say.

"God will save them," Will tells me. I look Will in the eyes and repeat a story I heard once.

"A man is lost at sea and as he treads water, he prays to God to save him. After some time, a boat comes by. The captain offers to take him on board, but the man refuses saying God will save him. When a second boat comes by, he says the same thing. Eventually he slips beneath the waves and dies. When he meets God, he asks why He didn't save him. God says, 'I sent you two boats, what more did you need?'"

"God will provide us with what we need, Lucy."

"I need Penicillin," I say.

"I don't know what that is," Will admits.

"It's a mould that makes people better." I sigh.

Will reaches into the bag he holds and pulls out a stale piece of bread.

"Like this?" He holds it out so I can see the blue and green moulds growing on the wheat bread. Penicillin was created by accident, but I don't know if it needs to be a certain type of mould. This looks different to what forms on the processed bread in my future life. I look up at Will.

"I don't know if this will work," I say hesitantly, "but we could make this into a tea."

Will leaves in search of a dark container. He comes back with a saucepan with water in it. I tear up the bread into small pieces and throw that in. The lid goes on and Will places it in the sun. We need it to be at the right temperature. If it gets too hot I think the mould will die. I'm hoping that around body temperature is what we need. The chooks will have to eat something else today.

"What if it makes people sick?" Will asks.

"If it's only given to someone with the plague it shouldn't matter. It will either make them better, or die faster," I say. At least we are trying something.

I check on the bread regularly as it soaks in the water trying to keep it at a constant temperature. It smells terrible. I guess it will take several days for it to work. I don't want to give something too weak and have it not work.

Archer's sore bursts the following day, leaving me to clean up the pussy dead flesh that spews out of the wound. The stench makes me gag. I apply honey to the open wound, but Archer is weakening, mumbling in his fevered state.

I try to make him drink more honey and lemon, but most of the time he is not alert enough to swallow. I fair slightly better with Elizabeth. She hasn't eaten for days, so I hope the drink will keep her strength up. I only wish Archer could find the strength to swallow.

I wake in the wee hours of the morning to Archer's screams. Mother and William join us in the barn with their faces covered in cloth like I've instructed them, while I cradle Archer to my chest. Elizabeth tosses fitfully nearby.

Mother holds her youngest child's hand as we sit in silence. William goes to fetch the priest, but there are too many dying in the village and he returns alone. I don't think it really matters. Archer is too young to have sins to confess. Surely, if there is a heaven, children are admitted automatically? Archer clings to life long enough to see in the new day, before slipping from our reach. No matter how hard we hold him, we cannot keep him with us.

The sexton arrives late morning to take Archer's poor body away. I keep myself busy burning the hay Archer has slept upon and my own stained dress, contaminated from holding Archer in his final hours of life.

William finds me crouched numbly in the field watching the flames destroy the remains of Archer's existence. He wraps his arms around my shaking body as I sob into his shoulder. We remain like that until the flames die down.

Elizabeth survives day four, five and then six. I have some hope now as most people die within three days or so. She starts to improve before my mould drink is ready. I don't give it to her in case it makes her worse.

We receive news that Mother's cousin has fallen sick and Mother wants to visit her. Will insists she stay to keep an eye on Elizabeth who is now improving. Orphan Maggie refuses to leave Mother's side and we don't want her near anyone sick.

I volunteer to go on my own, but Will insists on joining me and nothing I say will change his mind. He says my mouldy tea will save him if he gets sick and points out my treatments worked for Elizabeth. I'm not convinced. They did nothing for Archer. I think Elizabeth is lucky.

We take a container of my tea with us and I find Will has set up another batch in case it is effective. We detour via the church in the hopes of bringing the priest with us. William knocks on the door of his residence. After some time, we hear the sounds of footsteps from within. The maid cracks the door only enough to see who is there.

"My cousin has fallen ill and needs the services of the priest," Will says.

"He is not available," the harried woman tells us. I look into Will's alarmed face and realise he believed God would spare our priest.

"What of his assistants?" Will asks.

"They fled. They no longer believe their faith will save them."

"The sexton?"

"He succumbed to the pestilence yesterday."

"Who will take care of the dead?" Will asks.

"There is no one left. Families must take care of their own." The woman closes the door, leaving us to fend for ourselves.

When we reach the cousin Edith's house, we find it quiet. No one answers our knock on the door, so we tie cloth masks over our mouths and enter cautiously. We were expecting to be met by her husband, but there is no sign of him. I suspect he has fled.

We find Edith in bed. Once again I try to convince Will to stay away, but he insists on helping. It is the Christian thing to do. He rouses his mother's cousin and lifts her into a sitting position. She mumbles something we can't understand. I lift the container of the mouldy tea to her lips and dribble it slowly into her mouth. When she has swallowed, we lay her down on the bed again.

"How long do you think the tea will take to work?" Will asks me.

I have no idea. The doctor normally gives a packet of tablets and says 'take the whole course'.

"I think we have to give her some each day," I suggest.

"If it works, we need to make much more, so we can give it to everyone." Will doesn't need to pray in Church, God would see him coming and open the pearly gates.

We search the house and find some abandoned bread growing mould. We collect it to add to our own in case my cure has some effect. On the way out of the house, we are confronted by a young boy wandering around on his own.

His eyes are glassy and he has the beginnings of a fever. I give him some of the drink and lead him back inside his house. We find his mother dead on the floor and his father not far behind.

I step outside the house to catch my breath. The stench is almost as overwhelming as my memory of Archer's tortured body. William joins me, enfolding me in a hug while I try to pull myself together.

"Someone has to collect the bodies," I say. Leaving contaminated bodies will spread the disease, risking the lives of the healthy.

"We will do it," Will says.

"That's a terrible idea," I say.

"Who else will do it?"

I have no answer. Many of the villagers have fled. Of those who remain half are already dead or sick. Anyone who has been spared for the moment is tasked with not only their own occupation, but often trying to cover the gaps left by those no longer able to work.

I look into Will's eyes and know he will never stand back when he can make a difference. I swallow my fear of losing him and repulsion at seeing the dead. Can I separate their names from their lifeless corpses, to help those not yet afflicted?

"I'll do it," I say.

"I won't let you do this alone."

"I'll collect the bodies. If I die, I return to my other life. Besides, I need someone strong to dig the graves." My stomach heaves and settles into an uneasy queasiness. I can do this, for Will.

We collect shovels from various unoccupied properties. I stumble across bags of lime in one shed that I hope will help decompose the bodies faster. We haul our finds back to the Church. Some faces appear in windows as we toil, but the streets remain deserted.

Will begins digging in a patch of ground near the church. The cemetery is already full. I take my mouldy bread home and hitch up our horse to the neighbour's cart. The man won't object. He died last week.

I take the medicine with me in case I come across someone who might be saved. I discover that those who take it just as they are getting sick, have the best chance of survival. It's not a cure. It only gives the strong a better chance of survival. Many still die and I have to visit the sick each day to force them to swallow my putrid concoction.

I am sickened by the number of dead in our village during the first week of my new role, but there are only so many corpses I can handle before numbness sets in. My mind refuses to allow me to see the faces of people I knew on the contorted bodies of the dead. Even though the death rate increases as the days pass, it has less effect emotionally. Only someone really close to me like Will or Elizabeth could touch me now.

If a house is quiet, I check it for the sick. The dead I drag out and into my cart. It's odd how a lifeless body weighs so much more than a live one. It's a good thing I spent so much time working the fields with Will or I would never have the strength to do this job.

For the sick I give comfort and fluids in the hope they may recover, or at least be more at ease in their last hours. I burn everything I can that might be contaminated, especially bedding that can harbour rats and their fleas. It provides relief from the heavy lifting and makes me feel like I'm doing something constructive to combat the plague.

Death is a strange creature. I watch it pursue the weak relentlessly. Some fight it with every breath in their bodies. One or two even survive. Others simply surrender to it, too tired to keep going. They are the ones with nothing to live for. There is a peacefulness about them as they let go of life.

The mind does strange things when confronted with sights it doesn't want to process, sometimes leading to actions that would be deemed inappropriate at any other time. Kind of like in the song, One Week. *'I'm the kind of guy that laughs at a funeral. Can't understand what I mean? Well you soon will.'*

I drive my cart around the village, calling out, "Bring out ya dead," in my best Monty Python voice. Most of the time there's no response. Occasionally someone will drag a body from their house, but most are too afraid or sick to help me with my gruesome task.

One woman's hand twitches as her husband loads her onto my cart.

"I'm not dead yet," I mutter under my breath.

I glance at the woman's husband. There is no life in his eyes. The woman is unlikely to still be alive by the time I reach the church, so I don't make him take her back. I'd only have to collect her tomorrow. Am I being callous, or realistic? I'm not sure.

Further up the road I'm stopped by a woman running out in front of me. I pull on the reins and my horse rears up on his hind legs. By the time I have him under control, the woman has darted around the back and climbed into my cart. At first I think she is looking for a loved one, but I can't understand why she is rolling over the dead, infected bodies.

"What are you doing?" I shout at her.

"I'm making sure God takes me too," she says before jumping off the cart and disappearing. She must be crazy, I tell myself as I continue driving, but I'm shaken by the encounter.

On one of my trips I come across Robert. My back aches as I struggle to haul a tall man into my cart. A hand reaches over, giving me the fright of my life and throws the body onto my cart. I've almost forgotten what it is like to be faced with someone who is alive.

Robert, the town blacksmith, is fit for his age with tanned skin and short grey hair thinning on top. I met him many months ago when I went with Will to have a new shoe made for our plough horse. Robert gives a nod of his head taking up a position beside the cart and helps me load. As the days wear on, he becomes a regular by my side. I'm grateful for the help and glad of the company, even if we rarely speak.

Each load is taken to William's hole. I make him stand back while Robert and I unload, sprinkle the bodies in lime and cover them with dirt then Will goes back to work. I worry he will wear himself out, but thankfully he shows no signs of the sickness.

I lose track of the days. I've been handling the dead forever. I ache from the labour so at first I don't realise I'm ill. It's not until the headache won't fade that I realise I'm sweating and have a fever. I'm about to drink the last of the processed tea, when Robert calls out to me. He has found a four year old girl showing early signs of the sickness.

I look at the remaining liquid. There is not enough for both of us and the next batch is several days away. I want to stay here with Will, but I'm so tired. I want to sleep forever. I sit still for a moment with my head pounding. I slide from my seat and take the girl her drink.

I don't say anything to Will, but Robert realises soon after I do. He lets me keep working until I can no longer stand. I slump to the ground with my arms spread out by my sides hoping the world will stop spinning.

Robert takes hold of one clammy hand. I've seen many people suffer from hallucinations before they die. I need to tell him something while I can still think.

"I'll be gone soon," I say.

* * *

"She's crashing. Stand clear." Bright lights shine in my eyes. I can feel bodies pressing around me and for a moment I fear I'm already in Will's grave, buried beneath all the plague bodies. I can't breathe. I need to get them off me.

"Clear."

My body jerks.

* * *

"Lucy?" Robert waves his hand in front of my eyes. I blink. The world is dull after the bright lights from a few moments ago. Is this what it feels like to hallucinate? I struggle to focus on Robert's face. I wish I could see Will one last time. Feel his hand in mine.

"Tell Will I love him…"

* * *

I'm back in the bright world. Someone shines a light in my eyes. My chest feels heavy. I need space. I need to hold on. I've left something behind. I need to tell Will something.

"Pupils unresponsive."

"Give me one milligram of adrenaline."

* * *

"Robert. Tell Will to take care and I will see him in a few hundred years. Look after yourself."

I'm losing him. My eyes won't open. I can no longer feel his hand in mine. I will join the villagers in the mass grave dug by my friend. One more body among the many. I hope I have done enough so he doesn't join me there.

Disconnect

I wonder if I leave a body behind. In my mind, I imagine Will and Robert burying my remains, carefully so they don't catch the disease from my lifeless body.

I don't want to be added to the pile of unnamed dead in Will's hastily dug ditch. Maybe I vanish like I appear. I prefer that idea, but worry it might bother Will. Like I never existed in the first place. I don't like that idea after all.

This is what I'm thinking as I sit in the doctor's office staring blankly at the art on the wall, my fingers worrying the fabric on the arms of my chair. The picture is beginning to freak me out. The impression of a landscape has a skeleton in the centre made to look like a live horse. Is it meant to be real or dead? I can't drag my eyes away.

"When did this first occur?" the doctor asks.

"She was ten," Mum says from her chair next to mine. Her foot taps the carpet making me grit my teeth.

"Eleven. It was my eleventh birthday," I correct.

The conversation continues as if I never spoke. I'm not even in the room. I'm in a halfway place with the skeleton horse. Breathing is becoming difficult. I think I want my body to have vanished. I don't want to be another nameless pile of bones in a trench by a village church. I was there, wasn't I? It was so real.

The doctor studies the pages in front of him. There is something wrong with me. I don't fit in. No one likes me. I'm sad, all the time when I'm not with Will. Tell me why I am so different from everyone around me. Tell me what is wrong with me as a person.

I don't say these things out loud. The doctor and Mum aren't interested. They're looking for something they can see. Something that can be fixed.

"This is the third time this has happened?" The doctor's pen hovers over his note pad.

"Yes."

"No," I say at the same time.

I probably should keep my mouth shut so I'm not asked to explain, but I'm frustrated with being ignored. This is me they're talking about. I'm not invisible. I'm here.

"No?" the doctor repeats.

"Stop being difficult, Lucy." Mum turns to address the doctor. "Lucy has difficulty differentiating between reality and fantasy. After the first time she ended up in hospital, she told me a wild story about how she'd been living in Africa with a bunch of cavemen!"

I didn't think she remembered that. I fold my arms across my chest and glare at her. At least it's taken my eyes off the skeleton horse picture.

"So where were you this time, hanging out with the dinosaurs?"

"Like you care," I throw back at her.

"I think we are getting a little off topic here. There have been studies of people in comas living entirely different lives in their heads, but Lucy wasn't technically in a coma. She was asleep." The doctor shuffles his paperwork before looking up at us.

"Isn't there some sort of medication you can give her?" Mum asks.

"There is nothing to medicate. All her tests came back fine. I'll give you a referral to a neurosurgeon, but there will be a wait for an appointment. They're always extremely busy and Lucy's condition is not affecting her adversely."

The doctor types out the referral, prints it and slides it across to Mum who dabs her eyes with a tissue from the box on his desk. He glances at the door. I take the hint and stand. Mum continues to sit for a few more moments, reluctant to leave. She wants to fix me, but she can't see that part of me is not broken. I don't want my 'dreams' to be fixed. It's the only way I can see Will.

I have nightmares. Some nights I wake suddenly thinking Will, or Robert, or Elizabeth are lying in that hole as I shovel dirt over them. I know it's not real. That wasn't my job. It doesn't stop my mind playing tricks on me. That is the hardest part; not knowing if Will and my friends lived. If they were happy. If they missed me.

Sometimes when I feel really alone, I lie down on the grass in the backyard in the dark and stare at the stars. They've changed slightly in the last forty thousand years and are harder to see with street lights on, but it still makes me feel like Will is not so far away from me.

Going back to school is always difficult after one of my other lives. Trying to focus on studies when I've spent the last few weeks burying hundreds of dead bodies of my neighbours is a challenge. There is so much 'real' work to catch up on and none of it feels relevant.

This year's departure from reality is particularly bad timing. Because I've been away from school for the last two weeks, people throw insults at me as though I've been hiding after the bra incident. I'd forgotten about it. It happened a lifetime ago. I find my bra in lost property while trying to find a new school jumper. I must have left my old one at Shaun's house in my hurry to leave.

I'm behind in maths and none of it makes sense. The teacher suggests I borrow notes from Bianca. I glance around at my fellow students, but they all look away. None of them will offer their notes and I won't ask the question when I know the answer. I have two assignments due for other classes I didn't even know about. The teachers give me an extension, but now I have to catch up and do the current work at the same time.

I survive the first day back at school and then the second. I don't talk to anyone unless a teacher asks me a direct question. I do my homework in the library during lunch break. I feel safe there. La-a, Jennypha, Bianca and Tayla would sooner be caught wearing last year's fashion than be seen in a library.

In English class, I sit in the front row with an empty seat beside me. Bianca has been made to move away from La-a and sits behind me, next to Tayla who was late to class. Bianca tells everyone who will listen how she has met some cute boy who she is going to make her boyfriend. Poor boy.

I glance behind me. Tayla twirls a strand of her hair around her finger while staring off into the distance, not listening to the story. For a moment my face loses its sad expression. I wouldn't go as far as to say there was a smile, but it's probably the closest it's been for a while. Tayla catches me looking and turns towards her friend, faking interest in Bianca's words.

In the corridor, I trip over La-a's out-stretched foot on the way to the next class. I land heavily on my knee and drop my books on the floor. I look up to La-a and Jennypha smirking at me.

As I grab my books off the floor, a pair of distinct black boots approach our group. I glance up in time to see Emma slam La-a with a sly hip and shoulder move. La-a loses her balance and hits the wall with a thud loud enough to make everyone in the corridor look. Emma winks at me and keeps walking. I scramble to my feet and limp off in the other direction before La-a can brush herself off.

At the end of the day with my knee still aching, I walk to the storage racks to retrieve my bike. I pause a short distance away and stare at my chained up bike frame. My stomach sinks. Both wheels are missing. For a moment I convince myself it's someone else's bike and mine is further down the row. It isn't. No one else rides a bike as old as mine.

I break down in the school yard, large sobs shaking my body as I gasp for breath. Several passing students point at my bike and laugh. I sink to the ground and drop my head into my hands. I don't know how long I sit there for wishing the world would end.

"They work better with wheels on them." I look up to find Emma standing beside me.

"Really? I was wondering what I was doing wrong." I struggle to sound as casual as Emma, but it's hard to do with my nose running.

"I'd offer you a lift, but I was kept in and I'm late for work. You'll be right to get home?" she asks.

"Sure," I say. I'm going to have to walk.

"Frankly my dear, you should just not give a damn. They can't hurt you that way," Emma offers before leaving.

I pull myself together. I can be like Emma. I'm not going to give a damn from now on. I have no idea what I'm going to tell Mum. I'm going to have to catch the school bus. I almost start to cry again, instead I straighten my shoulders, brush away my tears and wipe my nose on the sleeve of my school jumper. Then I stand up and unlock the remainder of my bike.

I'm carrying my bike awkwardly out of the school gates when a car toots its horn at me. I keep walking, but the car pulls up beside me and the driver rolls the window down.

"Do you want a lift?"

I stop uncertainly. Hannah is a popular final year student. It's not that she is part of the 'in' crowd, she is just smart and friendly. I've never spoken to her, but I know who she is. The school is virtually deserted now, so she must have stayed back to study.

"The bike will fit in the back," Hannah suggests.

She is already out of the car and has the boot open. She proceeds to lower the rear seats while I stand by unsure how to react.

"I'm Hannah, by the way."

"Lucy," I manage.

"Having a bad day?" she asks.

"Something like that." I'm having a bad life.

Hannah takes my bike frame off me and puts it across the back seats. There is nothing else for me to do but slide into the passenger seat. I give her directions to my house when she asks. Hannah chats as we drive, but doesn't expect me to answer which is fine with me. She drops me off at the front of my place and doesn't comment on the crappy house and street I live on. She gives me a little wave as she drives off.

I carry my bike frame around the back and hope Mum doesn't find it. She'll give me the spiel about money not growing on trees, as if I didn't already know. I let myself in the back door and dump my bag in my room.

There's a bunch of flowers in a vase on the dining table. I glare at the arrangement. Yesterday a single red rose occupied the same vase. I picked it for Mum from our next door neighbour's yard. It's not even there. My flower has been replaced by a small white card with Frank's name on it. I resist the urge to smash the vase against a wall and instead start making dinner. I find my rose crumpled in the rubbish bin.

I catch the bus to school in the morning. I sit hunched in the seat as close to the driver and the door as possible, clutching my school bag and wishing I was as uncaring as Emma. I'm at the door before the bus comes to a complete stop. The door whooshes open and I leap down the steps, putting Superman to shame with my exit.

I cross the car park quickly and make it inside. I hope to get my books from my locker before the other girls arrive. I have to get through the day and the bus trip home before I can hide safely away in my bedroom.

After three days of this I am ready to stay home sick. The only thing stopping me is Mum. She's still worried there's something wrong with me and the only appointment she could get with the neurosurgeon is still months away. Who knows

111

what sort of medication she will try to make me take if I say I'm unwell.

"You know, if you hunch much more, you'll probably disappear into the floor." Emma appears beside me in the school corridor. Before I have a chance to reply, a boy yells out at us.

"Look, it's both the losers together."

Emma turns towards him and gives him a crazy death stare. She holds the expression until the boy swallows and disappears into the crowd. She gives me a friendly punch to the shoulder and walks off. It's one tiny moment of interaction, but it's enough to get me through the rest of a miserable week.

I arrive home from my paper delivery job on Saturday to find two bike wheels tied up with a piece of red ribbon by the front door. They're much shinier than mine had been, but they look to be the right size. I ask Mum where they came from.

"Your friend dropped them off. I don't know why you'd lend them to her all week and not tell me." Mum frowns.

"What friend?" I ask.

"The one who looks like she's on drugs," Mum pauses. "You're not doing drugs are you, Lucy?"

"No!" I exclaim.

"Good. I don't think you should be hanging out with people like that," Mum tells me. She walks away, the conversation over.

I don't have any friends or know anyone who does drugs. I kick at the carpet. Mum has no right telling me not to hang out with people she doesn't like the looks of, even if I don't know who she is talking about. I shake my head. I don't care if the wheels have come from a drug dealer; I won't have to catch the bus next week.

I roll the wheels enthusiastically around the back of the house and fit them to my bike frame. They spin much smoother than the old ones. I spin them again and again until my finger tips are tender, just so I can watch the motion.

On Monday, I ride hard to get rid of my frustration with life. Perhaps things will get better. After all, my bike is back in one piece. I'm still not keen for school, but at least I'm not riding the bus.

The first person I see when I arrive is Shaun. He normally rides a flash bike to school. I always make sure to place my bike as far from his as possible. Today he is dropped off by his parents. He also has a black eye. When he sees me, he glances away and hurries off. I stare at his retreating back.

I make sure both my wheels and bike frame are locked up before I head inside. An arm slung over my shoulder makes me jump.

"Nice wheels, girlfriend," Emma greets me.

"You got them for me?" I ask.

"You have other friends?" she jokes.

"That must have cost you a fortune!" I exclaim. I don't have anything to repay her with. Those wheels are much better than the ones that had been on it before.

"Don't be stupid. I just spoke to the little weasel who took yours. As he no longer had yours, I convinced him to donate the ones off his bike."

"How'd you manage that?"

113

"Let's just say I got one punch in before he realised he wasn't getting any nooky and then threatened to tell his mates he got beaten up by a girl," Emma says.

"Wow, thanks," I say. No one has ever done something like that for me before.

"No problems." Emma saunters off to class.

In English class, Jennypha stops beside me and slaps her hands on my desk. I flinch.

"Your friend's a psycho," Jennypha tells me.

"Sure is," I agree, trying to keep my voice steady. I stare at the whiteboard at the front of the class, avoiding eye contact with my tormentor. Jennypha stares at me for a moment before spinning on her heels and stalking off to talk with La-a and Bianca. I release the breath I was holding.

We're given the task of drawing a portrait of someone we admire for our art assignment. Most people are using a photo or a picture from a magazine. I don't have a picture. All I have is my memory and the sketches I have already drawn of Will from memory.

I draw him as I saw him last, William of England. I capture his cheeky grin and coarse tunic he wore in the fields. Time slips by unnoticed. I am alone with my page and pencils.

The ringing bell drags me back to the classroom. The portrait still needs work, but it's nearly done. The students leave the room noisily as I remain looking at Will's face. If I sit here long enough, I could will him into this life.

I glance up at a slight noise by my shoulder to find Bianca staring at my picture with her mouth slightly open in surprise. For a moment I think she is admiring my work. I think I've captured Will as he is in my mind. Bianca looks up and glares at me as if I have just kicked her dog.

"Slut," she hisses at me before marching from the room.

Tears prick the backs of my eyes and I hang my head until the room is empty. I slide my drawing under all the others at the front of the room. No one will see it at the bottom of the pile.

La-a, Jennypha and Bianca are waiting by my locker. I stop in the middle of the nearly deserted corridor. They are not in the habit of remaining at school after the final bell has rung.

They advance towards me. I could probably run, but they would only track me down later, so I wait for them to come to me. I have no fight left inside of me. Better to get this over with. Jennypha shoves me into the wall and La-a spits on me. Bianca grins evilly from behind them.

"Do you really think you could get a guy like that? You're pathetic," La-a says.

They leave me sitting on the dirty corridor floor, wondering what the hell they're talking about as they waltz away.

Emma finds me in the library during lunch. I've never seen her in here before. She drops a pile of books on the table with a thump and drags out a chair opposite where I am sitting. The librarian glares at us.

"I'm told you're good at history," Emma says.

"I guess so." I keep my voice low. It's best to stay on the good side of a librarian.

"I'm not. I don't like history and I need help with my homework," she tells me.

"Why are you taking the subject?" I ask.

"To annoy my mother." Emma grins.

"What are you stuck on?"

"The beginning," Emma replies. She opens her text book and slides it towards me. I shut my own books and push them to one side. History I'm good at.

We begin a new routine, meeting during lunch and doing homework. Sometimes Emma isn't interested in working so she just tells me wild stories about her mother's friends. I'm not sure if they're real or not, but I guess people would say the same if I talked about Will.

The disconnection I've felt since my return from England begins to ease. In the back of my mind I'm always counting down the weeks to my next birthday, but at the moment I feel like I can survive those long months ahead of me.

I ride my bike to school as usual. An athletic old man regularly walks in the opposite direction. He has sun-darkened skin and short grey hair thinning on top, reminding me of Robert who helped me collect the dead, only Robert would never wear shorts and a sleeveless shirt matched with a bum bag.

I like this man even though I don't actually know him. It is not because he reminds me of Robert, but because he looks at me and smiles as if he is happy to see me. It's a tiny interaction with another person, but it makes me feel real in a world where I'm usually invisible.

"Good morning," I say cheerfully as I ride past. He returns the greeting. Sometimes it's the only smile I see all day.

The almost smile remains on my face until art class. I hang back while everyone else collects their portrait. Mine is at the bottom of the pile where I hid it at the end of last class, contaminated by Bianca's scorn. I stand at the back of the line picturing the finishing touches it needs and attempting to push Bianca's negative response from my mind.

When I reach the teacher's bench there are only two drawings left. Both belong to students who have not come to class today. Will's face is not in the pile. I struggle to breathe. I check the pile again, but there are still only two drawings.

"My drawing's missing," I say to the teacher, my voice cracking as I once again search the two remaining sheets of paper in a vain attempt to find Will.

"There's a picture in the bin," Kate points out.

The teacher and I both look in her small paper bin. She fishes four scraps from the bin and lays them out on the desk.

"Is it yours?" she asks. I look at my Will with his face torn into pieces and tears slip silently down my cheeks.

"Don't worry, Lucy. I can mark you on what we have here. It won't affect your overall grade," she says.

I reach out to touch the pieces as though doing so will make them whole once more. My drawings are all I have and even those, people want to steal from me. Clutching the torn pieces against my chest, I walk out of the room. The teacher calls after me, but she can't leave her class unattended. I grab my bike and ride off before anyone can stop me.

I hang out on my rock by the lookout for the remainder of the day. I pull the ruined drawing from my bag and let the pieces flutter in the breeze. I consider releasing them, but even damaged I can't let Will go. I tuck the drawing back into my bag.

The wind makes me shiver, eventually forcing me to head home. I ride slowly, as though taking my time will ease the burden of re-entering the real, unloving world I live in. The house is quiet when I arrive.

I slide the drawing into the back of my sketchbook in my room, before running a hot bath. I leave the lights off and instead light two small candles sitting on the shelf above the bath, the flickering flame casting a faint glow over the room.

I drop my clothes on the floor and lower my tired body into the bath. I focus on my memory of Will's face in the moment by the house when he leaned in and I thought he might kiss me. I sink

118

beneath the water. If I could just stay here, the world would just disappear taking my problems with it.

The heat slowly seeps from the bath water and my eyelids grow heavy.

Dream

England 1553

"Lucy!"

Will's voice carries on the wind to where I lie among the spring flowers in the meadow. I open my eyes and stare up into the bright sky and wait for him to find me.

"Were you dreaming again?" William towers over me. I smile up into his warm brown eyes. His dark brown hair is disordered as though he ran much of the way.

"Perhaps," I say. I don't remember what it was about now. Only lingering feelings of despair and loneliness remain, gradually being blown away by the breeze across the meadow.

"I wish you wouldn't do that. You know how it makes you sad." William's brow furrows slightly. I hold out my hand and he pulls me to my feet.

"Race you back to the house," I say, taking off before I finish speaking. Despite his earlier exercise, he still catches me before we reach our destination. We arrive dishevelled and out of breath, earning us a scolding from the housekeeper.

"Get upstairs and change, both of you. Master William's cousins will be here any moment."

I laugh at Will's sheepish face and dash off to my room to do as instructed. The young maid struggles to comb the tangles from my hair and arrange it in a more ladylike manner before lacing me into a clean dress. The girl hasn't worked in the house long, but she is efficient. William is still ready long before I am and is waiting downstairs for me.

"Ready, Miss Lucy?" he asks. I drop him a practice curtsy and he laughs. The butler opens the door to the parlour and I follow Will into the room.

"There you are, William." Mother takes his arm and leads him forward to introduce him to Mother's cousin and her three daughters. The older girl, Mary is ushered into a seat next to Will.

"Where are your family from, Lucy?" Mary asks.

My mind goes completely blank. Have I not always been here? Fractured images flood my mind, disjointed and confusing. The conversation starts up around me in an attempt to ignore my lack of response.

"Excuse me," I say as I stand. I curtsy to the group and flee the room as politely as possible.

Will finds me some time later sitting in the window seat of the study with my slippered feet tucked up under my long skirt. The fading sunlight brings a chill to the room fended off by my shawl about my shoulders. Will positions himself at my feet, watching me silently.

"Is there something wrong with me?" I ask.

"Why would you believe that?"

"Where was I before here?"

"Do you not remember?" Will asks.

"I have these images in my head of different places, lives maybe. Each time you are with me except for one where you are not. I keep being drawn back to that one, but I don't want to be there."

"Why are you here?"

"To save you." It's the only thing I'm sure of.

"Will you stay?"

"I don't know if I can," I say.

"Father wants me to enter into marriage with Mary when I've finished my study. I'll say no if you'll still be here."

"I have no control over where I am." Tears spring to my eyes.

"I think you have more control than you think you do."

"What if I'm not good enough? I could never compete with someone like Mary," I say.

"No one is perfect no matter how hard they pretend they are, so don't compare yourself to them," Will says.

"What if you're here for another reason?" William throws himself down on the grass beside me, moving several paint colours to one side to make room. I study the canvas square I'm trying to capture the image of the lake on.

"Such as?" I ask.

"You said I don't exist in one life. What if each of these lives are designed to teach you a lesson so you have the tools to save yourself when you're alone?" His words strike a strange truth inside me. Do I need saving?

"You think?" I turn the idea over in my head. I've been thinking the purpose of my life is to save Will, which is why in the one time he isn't there, I have no purpose.

"What did you learn about your first life?"

I concentrate on sorting the images in my mind, but it is difficult to know what is real and what is dream. An image of Wu appears in my mind.

"I made the first ever bow and arrow so the clan wouldn't starve."

"Family," Will says.

"I don't have any," I say.

"The clan was your family."

"Why am I here now?"

"You have to learn to love yourself. How can others appreciate what you have to offer if you don't value yourself?"

"What about the other lives?"

"Let's see if we can work this out...?"

"What was she doing out in the storm?"

"Has the doctor arrived yet?"

Voices swirl around me as I lie cocooned in a pile of bedding. My thoughts struggle to surface in the thick fog inside my head as my skin burns and body shivers. I don't know how I arrived at this point. There was icy cold driving rain, but I can't recall why I was out there or how I arrived inside.

"Have you considered this might be a dream?" Will asks.

The thought had crossed my mind, but I pushed it into a pile of things I don't want to consider.

"What's the first memory you have of this life?"

I was lying in a field of flowers. 'Were you dreaming again?' Will asked.

"Where were you in the moments before that?" he asks.

There was water, lots of it, surrounding me, covering my head as I was consumed by loneliness and despair. I'm dreaming.

I open my eyes.

Losing It

I lie inside the claustrophobic white dome while the machine scans my head. My only thought as I lie here is they should have done this while I was asleep, to see if I'm still in my head. I'm not sure if I am.

When the machine is finished, I'm extricated from its clutches and the nurse assists me to sit up. My head spins and I struggle to breathe deep enough to stop it. I'm still feeling the effects of the pneumonia I developed after nearly drowning in the cold bath water.

The nurse directs me to the waiting room where Mum already sits. I take a seat next to her, pick up a magazine, rest it across my lap and flip through the pages. The repetitive action gives me something to focus on. Mum sighs and closes her magazine.

"Frank thinks you're doing this for attention," Mum blurts out.

My hands clench into fists. I'm none of Frank's business. When I don't reply, Mum huffs and continues to pretend she is reading her magazine.

My mind turns over too fast, like a tiny mouse is in there on his running wheel training for an Olympic sprint. When I was eleven, I was sure I'd been in Africa. The sights, sounds, and smells had all been so real. I even had the marks left on my body from the lioness attack, but now my mind doubts that belief.

This time something was off. It was dreamlike, even though when I was there, I was sure this reality was the dream. I never see Will except on the night of my birthday. So was I there, or is my mind playing tricks on me? A coping strategy to deal with my depressing existence. If I wasn't there, have I ever actually been present in Will's world? My stomach clenches.

"Are you hungry?" Mum asks.

"No."

I'm starving, but don't feel like I can keep any food down. Mum sighs and looks back at her magazine like she is the only parent in the world to have ever received a phone call regarding her daughter walking out of class.

It's sitting in the neurosurgeon's waiting room that I first begin to wonder about dying. I try to imagine who might miss me if I'm gone. The girls from school will find someone else to torment. Emma might think of me occasionally. She would have to find someone else to help with her homework. Mum will feel guilty, remembering all the times she wasn't there for me. I let my hair fall across my face as I rub the moisture from my eyes.

The receptionist calls my name and Mum stands. She frowns at me until I rise. She doesn't understand me. No one does. She ushers me ahead of her into the small consulting room. We sit down and the nurse rambles on about what happens next, but I'm not listening. Mum arranges for us to come back in a couple of days to discuss the test results.

Over the next few days, I slowly recover from my pneumonia. I become Lucy of the here and now once more. Nothing special. Just here. When Mum is out of the house, I curl up on the floor of my bedroom, clutching Wu the Lion and cry into the carpet until I can't breathe.

Mum insists I come back to the neurosurgeon with her to hear the results. There is nothing wrong with me. Mum leans forward over the doctor's desk and jabs a finger at the results printout insisting there is. No one sleeps for a week straight without there being a problem. She demands the test be repeated, but the doctor refuses. In their haste to discover the problem, they have overlooked the obvious. I don't want to be here.

I go back to school because it is expected of me. I forget to set my alarm and wake up as I should be leaving the house. I throw on my uniform and run out the door without breakfast. Because I'm late, I miss passing the man who always smiles and says good morning to me.

The first thing I see when I get to school is the graffiti on my locker. By the scribbled 'loser' I have a clear idea who is responsible. I have nothing to remove it with, so it stays there for everyone to see.

I continue the routine of moving from class to class, but I'm drowning. I've had more time off school for being sick, causing me to slip further behind. In the afternoon, I'm called to the careers teacher's office. The rest of my class had their appointments while I was away.

Our conversation is short. I don't see a future for myself. I can't image myself grown up. I'm struggling to see myself surviving the remainder of the year until I can see Will again. It's a distant vision, so far from my current reach.

My hand trembles as it reaches out to take the assessment sheet from the careers teacher. I don't say anything. My throat is tight. If I try to speak, my voice will come out high-pitched and I won't be able to hold back the tears. I don't want anyone to ask why I'm crying. I don't know. I just am.

I skip the next class and hide in the toilets. I sit on the closed lid with my knees tucked under my chin and focus on breathing. It is difficult when my nose is blocked from crying. I use the toilet paper as a tissue. I stay there until lunchtime when other people come in to use the bathroom.

Emma finds me sitting outside the library picking at my peanut butter sandwich.

"You look like shit," Emma tells me. I keep my head down so my hair falls over my face.

"Thanks," I say sarcastically. I washed my face with cold water, but it hasn't helped much.

"I heard you were in hospital?" Emma asks as we go inside and head towards our table at the back of the library.

"Yeah." One word and I am nearly bawling again. I bite the inside of my cheek and focus on the pain it brings.

"So what's wrong?"

"The doctors say nothing." I plaster a smile on my face as I say this. My voice only squeaks slightly.

"Yeah, they all say that, don't they?" Emma stares at the shelves behind me and drums her fingers on the table. I pull out my books and turn the pages occasionally.

Emma is away the next day. She often skips school. I wish I could predict when she was going to do it so I could stay home too. School is not fun when your only ally is not there.

The next few weeks of school are hell. My bag gets ripe banana squished into it and I find white powder around the edges of my locker vent. I open the door cautiously. As I stand in the crowded corridor, I can feel eyes on me, waiting for my reaction.

Someone has let a fire extinguisher off in my locker. Everything is covered in fine white powder. My sandwich is ruined so I have nothing to eat. I spend the lunch break trying not to cry as I clean out my locker. A teacher gives me detention for being in the corridor during break.

I leave school early and ride up to the lookout to spend the afternoon sitting on my overhanging rock.

The warm stone and the wind in my hair are calming. No one can see me cry up here.

There is a thought in my head becoming more regular. It's the only thing giving me a sense of hope. I could end my life. If I wanted to. I have no idea how I would do it, but the option is there. I don't have to hang around forever. I can always check out. I'm not going to. But I could.

When I get home there is a message on the answering machine from school regarding my attendance. I delete it. I go to school on Monday because I have history. For a brief moment during the day, I can pretend I'm normal and my world is not falling apart around me.

At lunch time, Emma suggests I hang out at her place after school. I've never seen her house and although she knows where I live, she hasn't been inside. I try to act cool as I agree as though people ask me over all the time and it's no big deal.

Emma doesn't live far from school, so I push my bike as I walk beside her. She lives with her mum and younger brother in a small two story townhouse. Her brother is away on a camp and her mum is out so we have the place to ourselves. I'm glad. I don't know how to act around other people's families.

A car toots its horn as it passes and the driver waves. The car belongs to Hannah, the girl who gave me a lift when my bike wheels where stolen. I'm about to return the action when I see the young man in the front seat. I'm sure I've seen his face before on a photo taped to La-a's locker. My suspicions are confirmed by La-a in the backseat with both fingers up in our direction.

"Can you believe anyone would date that idiot's brother?" Emma comments.

I make a mental note not to accept any favours from Hannah in the future. Who knows how much trouble I could get into if she is dating La-a's brother.

We talk about nothing in particular as we walk. Emma loves music and promises to play me some of her favourite songs. Mum has a handful of CDs, but they're all old so I never know the latest songs everyone at school talks about.

Emma is cool but animated until we reach the house and we are confronted by a shiny red classic car parked in the driveway. She stops in the middle of the footpath and I trip over her heels.

"No fucking way!" she says.

"What's wrong?"

"That's my dad's car. He's been in gaol for assaulting Mum. It looks like the idiot is going to take him back again." Emma shoves her fringe out of her face as she glares at the offending vehicle. Some of her hair remains standing up making her look young and vulnerable. I pretend not to notice.

"Stupid car. He goes nuts if the thing even gets dirty," she mutters.

She kicks the front wheel as she stalks by. I hover in the yard as Emma opens the front door and calls out. No one answers. She waves me in and I follow cautiously.

"I can go if you want," I say.

"Nah, let's put that music on."

She leads me up the stairs to her room. I move a pile of clothes out of the way and sit on the edge of her unmade bed. A poster of Miranda Kerr dominates one wall. I glance up at the glow-in-the-dark stars stuck to the ceiling. When she sees me looking, she pulls the blinds down, shuts the door and turns out the light. I lay back on the bed to take it in. Emma lies down next to me.

"It's beautiful," I whisper. Emma's put a lot of effort into her ceiling. The stars aren't randomly placed, but reflect the constellations in the night sky. It reminds me of Wu. Life was simple back then. A stray tear slides down my cheek.

"When I was little, I wanted to be an astronaut," Emma says.

"That's really cool."

"What about you?"

"When I was little, I wanted to have friends," I say.

"How's that working out for you?" Emma pokes me playfully in the ribs.

"Well, I've got you and Will." I don't realise I'm going to say his name until it slips out.

"Who's Will?"

"He's my imaginary friend." I brush the question off. Emma laughs.

"That's a relief. For a moment I thought he might be the same poor guy that dickhead Bianca is chasing. His name is Willie or Billie or maybe that's some cutesy nickname she's given him."

"He doesn't live here. He was in England last time we met," I say.

"You've been to England?"

"No."

"You're an odd one, Lucy."

Emma jumps off the bed and cranks the volume up until the music can be heard throughout the house and probably down the street. The sound vibrates through my body like a living creature.

"Come on, let's show my dad he can't just move back in," Emma yells over the sound.

"What are you going to do?" I yell back. She grins at me and disappears out the door.

I haul myself off Emma's bed and follow her into her mum's room. The music is less intense in here. Emma sings the lyrics as she hauls an old sports bag out from under the bed and then flings open the wardrobe doors. She rips her dad's clothes from their hangers and drops them on top of the bag. She grabs my hand, spinning me around to the music before diving back into the wardrobe shaking her arse along with the beat.

"Give me a hand will you, Lucy?"

I clap my hands and she turns around to give me the finger. Emma grabs a hairbrush from the bedside table and holds it to our mouths as the chorus repeats. I manage to get some of the words right as we belt out the song.

Emma flings clothes at my feet in between singing the rest of the song. I drop to my knees and shove the items into the bag. When we are done there, she grabs his things from the ensuite and we shove them on top.

We have to sit on the bag to zip it up which sends us into fits of laughter. After several attempts and the sound of something snapping, a toothbrush perhaps, we get it zipped up. Emma pushes the bag out of the room and to the top of the stairs with her feet in time to a new song. She gives it a kung-fu kick and we watch it thump its way to the bottom.

She jumps onto the rail and slides down on her behind. I try to copy and nearly fall off. The second go gets it, but Emma is doubled over laughing at my first attempt. Her laughter sets me off and we both sit on the floor giggling so hard I can't breathe. I wipe the tears from my eyes. I'm not sad.

"Any suggestions on where we should leave his shit?" she asks in between gasps. A set of keys lie on the table. Emma's mum is out and there is only one car in the drive.

"In his car?"

"Loser carries the bag," Emma squeals and we both dive for the keys. Emma trips on the rug and grabs my ankle to slow me down. I fall to my knees. I stretch my arm out, but the keys are just out of reach. Emma gives me a shove and a picture frame falls to the floor. She leaps over me and holds the keys triumphantly above her head.

"I win!"

"You cheated!"

"I don't recall there being any rules."

Emma dances out the door with her prize while I haul the bag outside. She unlocks the car and I shove the bag in the back seat. Emma slams the door shut and looks at me with a wicked grin on her face.

"We should take it for a spin." She jiggles the keys in front of me.

"No way! You'll get in so much shit!" I exclaim.

"Come on. Live a little, Lucy. Imagine it's La-a's new BMW Daddy bought for her birthday. We won't hurt it, I promise." She laughs wildly and swings into the front seat. I hesitate for a fraction of a second, considering riding my bike home and spending the evening on my own. I run around to the passenger side, jump in and do up the seatbelt. I take a deep breath and stare out the windscreen.

"Ready?" Emma asks.

"Shouldn't you lock the front door?" We've left the house open and the music on.

"Who cares."

She stomps on the accelerator, the wheels squeal and we swerve out of the driveway. The car zig-zags twice before Emma regains control. I squeal and grab the dash. Emma lets out a loud whoop. She reaches for the radio.

"We need some rocking tunes," she tells me. I need a sick bag.

She finds a station with loud songs we can sing along to. I swallow my nerves and join in when I can catch on to the chorus. She drums on the steering wheel as we drive down the streets.

"Who taught you to drive?" I yell over the music.

"No one," Emma shouts joyfully. I should be scared, but I don't care. I'm having fun and I don't remember the last time that happened. I wind down the window so I can feel the wind blowing my hair around my face. I lean back into the seat.

Emma slows as we drive through the main street. A row of cars are parked either side of the street, but the shiny black BMW parked outside the cinema stands out from them all. Four girls stand next to it preening, waiting for the world to envy them.

"Speaking of La-a's new car," I say.

"Dare me," Emma says. She slows for a speed bump as we creep closer to the vehicle. She turns to look at me, daring me to dare her to do something to the offensive black car belonging to the girl I despise.

"You wouldn't?" I exclaim, but I don't discourage her from her thoughts. We draw level to the shiny car as I speak. The moment has nearly passed. The car will go untouched because nothing bad ever happens to girls like La-a.

Emma swerves left and I scream as the parked cars rush towards me. We scrape the side of La-a's car, rip off her side mirror and dent my side door. I don't know if I'll be able to open the door when we park. I'll have to climb over Emma's seat. My heart is pounding, but I feel strangely elated. We drive off to the sound of four girls screaming after us.

"Oh my God, that felt good," Emma whoops. I look at Emma with fresh eyes. There is an incredible amount of satisfaction in seeing La-a's expensive car damaged.

"You know she's going to call the cops." Emma ignores my comment.

"I think we should wreck this car, too," she suggests recklessly.

"Not while we're in it," I say. She turns to look at me.

"Have you ever wondered what it would be like to end it all?" She sounds serious.

I stare at her wondering if she can see inside my head. Have I somehow given myself away? I have no idea how to respond. If I tell her what I'm thinking, I don't know where that will put our friendship. I don't want to ruin this afternoon. I don't know if I can let the words out of my mouth. They're stuck in my throat.

"I…"

A car honks loudly and we both jump. Emma swings her eyes back to the road to find we've crossed the white centreline. She pulls on the wheel to bring us back into our lane. My hand flies out to grab hold of my seat as the car bears down on us. For a moment we're out of control then Emma straightens up as the other vehicle slides past and disappears around the corner.

"That was close," Emma says.

I release the breath I've been holding and force my fingers to unclamp from the seat. I glance at Emma. She stares at the road looking as white as I feel.

"I need a change of underwear," she states and suddenly we're both laughing hysterically. The tears streaming down my face blur my vision and my sides ache.

"I don't think I've ever seen you laugh before today," Emma says. She looks at me again. It makes me pause to recall the last time I really laughed. I don't know when it was.

Gravel pings against the underneath of the car as the wheels hit the uneven edge of the road. Emma jerks the wheel, but she over corrects and we zig-zag across the road for several terrifying moments before the world rotates.

The sound of crushing metal hurts my ears until we are upright again for a second. Loose objects fly everywhere as we continue to roll. I have the odd sensation of being in a washing machine without the water. The bag I tossed in the back of the car hits my arm, a CD flies by and I smash my head hard against the window.

Everything stops moving. The music is no longer playing making the vehicle suddenly quiet. I'm partially upside down with my head at an angle due to the crushed roof below me. My seatbelt digs into me. I think we're in a ditch. My head hurts and I'm struggling to keep my eyes open.

"Emma?" I whisper.

"I'm in so much shit," Emma groans. "Are you okay?"

I'm not sure how to answer her question. It takes a few moments for my mind to process her words. Something damp trickles across my forehead and there is a metallic taste in my mouth. I can't tell if Emma is above or below me. I close my eyes for a moment.

* * *

"Are you injured?" William's voice is concerned. I think about his question. Didn't someone else ask me that question a moment ago? I don't remember what I answered. I can't move. Something is holding me where I am. I have a question I need to ask him.

"Where am I?"

* * *

"Lucy, you're in the car." Emma sounds stressed, but I can't remember why. My head is foggy. I feel her hands on me as she tugs on the strap across my chest. I'm going to have bruises.

"It hurts," I say.

"I'm sorry. I can't get the seatbelt undone."

"The car?" I ask. I'm trying to work out why Will is in the car with us.

My mind wanders as I try to think of a way to explain what a car is to someone who has never seen one before. Just as I think I've come up with an explanation it slips away, but he has gone quiet anyway.

"Where's Will?" My voice sounds strange to my ears, distant. Emma's hands pause for a moment.

"Your imaginary friend? How would I know? Please don't go weird on me now," Emma begs.

She must free the belt buckle because I suddenly fall sideways and hit my shoulder. By the yelp, I've also kicked Emma.

"Why can I smell smoke?" I ask.

* * *

"There's no smoke."

I wish my head would clear so I could recall the origin of Will's accent. He's right though. The smoky smell has disappeared. Maybe I imagined it. Maybe I've imagined my entire life and the only real thing is Will.

I try to crack one eye open, but the sky is too bright and I close it again. All I saw was a glimpse of Will leaning over me wearing a kilt.

"Did you fall off a horse, lass?" Will asks.

"A horse?" I repeat. I was going to tell him about the horses in the car engine. I wonder if the horses escaped in the crash and are wandering around Scotland. I frown. That doesn't make sense even to me.

"How did you get here?"

He's right. It's not my birthday. I shouldn't be here.

"The car crashed."

"What is a car?"

"It's a…" My mind is blank. What was the question?

"I think you should see a healing woman."

* * *

"Lucy! Wake up! I can't find my phone."

I can definitely smell smoke. Emma's hand connecting hard with my cheek makes me snap my eyes open. Now I can see the smoky haze forming inside the crushed car. Wasn't I lying in a field a few moments ago?

"Where are the horses?" I ask.

"What? I can't call for help. We have to get out of the car ourselves. Can you move?" she asks, tugging on my hand.

The doors are buckled beyond use so Emma kicks out what is left of the smashed windscreen. I watch her through partially closed eyes, but I'm drifting away. I'm sure I was somewhere better a few moments ago. A coughing spasm holds me in the present.

Emma tugs me towards the missing windscreen. I struggle to lift myself as Emma pulls my arms. The jagged edges cut into my skin, but she stumbles free and I collapse on top of her. She pushes me off and grabs my arms again, dragging me further away from the wreck. She pants with the effort.

When she lets go, I flop down on the ground. It's not as comfortable as Will's field, but I can't lift my body. Even the sound of the car erupting into flames a few metres away doesn't make me move. The heat is intense. My eyes are closed again. I'm drifting away.

"I can't find my phone," Emma repeats. "Don't leave me, Lucy."

Brave

Scotland 1746

The sky is bright, but cloudy above me. An icy wind blows across the moor making the grass sway around me. My skin is parched, like I've been standing too close to a fire. Underneath my woven dress, I am cold and burning at the same time.

Sitting up makes my head spin. I hold still so I'm not sick. Eventually, I realise I'm being watched. Will stands nearby studying me. I shake my head to clear it and immediately regret the action. I clutch my stomach. Will continues to watch me.

I'm uneasy as if there is something I need to do elsewhere, but my mind fails to hold on to the moments that led to this point. I reach a hand up to my forehead thinking I cut it, but there is no blood.

"Am I dead?" I ask Will.

"You don't look dead," he replies with his Scottish accent. It sounds natural to my ear as though I have spent my entire life in Scotland. It's disorientating. I'm sure I was someplace else only moments ago. Perhaps I was dreaming.

"Will you be alright then, lass?" he asks. He glances over his shoulder, impatient to be gone.

"I think so." I remain sitting on the ground studying him.

"The nearest village is that way." Will points out the direction. I glance briefly that way and then back at him. He picks up his axe off the ground, turns away and walks off. I sit there stunned for a moment until I realise he isn't coming back for me.

"Wait!" I yell out stumbling to my feet.

He keeps walking away from me. I move my legs to run after him. They are wobbly and the edges of my vision are turning black and creeping inwards. I need to reach him before I faint. I take a deep breath.

"Wait up, William!" I call in desperation.

He turns to look at me, so grown up with his axe slung over his shoulder. I stumble as I near him, blinking my eyes to repair my vision. With every breath I take my head is clearing. The heat from the fire is fading from my skin, being replaced by the chill in the air. I'm becoming one with this present.

"How do you know my name?" He frowns.

"I'm Lucy," I say.

"I have somewhere to be," he says walking away.

"William!" I yell. I run after him and grab his arm. He shakes me off. I stop where I am and watch his retreating back. I look up at the sky, close my eyes and let my body crumple to the ground.

I lie in the grass focusing on keeping my breathing even. The minutes tick by. I strain to catch the noises around me, but the rustling sounds only like the wind. It's cold out here. I was certain Will would come back for me. Do I not know this person he has become or is it me who has changed? I'm considering opening my eyes when I feel the grass move against my face followed by an exasperated sigh.

"I guess I'm heading back home," Will says.

Something hits the ground near my arm. It sounds like the axe he was carrying. Before I can react, he bends down and hauls me over his shoulder. For a moment, I am unsteady as he reaches for his weapon then we are upright and moving. His body against mine is warm and makes my insides do funny things.

I open my eyes to find myself facing Will's kilt covered behind. A slightly strangled sound escapes my lips before I can prevent it. Will pauses and I make myself as limp as possible until he continues walking.

"Are you going to make me carry you the whole way or are you planning on walking some of it yourself?" Will asks after some time. His voice startles me out of my daydreaming about his behind and I forget to play unconscious.

Will loosens his grip around my waist and I slide down his taut body until my feet touch the ground. Will grins at me and I realise my hands are on his chest. I pull back blushing.

144

"Feeling better now?" he asks. I clear my throat before answering.

"Much better."

"Good. You were getting heavy." Will shoots a teasing smile in my direction. I swallow as I try to resist the urge to put my hands to my heated cheeks. Will continues walking as though he hasn't noticed. I jog to catch up and keep pace beside him in silence.

We pause to rest on a craggy outcrop of rocks, the land laid out before us. I climb up beside Will and sit down. He sits soundlessly as though mulling an idea over in his head. Eventually I break the silence.

"Are you real?" I ask. Will shifts to face me and nudges my shoulder.

"I'm as real as you are."

"What if you're just in my head and you don't actually exist?"

"If that was the case, I would only ever do what you thought I would do." Will smiles before leaning towards me. His face is close to mine. My eyes drop to his lips. After several agonising moments, he closes the distance and kisses me on the lips. "Did you imagine I would do that?"

"I'm not sure, I might have. Is it the same thing?" I'm blushing. Will laughs.

"I'm definitely me. I'm not in your head."

"What if I only exist in your head? When I disappear, I don't think I leave anything behind. I imagine it's like I'm not even here in the first place. Not real." I can't shake the feeling that one of us is not actually here. Or there. Will reaches out a hand to inspect my head for injuries, but there is no sign of the wound I thought I had.

"Can your presence change the lives you interact with?"

"I don't know," I say.

"Maybe you need to work that out and you will have your answer. If I can make one person's life better by my being in it, than my life has been real and worthwhile."

Have I made anyone's life better by my existence? I didn't think I have. Certainly no one I know has made my life better by being in it, unless I count Will and I'm no longer sure I'm even here.

We continue on our journey, but the answer remains elusive, so by the time we reach the large stone house, I'm still no closer to knowing if I leave anything behind. Will puts his axe away before leading me inside. A woman greets us in the hallway.

"Where have you been all day, William? Your mother is in one of her moods. You'd better go in and see her."

I follow Will into a room where two young, ginger-haired versions of Will wriggle in their seats while a distracted woman attempts to sketch them. They glance up as we enter.

"There you are, William. I was worried you'd gone chasing after your father," she says.

"Of course not, Mother." William studies the floor. His mother's gaze settles on me. Something about her face is familiar, but I can't place why. Her eyes take on a glazed look.

"Come here child," she beckons. I walk cautiously over to where she is seated. Her work table is set up with several attempted miniatures of the twins. She places her hand on my cheek and looks through me.

"You shouldn't be here." Her voice has a faraway quality to it. "You need to go home."

"Mother, stop that. I brought Lucy here because she hit her head and was disorientated." Will lays a protective hand on my arm. His mother blinks at me several times and lets her hand drop from my face.

"You two can sit over there. Dougald and Duncan won't sit still long enough for me to finish their likeness." Mother waves us over to the chairs. The two boys scamper from the room as soon as they realise Mother has found new models.

"Shouldn't you check Lucy over to make sure there is no damage from her fall?" Will asks.

"She's fine, William," Mother insists. "Sit down."

We submit to her demands, allowing her to arrange us side by side on the seats vacated by Will's younger brothers. Our thighs press against each other and Will's arm is warm around my waist. Mother steps back from us and nods her approval.

"Stay like that," she instructs. I do my best to remain still, but I'm distracted by Will's closeness. I keep my eyes forward, but I can feel when he turns to look at me and his breath moves my hair. I lose track of time as Mother works.

My legs become numb. Tiredness overcomes me and my head drops down onto Will's shoulder. He nudges me awake and I realise we are done. We stand so we can admire Mother's work. I stare at the tiny image of Will's and my faces staring back at us. She turns the parchment over and writes on the back. William and Lucy 1746. Wherever I am in the future, I was here.

It is dark outside giving me a reason to stay the night. In my dreams I worry about the date. I am moving too quickly through time. There aren't many generations between now and my present. What happens when I run out of time? Is that the last I'll see of Will? My sleep is restless.

I can't find Will when I wake in the morning. I miss his presence like I am missing a vital part of me. In my search for him, I come across his younger brothers.

"Have you seen William?" I ask the twins. They glance at each other in a silent conversation before turning to me.

"He's gone to find Father, but it's a secret so don't tell," Dougald, or maybe Duncan tells me.

"Where's Father?" I ask.

"Dunno," he says. The two boys whisper to each other.

"The man who came with the message mentioned Culloden," the other twin says.

"Culloden?"

My body feels like it has turned to jelly. If I step forward I don't know if my legs will hold me upright. The boys giggle and nod as if we are all in on a secret. To them Culloden is only a place.

"How do I get there?" I demand. They shrug in unison and dart out of the room their attention having wavered from our conversation.

I glance around the room as though it will reveal the answers I need, but it doesn't. Adrenaline flows through my limbs spurring me into action. I run from the room searching for Mother. She looks up startled as I burst through the doorway.

"How do I get to Culloden?" I demand breathlessly.

"You can cut across the moor and then follow the road." Mother points out the direction. I spin around and race for the door. "Lucy, wait."

Mother reaches into the pocket of her dress and pulls out a locket. She hands it to me and although I am anxious to chase after Will, I pause to open it. The miniature of me and Will sits inside. I don't need to pull it out to know our names and year are on the reverse.

"For good luck," Mother tells me.

"Thank you," I say. I take one last look at this life and run after Will.

I don't normally run much, but adrenaline helps. Knowing Will heads towards a battle that will end in slaughter spurs me on. I find myself retracing our steps from where Will found me. Eventually I have to slow to a walk to catch my breath, then I'm running again. I don't know how much of a head start he has on me.

I finally catch sight of him ahead of me. I'm out of breath as I reach out for him. He turns around at the sound of my footsteps.

"What are you doing here, Lucy?"

"This is a bad idea, Will. We should head home."

"I'm not going to let Father fight alone."

"Some battles can't be won and this is one of them. If you fight, you will die."

"You can't know that." Will continues walking. I tug on his arm, but he shakes me off. I walk beside him evaluating my options.

I'm studying my feet passing over the dirt road so I don't realise we have come across anyone until Will calls out to the man by name. I glance up quickly, my heart rate increasing.

"What news?" Will asks as we approach. I hang back. I am a girl. I can see in the other man's eyes that I do not belong here. I stand small and still. I know how to be invisible, not to draw attention to myself.

"Our men are assembled, but Cumberland hasn't shown."

"It's his birthday," I say. Cumberland's given his men the day off to celebrate. I read it in a book. That and fifteen hundred men will die tomorrow. I keep my mouth closed. People don't like to hear their future. They might think they do, but they don't.

"You need to head home, Lucy. This is no place for you to be right now," Will says.

"It's no place for you to be either."

"I have to stand up for what I believe," Will says. "Be safe, Lucy." I let him go because there is nothing else I can do. When they are out of sight, I follow. I am invisible.

Darkness is falling by the time Will and his companion join the men camped by the moor. His father greets him although I see regret in his eyes at his son's presence. Sometimes it is better to run than stand and fight. Me, I'm a runner. Standing up to be noticed terrifies me.

I eavesdrop on the planned sneak attack on Cumberland's army. A group is selected for the mission, but Will is not allowed to join them. His father does though. They will leave later tonight, but they won't give themselves enough time to reach their destination before sunrise. I curl up on the ground out of sight and try to catch a few hours of sleep.

I wake as the first rays of light appear in the sky. I'm cold, stiff and tired, but I know sleep won't find me again in this life. My stomach rumbles. I search silently for Will. He is still sleeping. I stay out of sight.

The men return from their march weary, hungry and dejected. They didn't reach their destination in time to launch the sneak attack. Some lie down to sleep. Others go in search of food. There is none here. They expected to fight yesterday. I keep my eye on Will's location.

The sound of the drums makes my arm hairs stand up on end. I'm glad I haven't eaten. I would be sick right here if I had food in my stomach. The men rush to pull on boots, those that have them, and collect their assorted weapons.

I lose sight of Will in the commotion. I step forward and a grisly old man sees me. I disappear from sight, skirting the edges of the camp as the men rush to join Bonnie Prince Charlie's forces. Many have not arrived back yet.

I see Will a short distance from the others, heading to the moor with only his axe for protection. I run in his direction and throw myself at him. We both tumble to the ground rolling several times and losing the weapon in the process. Will lands on top of me.

"Lucy? What in Hell's name do you think you are doing here?" he demands.

"Preventing your death."

I use his confusion and loose grip to topple him. I roll on top of him. He is taller and stronger than me, but I hold his wrists above his head, press my legs to the sides of his and use my weight to pin him down.

"If you join the battle, you will die." I put as much conviction into my voice as possible.

"You don't know that."

"I do! I live in the future. This has already happened. Cumberland wins, lots of people die and Bonnie Prince Charlie goes over the sea to Skye. There is a song about it, bagpipes and everything."

"You're crazy." Will looks at me like he is worried I might hurt myself. I have to keep him here until it is too late to join the battle. I try to remember how long it will last. It will be short and bloody, but Charlie hesitates in giving the order to charge, waiting for the rest of the men to arrive. I can't let Will be one of them.

I lean down and kiss Will on the lips. He's taken by surprise, then we are rolling again and Will is on top, pinning me to the ground.

"That's not going to work, Lucy."

Will starts to rise, but I wrap my legs tightly around his waist locking my ankles together. I am a boa constrictor and he is my prey. At any other time I would enjoy being in this position with him, but I'm worried I cannot hold it for long enough to save his life.

"Let go, Lucy."

"Only if you go home."

"I'm not going to leave my father and clan to fight alone." Will relaxes his body, but I don't trust him not to break free if I do the same. My legs are tiring.

"If you stay, I stay and we both die," I threaten.

"I'll take you back to Inverness, but then you have to stay there," Will says.

"Fine," I concede. Hopefully the battle will be over by the time he gets back. I release my grip on his body. Will holds out his hand and hauls me to my feet. I don't let go. We're both going to walk away from this.

I set a fast walking pace, but we're still some distance from the town of Inverness when we hear pounding footsteps behind us. I spin around expecting an attack, to find it is our side fleeing. Will pulls me out of the way.

153

"Cumberland's men are going to come after us," I say. We begin to run as shouts sound in the distance.

Will pulls me to the ground, tucking us behind some rocks, our bodies pressed together as we lie as small and still as possible. Will's breath is laboured next to my ear although I don't turn to look at him. I have limited vision of the landscape in front of us. More men run by. People scream as they are cut down out of our sight. Will grips my arm.

"That's my father," he hisses.

A man lies low, trying to stay hidden some distance from us as sounds of pursuit reach us.

"I have to help him." Will struggles to crawl around me without giving away our hiding place.

The history book I read about this battle tells me these men don't care if they find men, women or children, fighting or fleeing. They kill anyone they find. I don't belong here no matter how much I want to. Only one option remains.

I shove Will roughly backwards. His head hits a rock and his eyes slide closed. I hope I haven't hurt him too badly. I pull the locket out of my pocket and place it in Will's hand.

"For luck, to remind you of me," I whisper.

I crawl clear of our hiding place and run. As fast and loudly as possible. Will's father sees me and uses the distraction to slip away unnoticed. I am the decoy. Leading the hunters away. I am unarmed. I know they are faster than me. I hope it will be quick.

Letting Go

I become conscious of the familiar hospital scent before I even open my eyes. I lie still trying to ignore the present, but is a bloody battle field really a better place to be? I don't belong in either. My mind ticks over, evaluating my situation.

I sit up abruptly opening my eyes. There was a car crash. I search my mind for details. Emma had been driving her dad's car. We damaged La-a's car and rolled further up the road. Emma helped me out through the windscreen. There was a fire and Emma couldn't find her phone. I hit my head. Emma had sounded scared but alive. I sigh in relief.

The sound fixes me in the present. Will slips away from me. I hit my head and lost consciousness. It wasn't real. I lift my hospital gown to check for injuries. I have marks on my torso that could be from Cumberland's men cutting me down, but they're not. I was in a car crash. That's where the marks came from. There is no

Will. My only friend is Emma. I take deep gasping breaths. The truth hurts. I am here and I am alone.

Mum arrives to pick me up from the hospital still in her work uniform. She brings me a change of clothes. The school uniform I'd been wearing when we crashed is ruined. I'm going to have to wash it and see if I can rescue anything, otherwise I will have detention for being out of uniform. I rub my eyes to remove the moisture forming.

Mum barely talks to me. She yells at me as soon as we're out of the hospital about how irresponsible I've been and how I'm never to see 'that girl' ever again. I'm also grounded. I don't think Mum understands the concept. You can't ground someone who has nowhere to go.

It's not until I've scraped together a uniform and about to leave the house in the morning that I remember I left my bike at Emma's house. I've been too busy thinking about what I'm going to say to Emma that I'm already down the back steps when it occurs to me.

I pause in the backyard. My bike sits in its usual place at the back of the house. I stare at it suspiciously for a few moments, but it doesn't disappear. It's definitely my bike and it's where it should be.

Something white is taped to the handlebars of the bike. I peel it carefully away to reveal Emma's mp3 player and a scrap of paper with my name on it. There is a note squeezed in underneath.

I asked your mum to give you this but she told me to f-off. Hope you get it - E

I unfold it and read the words inside.

Turns out I give a damn after all. Bye, your friend Emma.

I stare at the mp3 player and note. Has she taken Mum's threat seriously, that we can't see each other again? Mum doesn't control what I do at school. I unwind the headphones and search the playlists, until I find one labelled with my name. I hit play as I wheel my bike out the front and ride off. I need to see Emma.

'If I lay here, if I just lay here, would you lie with me and just forget the world...'

There is a weird vibe at school when I arrive. Students whisper to each other and no one speaks to me or even shoves me in the hall. One girl bursts into tears and runs off past me. I have no idea who she is. I feel like I'm in a strange dream where I'm expected to know what today is, but don't.

I go to class and again I am ignored. There isn't even payback for damaging La-a's car. It makes me nervous. The teachers struggle to hold the attention of the students and many give up, suggesting we work quietly on catch-up projects.

Throughout the day students are called out of the room one by one. Some return looking like they've been crying. I've missed something important, but Emma is the only one who would probably answer my questions and I haven't seen her around today. I have to wait until lunchtime to go looking for her.

157

She's not at school. I've looked everywhere. I eat my sandwich, but it tastes like cardboard in my mouth. I throw the remainder in the bin and go to our usual table. Why is she not here to make my day easier? We're meant to be friends. I consider riding over to her house after school to see if she is home. I'd have to make it quick so Mum doesn't find out.

I'm called for during afternoon English class. A student from another class taps timidly on the door and says my name when the teacher asks. The girl won't look at me as I step outside the room. She stares at her feet and tells me I have to go to the school counsellor's office. The student leaves me there and disappears in the other direction.

My palms sweat as I walk the empty corridors to the administration building at the other end of the school. I pause to read the name plates on the doors before tapping hesitantly on the counsellor's door.

"Come in."

I ease the door open and hesitate at the threshold. My knees are weak. I want to sit down, but not in here. The room is small with a desk and two chairs opposite the counsellor for students and parents to sit in. The woman behind the desk is young. I've not spoken to her before and I don't think she's been at our school for long. This is probably her first proper job out of university.

"Take a seat," she tells me.

I do as she says leaving the door partially open. She stands, taking her time walking over to close it, trapping us in the room. She comes back and sits in her chair with the desk separating us. She picks up a pen.

"How are you?" she asks.

Her pen taps her notepad repetitively. I want to reach out and stop the motion, but I don't. I feel like I should be the one asking her how she is.

"Fine," I say when I realise I have to speak. Sometimes I think things in my head and don't realise I've stayed silent. I wonder if I keep all my answers to single word responses, I can get out of here faster. I slouch in the uncomfortable chair, not offering anything else.

At first, when I entered the room, I wondered if she suspected how I've been feeling. I've not yet decided how I might do it, but the idea is certainly looking like a better option than continuing like this.

I've seen lots of students called out of the class today. The counsellor appears to be speaking to everyone, at least in my year level. This is not about me. I'm not going to offer up my problems if she doesn't ask.

"Lucy, is it?" She glances at her list. I nod. "You probably know why you're here?"

"No."

She glances up at me. The pen stops for a moment before continuing at a faster pace. She opens her mouth, closes it again and looks back at her list. She has a script prepared for all the students and I've given the wrong answer. I'm meant to know what this is about.

"I've been in hospital for the last week," I offer.

159

"Hospital?" she repeats as though she has no idea what one is. This isn't about me.

"I was in a car accident," I tell her. I don't mention being unconscious for the whole week. She doesn't look like she can handle that amount of information.

"Oh," she says. The pause drags on while she shuffles her list of student names as though they might hold the correct response. "Well, I'm speaking to all the students to see how they are coping in the wake of this terrible tragedy."

"What tragedy?" My mouth is dry.

She glances up at me to see if I'm serious or just trying to make her repeat the news of the 'terrible tragedy'. Her pen stops its repetitive motion. Now she spins it around on the desk with her fingers.

"Several days ago, one of our students... died. You probably didn't know Emma Casey. She wasn't in any of your classes and she didn't have any close friends. We want to make sure none of our students have been adversely affected by this event."

My face turns slack. I couldn't find Emma today because she isn't here. Emma is dead. My whole body is numb. I want to uncross my legs, but I'm afraid of making a noise and drawing attention to myself.

She wasn't badly injured in the crash. She got me out of the car and was worried about losing her phone and not being able to get help for me. She was fine. I was the one who hit my head and ended up in hospital.

A coldness seeps through me, but my eyes remain dry. Why am I not crying for my friend? Am I heartless to still be sitting here calmly, or am I in some kind of shock? There is only emptiness inside of me. A dry, tearless emptiness.

"How did she die?" The words leave my mouth without me realising I moved my lips.

How can my friend drag me from a wreck one day and be dead only days later? The counsellor's expression is one I would expect from a person asked if they would help me bury a body.

"That's not what's important," she says.

I think back to all the whispering in the halls. In the car, Emma asked if I'd ever thought about ending it all. I froze thinking she could see inside my head, but she was talking about herself.

"She killed herself," I say. It's not a question. I've never felt so alone in my life.

"We don't talk about things like that!" the counsellor gasps.

Suicide is a dirty word. People don't talk about it. She is here to make sure no one follows Emma's example, but she can't see I'm already there.

"When's her funeral?" I ask.

Showing my support for Emma, even in death, is the least I can do. If she is looking down on us, I want her to see someone cares she is gone. She left a friend behind.

"Her parents have requested a private burial. It will be immediate family only," the woman informs me. Are her family ashamed of her? I'm not going to have a chance to say goodbye to my only real friend.

There is nothing this woman can do for me. I stand and she gives me the name of the next student she needs to see and allows me to leave. I walk back towards my classroom feeling nothing. I glance at the card the woman has given me 'in case I needed to talk some more'. It looks so impersonal. I toss it in the first bin I pass.

I place one foot in front of the other. If I pause, I don't think I'll know how to start again. I don't focus on anything. I am on auto-pilot going where my feet take me.

I hold myself together until I reach the lockers. Someone has written 'slut' in permanent marker across Emma's locker door and a wave of fury sweeps over me. I slam my fist into the offending words.

The first punch is for whoever graffitied her locker. It breaks the skin on my knuckles. It is followed by several more for everyone who has ever bullied someone to make themselves feel superior. I swear under my breath with each strike.

My anger turns to Emma. I hate her for leaving me here on my own. Now I have no one. I stop punching the bloody locker door and slide down to the floor cradling my torn hands to my chest. The tears are finally streaming down my face. I can't breathe.

Did I do this to her? Would she still be here if I hadn't disappeared into dreamland? Surely she knew I wasn't dead while I was in the hospital. I don't want her to have blamed herself for my comatose state. Emma might still be here if I wasn't broken, if I'd stayed, if I'd woken earlier. It's my fault she's dead.

"Lucy? Are you alright?"

I look up through my wet lashes to see Tayla hovering in the hallway, coming back from the bathroom. Without her bully friends, she has no mean retort to throw at me. I pull myself to my feet and glare at her. She steps towards me with her hand outstretched.

"Get the hell away from me," I scream.

A plastic rubbish bin is wedged between the banks of lockers minding its own business. I rip it from its nook and throw it at Tayla. It falls short of my target, rolling across the floor spewing rubbish as it goes. Tayla backs up several steps.

"Hey! What's going on here?" A teacher appears in a doorway and suddenly the corridor is claustrophobic with people standing in doorways. Phones not allowed in class appear in their hands. I am a circus freak putting on a show for their amusement. I bolt from the building taking nothing with me.

I'm not at school this week. I stalk the local cemetery and today there is a freshly dug grave set out for a funeral. It reminds me of all the bodies we dumped in the mass grave during the plague. Of course that wasn't real. It was just in my head.

I loiter around the older graves not wanting to draw attention to myself. Eventually a couple of cars arrive. There aren't many people to say goodbye to her. It makes me wonder if I'm the only one who actually misses her.

If I'm the only one for Emma, will there be anyone for me? I picture Mum being the only one standing by my coffin. No one will notice if I'm gone. It will be as though I never existed. I've left no mark in the world, nothing to say I've been here. I will vanish the same way I do from Will's world.

I wait until the funeral is over and Emma's parents and brother have left, before I go say goodbye. I don't have any flowers, but I spent last night drawing a mixed bunch of all my favourites for her. I leave the piece of sketch paper by her grave with a pebble on top to stop it blowing away. I've signed it with my initials – LJP.

"I miss you, Emma," I whisper.

I ride my bike up to the lookout and sit on my rock out of sight. I consider methods of how I will end my life. I've lost the will to live and have made the decision to leave when the time is right.

It's not like I'm going to do it tomorrow, but I see it as an event in my near future, waiting like an old friend. I run different options through my head until my backside becomes numb from the cool stone. I stand awkwardly and ride home.

A sense of relief settles over me after my decision. Every time I am shoved or tripped or have belongings stolen throughout the school day, I remain calm. There is an end to this. One day, this push will be the last.

In history, I picture my desk sitting empty sometime in the near future. At some point during the class, Ms Miller smiles at me. I force the corners of my mouth up in response. It takes a lot of muscles to smile, but until all happiness is drained from your life you will not notice.

"What event brought the Americans into World War II?" Ms Miller asks the class.

We are studying wars at the moment. I've missed a lot of it being away over the last few weeks, but I have read about the important stuff and almost survived the Battle of Culloden.

"Yes, Ladasha?"

La-a has her hand in the air. I've never seen her volunteer an answer before. She has something on the desk in front of her that she clearly wants to share with the rest of the class. Beside her, Bianca stares jealously at whatever it is.

"The bombing of Pearl Harbor," she states.

"Can anyone tell me the date?" She pauses. I'm staring at my desk, so I jump when she says my name. "Lucy?"

"7th of December, 1941." I rattle the date off the top of my head. I've always been good with dates.

To be honest, it doesn't really matter. What is the point in studying history when it doesn't change anything? Knowing how a war started won't give meaning to my life. No one is going to stand at my funeral and say at least she knew what day Pearl Harbor was attacked. It's not important.

"My parents and I went to Pearl Harbor when we were in Hawaii over summer," La-a interrupts. "I've brought in some photos for the class to look at."

She has everyone's attention now. No one else has been to Hawaii and she makes it sound so exotic. Half the students didn't even know where Pearl Harbor was. Our teacher suggests La-a pass the photos around while we continue the discussion. La-a is centre of attention and everyone is jealous of her overseas holiday. That's the way she likes it.

I look at the photos as they reach me one by one. I'm the last to receive them so I have sat listening to everyone else exclaim over them. There's a photo of an artist's painting of the attack with the battleships sitting in neat rows, giving the area the name of 'battleship row'. The class discusses the reasons behind the vessels, as well as the aircraft, being set up in a way that made it very easy to be bombed. No one expected an aerial assault.

I stay quiet. Is this any more important than the attack on Darwin ten weeks later by the same Japanese fleet? One was publicised, the other kept quiet. Emma and I are Darwin. No one talks about it, so no one knows. The dead are buried quietly.

I trace my finger over the last photo of an aircraft hangar. The glass in the building is original from 1941, with bullet holes still present. Somehow that makes the whole event feel more real to me, like looking into the past.

I sometimes wonder why certain people have everything while others have nothing. I've heard people suggest they must have done something bad in a past life. I don't think I have though. I've seen me in the past, even if it's not real. I hope there isn't another life after this one.

Last night I drew a picture of Emma as I want to remember her, smiling and singing into a hairbrush as we wreak havoc on her father's wardrobe. When I'm done, I rip the pages from my sketch book and surround myself with them. Wu with his spear. Walker travelling across continents with his family. Villius sitting on the stone steps of Pompeii's amphitheatre. Wilhelm of Europe. William working in the English field before the plague arrived. Scottish William in his kilt holding his axe. In the middle I place Emma. I curl up in a ball on my bedroom floor and cry myself to sleep.

The mornings are the hardest. Summoning the energy to crawl out of bed is a monumental effort. I do it only because it's expected of me and to stop would raise questions I don't have the energy to answer.

I go through the motions of sleeping, eating, going to school, going home, cooking dinner and going to bed. I tell myself I just have to get through each day. One at a time. I've made the decision to die, but I'm waiting.

It's still months away from my seventeenth birthday. It will be the last time I'll see Will. I need to tell him goodbye before I leave for good. It's silly, I know. He isn't real. It's all in my head as Mum constantly tells me, but I need to let go of Will so I can let go of me. I just don't know if I can hold on that long. I wish there was a way to find him sooner. I need to end this hell.

This morning I removed the four torn pieces of my art assignment picture of Will from the back of my sketch book. At my favourite spot up by the lookout, I pull out the pieces of my drawing from the pocket of my jacket and stare at the ruined image.

Standing on the edge of my rock, I let the wind whip my hair around my face. I hold the pieces of my drawing in the air letting them flutter in the breeze. I force my fingers to open one by one and watch the pieces fly away as tears stream down my face.

I have decided how I am going to die. I have also settled on when. I just need to find a way to reach Will without it being my birthday. I can't hold on that long. The next visit will be my last. Then, if I wake from my dream, I will end this life.

It's Mum's birthday, the last one we will ever share together even if she doesn't know it yet. I want to make it memorable, an apology for the fights we've been having, just the two of us like we used to be. I ride my bike to the shops after school. Mum isn't working tonight so I'm making her a special birthday dinner.

I've been saving my money for several months now so I can make Mum's birthday special. I'm going to cook her a fancy roast dinner to be waiting for her when she gets home from work. I lock up my bike outside the supermarket and head inside.

I pick up a roast chicken, vegetables and gravy. As I walk through the juice isle, I pause by the fancier bottled juice. Mum has always loved the ruby red grapefruit juice, but we never buy it because of the price. I hesitate for a moment weighing up the cost against the money I have. I grab the glass bottle off the shelf. It's her birthday. She deserves a special treat.

I head to the check out with my goodies. I feel almost content. I don't have a present for Mum, but we are going to have a nice dinner and spend the evening together. I count out my paper delivery money at the counter. I have sixty cents change. I drop it in the Guide Dogs donation container by the register and walk out of the shop.

I don't see La-a with her father until she is right in front of me. She shoves me and I stumble. My shopping bag splits, sending the glass bottle of juice rushing towards the pavement. It shatters on impact. I put my hand out to stop my fall and land on a piece of the glass. It cuts the palm of my hand. Grocery items roll over the wet footpath.

"Loser," La-a states in passing. Her father glances at me like I am a stain on his carpet and keeps walking. His daughter follows behind.

I choke back tears as I pull a piece of glass from my hand. I stare at the mess on the ground and burst into tears. I don't have the money to replace the drink. I bend down and retrieve the chicken and vegetables from the soggy mess.

I am invisible. People step around me as I crouch crying on the street, trying to rescue Mum's birthday dinner. A young woman reaches down to pick up a potato that stopped at her feet. She passes it to me with a sympathetic smile and continues on her way.

The shopping bag is ruined, so I shove what I can into my school bag and hold the rest. Someone has let the air out of my front tyre. I trudge home wheeling my bike, all my optimism for the evening gone.

The misery of the encounter envelops me and I am unable to shake it off even after I reach home. I retrieve the tweezers from the bathroom to remove the remaining glass splinters, wash the blood from my hand and cover the wound with a band aid. It doesn't stick properly no matter how much I press on it.

I stand at the bathroom sink taking deep breaths. After several minutes of trying to rid myself of the tightness in my chest, I splash cold water on my face. It does little to hide my red eyes. I stare at my reflection in the mirror until it blurs.

In the kitchen, I unpack the groceries. My school bag and books need cleaning, but I toss them to one side and focus on chopping the vegetables. The onions make me cry again, giving me an excuse for having red eyes.

I put the tray of food in the oven on high heat so it will be ready when Mum gets home. I sit down on our old saggy couch and turn the television on. I need the noise so I'm not sitting in silence.

The sound of the front door knob turning is followed by Mum's voice. She's home early. I stand to meet her hoping she hasn't invited anyone over for dinner. We don't see each other much these days and I only have enough food for two. She enters the lounge room followed by Frank. I deflate even further.

"Hi Lucy. You remember Frank." She turns to her boyfriend. "Give me ten minutes," she says.

She leaves me standing in the hallway being overwhelmed by Frank's cologne. We stare at each other not saying anything until I get really uncomfortable. I squeeze past him and follow Mum to her room. I find her standing in her underwear trying to choose an outfit while applying makeup.

"What's going on?" My voice cracks and I clear my throat.

"Frank is taking me out to that new Italian restaurant," she says.

"But I'm cooking a birthday dinner for the two of us," I say.

"That's really sweet, darling, but you should have said something earlier." Mum beams at me like she expects me to be happy for her. Tears prickle the back of my eyes for the third time today. I take a deep breath.

"It was meant to be a surprise," I whisper.

"We can have dinner anytime. Frank's already made the reservation and it's my birthday. I deserve a night out." Mum slips a black dress over her head, leans over to give me a kiss on my cheek and swipes lipstick across her puckered lips.

"What about the food I'm cooking," I say.

"You'll eat it," she says.

I no longer feel hungry despite not eating since my sandwich during lunch break. The dinner is meant for Mum and me to share.

"How do I look?" She doesn't wait for an answer which is good, because I'm unable to give her one.

My reflection in Mum's mirrored wardrobe door is miserable and lost. The eyes are blank. I break contact with my image and follow Mum towards the front door. Frank grabs her around the waist and kisses her hard on the lips removing half the quickly applied lipstick. Mum giggles and swats at his roaming hands.

"Don't wait up," Mum calls over her shoulder. Frank glances back at me standing forlornly and smirks. They leave me standing there, staring at the closed door with tears rolling down my face.

In the end, it's the headache forming in my temples and the desperate need for a tissue that makes me move. I can't find any tissues so I use the toilet paper from the bathroom. I shove a few spare squares into my bra for later and I go search for pain killers.

I go to my room and rummage in my drawer for a packet of Panadol. I take two tablets and lie on my bed willing the headache to fade away. I stare at the ceiling as stray tears slide down the side of my head.

There's a crack in the ceiling and a cobweb in the corner of the room. I squeeze my eyes shut, but I can still see the crack in my mind. It's been there since we moved into the house. It's never going to get fixed.

The headache is not easing so I roll off my bed and stagger into Mum's room, with my hand pressed to my forehead, in search of something stronger. In her hurry to leave the house, she left several discarded outfits on the bed. The only thing I find in her bedside drawers is a box of condoms. I slam the drawer shut and wince at the sound.

I find the tablets on a shelf in the closet. As I'm about to shut the door, I catch sight of a bottle buried beneath clothes on the closet floor. I grab the neck and pull out an almost full bottle of vodka. I brush the dust off it and read the small gift card tied to the neck. It simply says 'good luck' from a name I don't recognise.

I sit on the end of her bed, unscrew the lid, and throw back two painkillers with the vodka. It burns my throat and I choke. I remember there is a bottle of orange juice in the fridge. I take the vodka and tablets with me.

The vodka is better mixed with the juice although it still burns. I take the drinks to the lounge room and lie down on the couch. I mute the television, but the bright screen makes my head feel worse. I turn it off again. My headache doesn't improve so I take a few more pills and fill my glass again.

My head starts to feel foggy. I splash the juice when I refill my glass. I think I take another painkiller, but it's getting harder to focus on thoughts. I want the pain to stop.

I smell smoke. There's something I was meant to do. I drop my feet to the floor and walk into the kitchen. As I stand in front of the oven reaching out to turn it off, I jerk awake. It's all in my head. I haven't moved from the couch.

I try again and my arm knocks the table and flops down to the floor. My glass falls and shatters on impact. I'll deal with it later. I'm finally drifting into blessed sleep when the smoke alarm sounds. The beeping is far away so I don't worry about it. It's too difficult to move. I don't remember anything after that.

Speak Up

Hawaii 1941

When I open my eyes, I'm sitting on grass under a palm tree. The weather is warm and people frolic on the beach in the afternoon sun. A few men wear military uniforms, but others have floral Hawaiian shirts. They are happy and carefree. Calmness settles over me. This is my last adventure.

"What's a pretty little thing like you doing all on your own?" The American voice next to me makes me jump. He is part of a larger group. The two girls already have their chosen man on their arm. There are three single men including the one speaking to me. Will is not among them.

"I'm waiting for a friend," I say.

"I could be your friend," he suggests.

"Sorry, I'm not available."

He leans over me and I smell his alcoholic breath.

"How about we just play around for a bit until your 'friend' gets here?" he suggests. I cringe away, glancing around me in the hopes Will is nearby.

"Leave her be, Freddie. You can do better than her," one of the girls giggles.

He continues to stare at me as though about to say something further. One of the guys slaps him on the shoulder and points down the beach.

"Isn't that Mary?"

Freddie's attention waivers and the group sets off after a new target leaving me alone. I've lost the peacefulness of the day. I leap to my feet and head in the opposite direction looking for Will. I know he is here somewhere because I am.

I find him seated in an open air bar. I stand on the beach watching him socialise with his friends. A young man slaps him gently on the back and they both laugh over something I can't hear. I will never have that. No one will miss me when I am gone.

I turn and walk back down the beach, my bare feet digging into the soft sand. In my mind I see the pieces of my art assignment fluttering from my fingers. I will never see his face again.

I don't get far when I stop, scrunching my toes in the sand. I turn, treading back over my footprints. I have to say goodbye. I won't get another opportunity to do so. I can't leave until I have.

I reach the last footprint near the bar. He doesn't know me yet. Is it weird to introduce myself so I can say goodbye? Is it fair on him? I've never had this dilemma. I always planned on staying. I huff out a frustrated breath and trace my steps back down the beach.

I've known him since I was eleven. We have shared so much in our lives together. Whether he is real or not, I have to see him one last time.

I've walked back until I'm standing in front of the bar once more and lift my head. Will watches me as though wondering why there is a crazy girl marching up and down the beach. His friends head to the bar leaving Will to mind the table. It's now or never.

I take a deep breath, wipe my palms on the lower half of my dress and enter the bar. I slide into a vacated seat opposite the young man I've known for almost six years. He studies me with a look hovering between confusion and almost recognition. Déjà vu.

"Hello, Will," I say.

"My name's Bill." His accent is American.

"You've never been a Bill before," I say.

"Do I know you?"

"I'm Lucy," I say. The confusion doesn't leave his face.

"I'm sorry, I'm not looking for a good time with a pretty girl. I have a girl waiting for me back home," Bill says.

For a moment I struggle to breathe. I have always belonged to this boy and now he has someone else. I take a deep breath and try to hold onto my purpose. I am here to say goodbye, because I am already gone. I want Bill to be happy.

"Is she nice?" I don't care about her looks. Bill deserves a good person. Like him.

"Yes, she is."

I stare at the table tracing circles in the condensation left from the empty glasses. I'm quiet for a moment, ordering my chaotic thoughts. This truly is the end. I have nothing left. Mum would be pleased I'm letting go of dream lives, but it leaves a gaping hole inside me.

"I came to say goodbye," I say. Tears try to form in my eyes and I blink rapidly to hold them back. I dig my nails into my palms.

"We just met."

"I've known you for years."

Before he has a chance to respond, Bill's friends return with drinks and girls. They are loud, overwhelmingly happy and carefree. I want to get away from them. I could never fit in to a group like this. I don't belong.

"Finally got yourself a new girl, hey Bill?" one friend jokes.

"I'm sorry. I shouldn't have come here." I stand suddenly, knocking the chair over. I don't stop to pick it up. I run out onto the beach in the fading light of the evening.

"Wait up!" Bill shouts.

I try to keep running, but it's not easy to do on sand, and I can't breathe and cry at the same time. I slow to a walk and wipe my face unsuccessfully on the short sleeves of my dress. Bill catches up and walks beside me for a moment before speaking.

"Are you okay?" he asks.

"Sure," I manage. I'd be better if I had a box of tissues instead of my sleeve. Bill looks at me doubtfully.

"Are you staying nearby?"

I don't answer. I haven't considered it. I could sleep on the beach. If I get murdered in my sleep at least I've spoken to Bill one final time.

"Here." Bill pulls his wallet out. I begin to stop him, when I see the gold chain attached to it. I reach out and cradle the tarnished locket in my palm.

"You should look after this better. It must be nearly two hundred years old by now," I say. It is a beautiful thing. A sign I existed before today, even if only in my dreams.

"How do you know?"

"The back of the picture is dated. William and Lucy, 1746," I say. Bill takes the locket in his hand and snaps it open. By the look on his face I'd say he hasn't opened it for some time. He looks quickly up at me and then back at the picture, before holding it up next to my face. He has no recollection of sitting for the portrait like I do. With shaking fingers, he pries the aged picture from its housing and turns it over. I watch him read the writing on the reverse.

"Your family came to America from Scotland. They fled on boats after the battle of Culloden," I say.

"How do you know that?"

"I was there."

"This is my several times great grandfather William, who I was named after."

"Sitting next to me. This is a dream for me. I won't even be born for another fifty years. I appear in a time where you are and then disappear and wake up back in my present. I have no control over it," I tell him.

"That's not possible." Bill looks at me like one of us might be a crazy person and he doesn't think it's him.

"And yet I'm still here."

Bill is silent for a while. He leads me to a quiet spot on the beach where we sit and watch the colour fade from the sky.

"Do you have anything as beautiful as this where you come from?" Bill asks.

"I have a spot I like to sit and think," I say. I tell him about my hidden rock up by the lookout over the valley. I've never told anyone about it before. Bill listens as though there is nowhere else he would rather be than sitting on the beach hearing me talk. I finish my story and we sit in silence.

"Why me?" he asks.

"You're the only person who has ever bothered to get to know me. I couldn't leave without saying goodbye."

"Where are you going?" Bill looks at me. I stare out over the dark ocean. I don't say anything for some time. I open my mouth, but the words are not there. I say them over in my head several times to see how they sound, willing the words to be heard. Bill is silent, waiting for me to make the first move.

"I'm going to throw myself off my rock," I say quietly. It seems like the best way to go, looking out at the view as I die.

I wait for Bill's reaction to the thoughts I've never said out loud. I didn't say them to get a reaction. I think I said the words, because Bill is the first person I've met who is genuinely interested in what I say. He listens without judgement. I feel strange, lightheaded. Bill is the first person I have admitted this to.

"Why?" he asks.

I shrug as if it doesn't matter, but it is too late to take the words back. I don't know if I want to. They needed to be out in the open. Bill waits for me to speak. He is my only friend, even if I have only met this version of him a few hours ago. I open my mouth and tell him my story starting with my eleventh birthday. He sits on the beach and listens. He doesn't tell me I'm crazy or that it's all in my head.

"I don't think you should give up on life," Bill says once I've fallen silent. "Life is full of ups and downs. You might miss something amazing if you back out now."

"You're seventeen years old, Bill. You've barely lived yourself. You can't tell me it gets better. You don't know."

"What if I did know? Would you listen to me?" he asks.

"I always listen to you."

"I'll make a deal with you. If you really are from the future, wait for me to find you. I'll tell you how beautiful life is if you hang on to it," Bill says.

"You'd do that for me?" Tears spring to my eyes again. In my head I'm making a deal with myself. An escape clause from my death sentence. If someone cares enough to reach out to me, I will consider staying.

"Sure, what are friends for? Now do you have anywhere to stay tonight?"

I'm dreaming about swimming in the depths of the ocean off Hawaii. I glide through the water as the fish dart away from me. A dark cylindrical object moves stealthily towards the ancient string of volcanos rising from the sea bed. It pays me no attention as it is propelled towards its target.

A shadow drifts over me. The steel creature on the surface senses the one beneath the water. An object shoots from above leaving a trail of disturbed water in its wake. The stealthy Japanese submarine explodes as the torpedo strikes it. The pulse of energy through the water feels like my heart exploding in my chest. The shadow on the surface moves on.

I sit bolt upright from my dream. I'm on a mattress on the floor next to Bill's military issue cot. In the room someone snores, another turns in his sleep, otherwise the room is quiet.

Bill, an aeroplane mechanic in training to be a pilot, snuck me into the barracks he shares with the other men at Wheeler Airfield. His friends teased him mercilessly about it, but they didn't tell. I think Bill was worried about leaving me on my own after my confession.

I glance at the clock on the wall. The big hand ticks over to 06:54 am. Tick, tick, tick in the silent room.

"Did you hear that?" I whisper to Bill.

"Hear what?" He looks at me groggily.

"The explosion." It had been so loud in my ears I was sure the whole world had heard the submarine sink.

"You're dreaming. Go back to sleep," Bill tells me.

I lie down on the mattress and close my eyes. My stomach is in knots. I open my eyes and glance at the clock again. The moving hands are making me nervous. I sit up and crawl over to Bill's bed. I lean on the mattress and shake his arm until he opens his eyes.

"Why are you still asleep?" I ask.

"It's Sunday. We get to sleep in on a Sunday," he mutters before rolling over.

The hairs on my body are standing on end and I'm cold in the warm room. Outside the window a bird tweets calmly.

"What's the date?" I hiss, shaking him again. I glance around the room, but I can't see a calendar. Bill squints at me as he thinks about my question.

"It's the 7th," he eventually decides. I shiver.

"Please tell me it's not December?" I beg. Bill rolls his eyes.

"It's December 7th, 1941. Now can I go back to sleep?" he says.

"Get up," I hiss.

"It's Sunday. I don't need to be up yet," Bill groans, pulling the sheet over his head.

I leap to my feet. I'm still wearing my dress from last night. It's crumpled, but I doubt anyone will have time to notice. Bill's trousers are folded over the end of his bed. I throw them at him.

"You need to get out of bed." I rip the sheet off him.

I glance at the clock again. The big hand advances. I don't know how much time we have, but I don't think it is much. The attack will happen this morning and none of the planes are ready. I look back at Bill. He is sitting up, but hasn't got dressed yet.

"Get up!" I scream.

The note of hysteria in my voice frightens me. Bill jumps at my outburst. The snoring stops abruptly as everyone in the room is suddenly wide awake looking groggily in our direction.

"Bill, shut your girlfriend up. We're trying to sleep."

I ignore the pilot and focus my attention on Bill. He has reluctantly pulled his trousers on over his white shorts. I'm trying to formulate a plan, but all that is running through my mind is that we are out of time. I picture La-a's photo of the hangar at Pearl Harbor with bullet holes in the glass. We are based at one of the primary targets that will be destroyed this morning.

"What's wrong, Lucy?" Bill asks.

My breathing is erratic, making me light headed. I need to focus. I wipe my sweaty palms on my dress. Several men glare at us and someone throws a pillow in our direction.

"The Japanese are about to attack. Two and a half thousand men are going to die today. I need you to get the planes in the air." I talk quickly, tripping over my words. My mouth is dry. I'm shaking. I should have found out when I was last night, but I was too involved in my own problems. I need to focus on keeping Bill alive.

This time feels more terrifyingly real to me than any other I have visited. Perhaps it is because it is so close to my present. I have seen photos of the damage about to happen. I could almost reach out and touch it. There is a minute possibility that some of these men might still be alive in my present. Old, but alive. If they survive today and the rest of the war. I glance at the clock again. Tick, tick, tick.

"We're in the middle of the Pacific and we're not at war with the Japs," Bill assures me.

"Their aircraft carriers are north of O'ahu right now. Their planes are probably already in the air." My voice cracks. "The declaration of war won't come through until the end of the attack. You need to get the planes in the air."

"She's crazy," someone mutters. Something inside me snaps. We're all going to die. I grab the nearest item off a shelf and throw it against the wall above Bill's head.

"Get up!" I screech.

"You need to calm down, Lucy." Bill reaches out to stop me grabbing anything else. A couple of men are getting dressed. Maybe they want to escape the room in case I start throwing more items.

"You need fuel and ammo in the planes right now," I insist.

I look at all the faces in the room. They glance at each other. No one moves to do as I say. They don't believe me.

"Get the fucking planes in the air!" I scream at the top of my lungs.

I can hear running in the corridor outside, pounding feet heading in our direction. I've woken other people in the building. One of the men in the room grabs me from behind and holds my arms. They are afraid of me, of how I might act. I am just afraid.

"Now hold on a minute. She hasn't done anything," Bill protests.

"Stay out of this, Bill," one of the men answers.

Bill looks at me like he wants to believe, but the evidence says otherwise. Outside is a quiet Sunday morning if you ignore the girl screaming inside. I am in a war zone, but am the only one who knows it.

The clock on the wall keeps ticking, ignoring the struggle in the room. In another ten minutes it will be nearly eight o'clock. I think I hear planes in the distance, but the room is too noisy now. I could be imagining what I expect to hear. The men argue about what to do with me. Others have joined us to find out what the commotion is about.

I repeat the words over and over like a mantra. *Get the planes in the air.* No one listens. Outside the bird is silent. I'm holding my breath.

The explosion sounds faintly in the distance. We are some way from the first target: Pearl Harbor. Everyone in the room stands still as the unexpected sound continues one after another. Bill darts over to the window. I shake myself free and do the same. Plumes of black smoke rise over Pearl Harbor.

"Shit," Bill says.

"The Japs are here," I say. My heart pounds. We're out of time.

"We're under attack. Get the planes in the air," Bill yells.

"That's what I've been trying to tell you," I mutter as the room erupts into chaos.

People trip over themselves to do as Bill says. The men grab guns as they race from the building. I'm ignored in the confusion. I run after Bill as he yells instructions to people on the way to the hangars. I'm afraid to lose sight of him, overwhelmed with fear if I take my eyes off him I will never see him again.

Bill is joined by several other men running to ready the planes for take-off. The ammunition isn't kept on the planes so it can't be sabotaged. I help a young man use a crowbar to break the locks on the munitions storage. Bill passes me some items and we race for the planes.

We're under the first plane when the attack begins. War is noisy. The approaching Jap planes are loud and terrifying, but nothing compared to the ping-ping sound of bullets hitting the tarmac as they fly overhead.

Haste makes us clumsy, but I continue to fetch and carry for Bill as he and the other men ready the planes. A pilot throws himself into the first plane and trundles slowly down the runway. I pause to watch, willing him into the air. Please, please, please. More planes fly overhead and our plane erupts into a fireball, still on the ground with the pilot trapped inside. I swallow the bile rising in my throat and run back to the hangars for supplies.

A young man hands me a load of ammo and grabs his own. He follows me back into the open. I search the tarmac for Bill, taking a step in his direction when I hear the gasp behind me. I turn in time to see a red stain spreading across the chest of my companion. The life leaves his eyes like a torch being switched off. His body drops to the ground. I fight back a scream and run.

A loud boom is followed by the sound of glass shattering. I'm covered in sweat and my legs sting. I reach Bill's side. We get the next planes ready as others explode into flames around us. I choke on the thick black smoke.

A few of the men have got the guns in place and are firing back. The sound is horrendous. I can't tell who is firing. One man stands in the open in his shorts with only a shot gun. My ears ring and I'm sure I'll never be able to hear again.

Several more planes roll down the runway under heavy gunfire from both sides. Two lift off the ground, but I can't stop to watch their progress. As I turn away I see the enemy planes on their tails.

We're running across the open space when Bill stumbles and falls. I almost trip over him. My first thought is he has stumbled on the torn up concrete. He rolls over and looks at me with surprise on his face. A red stain spreads across his shoulder. For a second I'm frozen with the vision of the lifeless man's eyes. A second row of bullets passing inches from Bill's head makes me scream.

I grab his arm on his uninjured side and drag him across the pitted concrete. I make it to the door of a hangar and pull Bill inside. For the moment we are both still alive. I rip the hem off my dress. My legs are covered in cuts and trails of blood from the concrete shrapnel thrown up by the bullets. There is a large gash across my upper thigh. It looks like I've been grazed by a bullet, but I didn't feel it.

I press the cloth into Bill's shoulder. He winces, but I'm worried he will bleed to death before the raid finishes if I ease the pressure off. I kneel on the wound so I have free hands to make his shirt into a bandage. I tie it around his shoulder, but it is only successful to a point. I continue to press with my hands.

I'm covered in blood and I can't tell how much is his or mine. I'm shaking. Bill has never been this close to death before. I have always believed I am here to save him in whichever life I find him. Now I am failing in my one task. I wanted to say goodbye, to let go, so I could leave my life. Is his death my mind's way of destroying our connection so I have nothing left to live for? My head tells me this isn't real, but my body refuses to believe it.

"I need to get help," I say. The bombing continues around us. The glass has several bullet holes. It's funny really, I remember there being more in La-a's photo, but it could have been a hangar at Pearl Harbor.

"Lucy, don't leave me," Bill groans.

We are the only ones here. If it wasn't for the occasional piercing scream from outside, I'd think we were the only ones left alive. There is no one to help Bill. All I can do is keep the pressure on and hope he doesn't bleed to death before someone finds us.

"Don't die on me, Bill," I sob. *I'm sorry. I was wrong to come here to say goodbye. I don't want to lose you.* The words remain in my head.

"I'm not going anywhere," Bill gasps. I lean over him to hear the words. "I made you a promise."

"What?"

"I'll find you in the future… and tell you how," he gasps again, "…beautiful life is."

I'm sobbing now, the uncontrollable kind that shakes a body to its core. I keep pressing on his shoulder. If I let go, he will die. If he dies, I have nothing. I'm not ready.

"I'm scared," I whisper.

I need help to arrive. Bill needs to get to the hospital. I sit up to listen for the cease of the attack. My ears are so numb I don't hear the plane flying towards our hangar at first. Rapid gun fire sounds as a shadow passes over the glass. I'm staring at one of the panels when it cracks. Time slows down as the bullet pierces the glass leaving a hole in its wake. I need to move, but my body won't function.

As the bullet hits me square in the forehead, I know I have failed Bill. I fall across his body and am gone.

Coma

I sit in the psychiatrist's chair waiting for her to say something. I refuse to be the first to speak. I wait for her to notice. I have been waiting for months now, for anyone to notice. No one has. They are so obsessed with figuring out what is wrong with me, they cannot see the actual problem.

I watch her sitting in her chair with her notebook. I don't remember much about the last week. I woke with a red mark on my forehead and another across my upper thigh. My head feels like it has been cracked open and my ears hurt. I jump at loud noises.

"Do you dream when you're asleep?" she asks me. I flinch at the question. She is the first person to ever ask. I consider lying, but I pause too long. She looks at me and I have to answer.

"Sometimes." I shrug. I imagine walking across the grey carpet, opening the door and leaving this room. I don't. I sit in the square chair, a girl without a voice, unable to act.

"Tell me about your most recent dream."

I want to go home and curl up on my bed. I've said goodbye, I've lost Bill. There is nothing left for me now. I open my mouth and say the first thing that comes to me.

"I was in Hawaii." Can no one hear how sad I am?

"What were you doing?" she asks.

"Oh, you know, checking out the hot guys, Pearl Harbor, touristy things mostly." I no longer care. She won't believe anything I say.

"Have you been to Hawaii before?"

"Just this once," I reply. She gives me an assessing look from behind her glasses.

"Did you like it there?" More leading questions.

"Not really," I admit.

"Why?"

"Too many Japs." I regret the words as soon as they are out of my mouth. I shouldn't have used the wartime slang.

"Do you have an issue with Japanese people?" she asks.

"Only ones that fly planes."

She sighs and glances at the clock. That makes me nervous. I glance at it as well, but it's the afternoon. I take a deep breath and try not to grip the arms of the chair like a crazy person. Good thing I've never owned a watch.

"I think we are done for the day. Get your Mum to make an appointment for next fortnight and Lucy, be honest with me. I cannot help if you don't talk to me."

193

I flee the room. I don't think Mum will make a second appointment once she receives the bill for the first one, especially after the quote to repair the smoke damage to the kitchen. I'd be working a long time to pay for that, if I was to stay.

I hold it together until Mum and I are outside. The door shuts loudly making me jump. A light plane flies low overhead towards the local airport.

I cower in the doorway with my left hand gripping the stair railing. The plane disappears into the distance. My heart pounds. Mum turns around to see why I'm not following.

"Come on, Lucy. We don't have all day," she scolds.

I pry my cold fingers off the railing and follow her to the car.

I go back to school because it passes the time. If the girls continue their taunts, I don't register. I'm an empty shell. There is only one reason I'm still here and it's not because I'm waiting for Bill. He's not coming for me. He died sixty-five years ago, never having the chance to live the life he believed was so beautiful. That's if he ever existed outside of my imagination in the first place.

The truth is, I'm waiting. Mum is still seeing Frank and it's nearly his birthday. I overheard them planning a big night out while I was still at the hospital. They don't want me around.

This is the day I have chosen.

There are two reasons why. I will be on my own, so it will be easier to leave. No one will know until it's too late to stop me. I also don't want Mum

194

to turn to Frank when I am gone. I don't want the memory of his birthday to be a happy one. It may sound selfish, but I don't know how else to tell her she deserves better.

I count down the days until I die.

Eight more days. Monday I pass a dead cat on the side of the road as I ride to school. It stares at me with the same dead eyes as the airman at Wheeler who stood behind me as he was shot.

I turn my head as I ride, unable to drag my eyes away. An annoyed ding of a bell makes me swerve to avoid another cyclist. The cat loiters in my memory as I continue to school. It's still there when my history teacher asks me to stay back after class. The in-between time is blank. I didn't pay any attention to the day.

"Is everything alright?" Ms Miller asks.

"Sure," I respond automatically.

"You just don't seem yourself at the moment. Is everything fine at home?" she presses.

"My cat died," I reply. I don't have a cat.

"I'm sorry, Lucy. If you ever need to talk, my office door is always open."

I nod and escape from the room. She's the first person to reach out to me, but it's too late. I'm already gone. Perhaps if the offer had been made a few months earlier, I could have acted on it. I do appreciate her offer though. It's nice to know someone might notice if I'm not around anymore.

Wednesday my English teacher greets me as I take my seat.

"You're looking more cheerful than usual, Lucy," she smiles at me.

My face relaxes into something that may be mistaken as a smile in response. Acceptance brings calmness with it. It's almost over. I haven't cried for days.

Class begins with an assignment. Mrs Carmichael has found a writing competition she wants us to enter. We have to work in pairs to write a short story about how we see the future. She will pick the best ones to submit to the competition.

My mind considers what my future may hold. Is there an afterlife, heaven or reincarnation? I don't know. All I can see before me is darkness. Perhaps the darkness in my mind is a reflection of what I desire. Nothing. An end to life. I don't want there to be anything after this.

There are an uneven number of students in the class. I am the odd one out. The one who never gets chosen. It doesn't matter to me like it used to. I won't be here by the time it's due. There is no future for me. I shove the assignment to the bottom of my bag while my classmates squabble over who will work with who.

Thursday I sit at a computer in the library staring at the default library catalogue browser. Someone swings into the seat beside me. I don't look at them as they type rapidly into the search box. A few minutes later, they leave. Most likely with the information they were after.

I wish it was that easy. To find the information I need.

I open Google. The search box stares back at me. My fingers hover over the keyboard. The librarian hushes a noisy junior student who hasn't yet discovered not to get on their bad side. A book is dropped on a desk with a thump.

I glance at the time at the bottom right hand side of the screen as the minutes of the lunch hour slip away. I avoid looking at the clock on the wall.

I type Bill's name into the search box with my finger hanging over the enter button. I hold my breath. The bell rings. I sit still as students file out of the library. Bill's name stares back at me on the screen. I close the page without hitting the button.

I don't know what would be worse. Bill's death in print or nothing at all. He never existed in the first place. It's all been in my head.

Fridays should be good days. The last day before the weekend. A celebration of surviving the first four days of a week. I don't know if it is different any more. Each day is the same to me.

Our art teacher gives us the assignment of creating a drawing depicting emotion. I think about a noose hanging from the tree, but that creates more of a lack of emotion for me. I also don't want to end up back at the psychiatrist's office.

My mind wanders to Bill as it often does these days. My journey had been the briefest yet, but I can recall every detail clearly. The overriding emotion is one of pain. I rub my dry eyes and begin drawing.

I use pencil so the drawing is in shades of grey. I focus on the glass panelled wall of the aircraft hangar. There were numerous bullet holes already in the glass when I first glanced at it. With my pencil I capture the moment I looked up and saw the glass crack under the force of the bullet. Behind the glass is the shadow of the passing Japanese Zero.

My arm reaches down to press into Bill's shoulder, visible in the lower section of the page. His face is hidden. I pick up a red pencil, to highlight the blood on my hand and Bill's shirt. Finally I add a touch of gold to the tip of the bullet speeding towards me.

When I am done I stare at it until the bell rings. I hand it in to the teacher. I won't be here next class. I wonder if someone else would see the emotion I felt from this sketch.

Saturday: three more days. I wander aimlessly along the street. I felt the urge to escape the empty house this morning. I walk towards the park by the shops so I can sit on the grass under the trees and watch the world go by like I used to do when we first moved here. This is my last chance to feel the peacefulness of the park. I walk faster. I need to hold onto the calm that has fluctuated through my body these last few weeks.

I have the image of the bullet stuck in my mind, swamping me with the familiar feeling of despair at my failure to protect Bill. It makes me question if I saved Wu, Villius or William. My dream-like realities have given my life meaning. I had a purpose in saving my friend, but real or not, Bill died leaving me with nothing.

A cyclist hurls abuses as he rides by. I have been walking without registering where I am going. There are no planes or broken glass. Bill is not dying under my hands. I reach the park and stand on a patch of grass watching the people around me. They all look so happy to be in the park on this warm, sunny day.

A loud bang sounds behind me. I throw myself under the nearest tree and cover my head with my arms. My heart tries to break through my chest. When I don't hear answering gunfire, I raise my head to look around me.

Everyone calmly goes about their business. A small boy stares at me. I glance at the nearby road and realise a car has backfired. I climb shakily to my feet and brush the leaves from my clothes.

That is when I see him, the man who looks like Frank. He has his arm slung over the shoulders of a scantily clad girl who is probably only a few years older than me. From this distance, it looks like he is attempting to clean her ear with his tongue.

The man looks up in my direction. The hairs on my arms stand on end. Frank pushes the girl away from him and starts towards me.

I run. I've never liked Frank and I don't want to hang around to find out how far he would go to prevent me from telling Mum he's cheating on her.

I need to be near people so there are witnesses. I jump a garden bed and throw myself across the street. A car honks loudly.

I bolt through the doors into the main shopping mall, nearly colliding with the slowly opening glass panels. I push past a couple of mums with prams to get to the escalator. They call me names behind my retreating back. I pause halfway down to look back. Frank is a short distance behind me with a look of pure hatred on his face.

In my mind, I am running from the Japs again. If I stop, I will be shot and Bill will die. The noises around me blend to the sound of jets flying overhead. I have to escape so that Bill might survive, even if it is only in my own memory.

It was a mistake to enter the shopping centre. It's loud with lots of sudden noises and happy teenagers squealing at the tops of their lungs. Would any of them help me if Frank catches me? I don't believe so. I am invisible. No one cares what happens to someone like me. I'm shaking and struggling to breathe. I need to get out of here. I have to lose him.

I leap off the escalator, nearly bowling over a young child. I dash through the shopping centre like I've stolen something, making it to the other end of the mall and nearly colliding with the sliding doors again. I skid to a stop, taking deep gasping breaths.

After an eternity, the doors slide open wide enough for me to slip through and I run out onto the main shopping strip. I glance over my shoulder to see how much distance I've gained and crash into someone. We both fall to the footpath in a pile of tangled limbs.

"Get the hell off me," Jennypha yells as she attempts to extricate herself from me. I struggle to get up, but as soon as I'm nearly upright, Bianca pushes me back down again. I've run into the girls from school.

I crawl backwards on my hands and knees until I have space to stand. All four of them glare down at me – Jennypha, Bianca, La-a and Tayla. I take my time to rise to my feet. I might be able to charge through the group if I take them by surprise.

I look back the way I came. Frank hesitates by the door I exited. Without knowing it, the girls are protecting me from him. Pity there is nothing to protect me from them. I have nowhere to run. The fight leaves my body as my arms hang loose by my sides.

La-a grabs my elbow hard and shoves me towards Bianca. I'm still watching Frank, so I lose my footing and twist my ankle. Bianca unintentionally prevents me from falling to the ground. I imagine myself as a ragdoll being tossed around.

"You don't assault my friend and think you can get away with it, bitch," La-a screeches at me.

"Loser Lucy," Bianca yells as she shoves me. Tayla steps out of the way and I hit my head on a signpost.

"I don't think she meant it," Tayla says. The other three glare at her.

"Whose side are you on?" La-a demands. She doesn't wait for an answer. There is only one correct response unless you want to be like me. Tayla says nothing.

I haul myself up using the pole I hit and back up until my heels hang over the curb. I have nowhere to go. A vehicle honks as it passes. Adults give our group a wide berth and avoid eye contact. My heart thumps in my chest. I feel like I am watching a scene from outside my body.

I can hear a larger vehicle approaching. It could be a four wheel drive or small truck. In my mind it is a Jap fighter plane. Its droning noise is bringing me closer and closer to Bill. Three more days. That's all I had left.

La-a urges Jennypha to push me. I look at Jennypha and realise I haven't cared about her liking me for a long time. I hated this girl for so long. Now there is nothing. I am empty of emotions. She and her friends will suffer like I have. It's only fair they understand.

I look Jennypha directly in the eyes, almost daring her to push me. A slight smile crosses my face. I'm surprised I remember how to; it's been so long. My expression infuriates my tormentors. La-a calls me every nasty name in her vocabulary.

She pushes me sideways into Jennypha. I'm still on the edge of the curb. Jennypha shoves me with enough force to make me stumble. I step backwards, allowing the force to throw me into the path of the approaching delivery truck.

The screeching is followed by unimaginable pain. Someone screams, but I can't tell if it is me or Tayla. For a moment I am flying free, then I'm lying on hard concrete with my limbs at strange angles.

I've read stories that say at moments like these, your life flashes before your eyes. I remember lying beneath the huge paws of a lioness as it breathed its rancid breath into my face. I hope my sacrifice gave Wu the chance to survive. It would give my life some meaning I've never found in reality.

"Lucy? Talk to me." Tayla sounds hysterical. A paper bag will fix that, my mind says. There are no words. I can't answer even if I wanted to.

Everything is fading away. I can't feel my arms or legs. Even the pain is dull now. Tayla's voice continues, but it sounds like it's in a tunnel drifting further away.

I've finally done it. It's all over.

I'm scared.

Sirens sound in the distance. They're coming for me, but I will be gone before they reach me. I hope Bill is waiting for me somewhere.

Hell

Sydney 2084

It's completely dark. I shut my eyes and open them again, but it makes no difference. My mind is as blank as the vision before me. The last thing I remember is stepping in front of a moving vehicle. Now I'm lying on my back against a cool, smooth surface, completely unlike the rough road asphalt. I try to sit up, smacking my head on a low flat object in the process. This is not what I expected from death.

I throw my arms out to find I'm in a confined space not much longer or wider than me. I strain to hear my surroundings, but there is only silence and a faint whirring sound I can't place, but could be my ears reacting to the sound of nothing. My breathing accelerates and my palms become sweaty.

"Oh my God, I'm in a coffin." I say it out loud just so I can hear the sound of my voice.

I consider screaming, but I doubt anyone would hear me from six feet underground. I don't want to be buried alive. It will be a slow death and I will have plenty of time to think. I don't want to think anymore. I just want to be gone.

As I lie in my coffin, whimpering and hyperventilating, there is a faint sound of something going whoosh followed by what sounds like two sets of footsteps. My overactive mind quickly produces two solutions: I'm hallucinating due to lack of oxygen or I'm not in a coffin under six feet of dirt.

With the sounds come a hint of greyness in my dark world. One set of footsteps stops near my feet while the other set shuffles nervously by my head. Someone speaks.

"When will the new Monitor arrive?" a nasally woman's voice asks. I'm hallucinating. Why else would I be hearing a conversation about computer screens?

"I sent the request as soon as the rebel was discovered. Our replacement should arrive any day now," the second voice replies somewhat nervously.

"Good. I don't want any more problems. We lose control of desalinators and we lose the war. Let me know when the girl arrives at the training base. I need to ensure she keeps the Carter boy and his girlfriend under close watch."

"Yes, ma'am."

Footsteps retreat, while the other set paces for a few minutes. I lie perfectly still in my hiding place. Eventually the second woman sits down above me. I hold my breath. I'm beginning to think I'm under a bed.

I'm confused. I doubt Heaven or Hell begins under someone's bed. How did I get from lying bloodied on the road to under someone's bed? What if there is no escape and life just continues in a different form? On and on and on.

My heart skips a beat and resumes its erratic pace. What if I'm in the past with Will again? I'd accepted I would never see him again, but the slightest glimmer of hope has me wanting to crawl from this space and search for him.

The woman takes a while to get comfortable, but after tossing and turning for some time, the room goes quiet and dark. I try to assess my surroundings before I dare venture further. I'm under a bed and there is a possibly a door nearby that goes whoosh as it opens. That's all I've got.

After some time, I catch the faint sound of snoring. I try to move, but my leg has gone numb. I bite my lip as the pins and needles peak and finally recede. I move my left arm out and search along the surface. It feels like there are plastic boxes trapping me under here.

I give one a push. It makes a slight grating noise as it moves and I freeze. The snoring continues. After a few moments I move the box a little further. I'm not sure how long it takes, but I eventually have enough space to wriggle out.

Using both hands, I move the box back into place as quietly as possible. I stay completely still letting my eyes adjust to the darkness. There is no natural light, only several small red lights from technology in standby mode allow me to get an idea of the room layout. It is small with virtually no furniture except for the bed and a chair.

I crawl carefully across the room to where I think the door is and slide my hands up the wall. I touch a protruding panel and the door whooshes open. I get off my knees and step out quickly, then realise I didn't check for danger. The room may be the safer option. Then again, does it matter? I'm already dead.

I glance around, but I'm alone. The door slides shut, leaving me in a corridor with a faint green light at one end. I edge quietly towards it. There is a dimly lit stairwell at the end.

"Will?" I pause to listen. "William?" I call out softly.

The long stark corridor remains silent. He's not here, or if he is, he would be asleep in one of the rooms and I would never know. Continuing to stand here won't achieve anything. I hesitate before following the stairwell to the bottom. It's a long way down.

At each level I stop to call out Will's name quietly. There's no response. It's probably a pointless exercise, he wouldn't hear me from any of the rooms, but I'm trying to overcome an irrational fear that he's not here. What if I'm not even in one of Will's worlds? What do I do then? Am I dead or not? If I die here, will I wake there?

I come out at the ground floor facing another door. The corridor behind me is as empty as every other one above. My hand hovers over the control panel. The level of technology scares me. I'm not in any past era I know about. I need to see outside this building. I touch the panel and the door slides open.

I step out into the dim night outside. I'm in a tiny courtyard with a barbed wire fence a few paces in front of me and a small gate set into it. Beyond that is a semi-abandoned third world city. I turn back to the building, but the door has shut behind me. I touch it, but the panel doesn't respond. It needs some kind of security pass. I'm trapped.

I stand in the shadows with my back against the wall while I try to get my heart rate under control. I can't get back into the building and staying in this dirty, little compound is probably not a good idea. That only leaves walking out the gate. What's the worst that could happen? I've already thrown myself under a truck.

The smoggy air is dry, making it difficult to breathe properly as though this city hasn't known fresh air for some time. I need to find out where I am. If I'm in a dream, I will run into Will at any moment now, like I always do. If I am dead, I have no idea what is going on.

It's a warm night, but I leave on the course brown jacket and trousers I wear over skin tight black clothing so I don't have to carry them. I pull at the collar to stop it scratching my neck and creep up to the gate. I find the panel to open it and slip silently into the city.

I keep to the shadows of the dilapidated high rise buildings. Every now and again, the light of the full moon threatens to break through the clouds. My feet kick up dust as I walk. I keep moving. I catch whispers of movement in the distance. A skinny child, with cracked and bleeding lips, steps out in front of me, making me squeal.

"Spare a fifty for a water?" He holds his filthy hand out towards me. I stare at him trying to make my mind function.

"I don't have any money," I manage.

"There she is!" A voice shouts somewhere behind us. I can't see the person, but his aggressive tone is terrifying, as is the sound of multiple pounding feet.

The boy vanishes silently into the darkness. I throw myself to the ground and wriggle through a small gap in a corrugated iron wall. My clothing gets caught, but I manage to tear myself free. I'm wedged between the corrugated iron and a crumbling brick wall. I stay still in my crouched position and peer through one of the many holes in the wall back towards the way I came.

I hear the girl before I see her. Her boots pound the ground as she sprints towards my position. She has dark hair and wears loose clothing that flaps as she moves. The night air carries the sound of her laboured breathing as she nears. She twists her ankle on the rough ground and falls to her hands and knees.

The three men are on top of her in an instant. They grab at her clothing, ripping the jacket to reveal tight black clothing underneath. In the dark we could be mistaken as each other. She tries to break free, but she is no match for the bigger, heavier men.

I expect her to scream for help, but she stays quiet. She knows her fate before I do. The knife slides in and out of the girl so fast I almost don't see it. Her body goes limp in the arms of her assailant. The knife is wiped on her sleeve and the three leave, dragging the dead girl into the shadows.

I bite the fist I hold to my mouth. My whole body shakes and my legs cramp. I hold my position for as long as I can before I move. I haul myself back through the gap in the corrugated wall ripping my jacket in the process. Blood stains the ground where the girl fell.

I run. I don't know where to, but I need to get there as fast as possible. I'm no longer certain I'm in Will's world. I think I'm in Hell. I head in the direction the girl had been taking down winding streets – away from the three murderers.

I stop when I can no longer breathe. I bend over and place my hands on my knees as I suck air into my burning lungs. Under my feet, weeds struggle to grow from the filthy concrete. Rubbish litters the ground and a scrawny black rat darts in front of me. I start coughing, trying to smother the sound in my sleeve so no one hears. I gasp for breath until my head spins. I crouch so I have less distance to fall if I faint.

When I can breathe without choking, I stand. The faint light of the moon in the smoggy night sky illuminates an odd collection of buildings. When I arrived the dilapidated building could have been from my own time, but some of them where I now stand are stone and look to be from the past.

I'm near the water's edge and creep closer for a better look. A rock wall keeps the dirty harbour water at bay. Garbage floats on the surface attempting to hide a dead, bloated animal. Above me, the rusty arch of a wide bridge connects two shores. Across the water under the opposite end of the bridge, the shadowy face of a semi-submerged structure grins scarily at me.

I turn around slowly. The scrawled black words, *'nor any drop to drink'* mar the damaged, once white sails of the Opera House. A low wall keeps the tides from destroying what remains. I'm in Sydney, sometime in the future.

I choke on my panic as my pulse beats in my temples. I scream when something grabs my arm, but the sound is muffled by the hand covering my mouth. I'm yanked away from the harbour front.

"What the hell are you doin' out here and showing your skins while you're at it? You trying to get yourself killed?" the man hisses in my ear.

He marches us quickly away from the water towards the old buildings, pulling me inside one that doesn't appear to have been lived in for years. He removes his hand from my mouth and leaves me standing in the small, dirty living space while he rummages through a cupboard. He returns with a roll of tape.

I flinch as he nears me, but there's no fight left in me. I wouldn't get far before he caught me. He reaches out and tapes the tear in my outer coat.

211

"We need to get moving if we're to make the next bullet south," he says, moving back to an assortment of gear sitting by the cupboard.

"Who are you?"

He pauses the packing of two identical bags to stare at me. Perhaps it should be obvious who he is. He was waiting for me, or the dead girl who looked like me.

"They didn't tell you or you've been wiped?" He stares at me.

I stare back unsure how he will react if he discovers I'm not the person he was meant to meet. I'm caught in the middle of something I know nothing about. He swears.

"They're so damned worried about protecting themselves. We'd agreed you'd be more use if you had your memories intact. I guess I'll have to fill you in as we travel. You can call me George, like the last king of Britain," he says.

"Queen Elizabeth's father?"

"No." George gives me a strange look. "George the seventh, Elizabeth's great grandson."

"Oh." I gnaw on my lip. "Do you know a boy about my age called Will?"

"Never heard of him," he says. I sink into the only chair in the room. It creaks as it adjusts to my weight. What if Will isn't here?

George holds a small black device up to my face and presses a button. A light blinks on and off. He turns his back to me and fiddles with something sitting on the table against the wall.

"Name?"

"Lucy," I say, before it occurs to me someone might know the other girl's name.

"None of those airs, girl. You are a Monitor now," he tells me. I keep my mouth shut not sure what I've said wrong. Tiredness seeps into my body. There is nothing left for me. I tried to end my life and instead ended up in a place that is neither my world nor Will's. I want it to stop. My eyelids droop as I lose the fight that has kept me going for the last couple of hours.

My eyes snap open when a bag is dropped at my feet. George hands me an ID lanyard with my picture on it. I look startled in the image. Underneath it states my name as 'Luce', no surname.

"You spelt my name wrong," I say. No one ever misspells my name.

"Monitors have single syllable names. Whatever you were before, you're Luce now."

I've completely lost my identity. I'm here in place of a dead girl who I don't want to mention in case I am left out in that world on my own and now my name has been taken from me. If I'm in Hell, is it possible to die here? Where would I end up then?

"Look lively, girl. We have to be out of here before the Raids."

George lifts a tattered rug from the floor and motions me forward. I follow him across the room. He lifts several floor boards creating a space just wide enough for us to crawl through.

"Down you go," he says.

I get down on my hands and knees and wriggle through the gap. I've got nothing better to do. My feet touch the bottom before my shoulders are through. I twist my body until I'm on the other side in a narrow crawl space carved through rock. George drops both bags and a torch down to me.

"Keep moving," he says.

I push one bag in front of me leaving the other for him. The torch is tiny but bright, lighting the long and straight tunnel. I crawl forward as George drops down behind me and adjusts the hidden doorway above his head.

We crawl until we reach what looks like a dead end. I never thought I was claustrophobic, but the carved stone feels like it is closing in on me. I don't have enough room to turn around easily and George is behind me anyway. I try to convince myself there is another hidden door at the end of this tunnel and we aren't trapped.

There isn't. It's a T-junction. I come to a stop and look in each direction. They both look like identical small tunnels like the one I'm coming out of. George runs into my heels.

"Oh, we're here. Turn left." I do as he says.

I watched the movie "The Great Escape" on television once. All those men escaping down the tunnel to what they hoped was freedom and most of them dying. I wonder if the actual men the story was about felt anything in the end. Did they just die or did they go somewhere?

I pause when I find a water droplet painted on the stone wall. It's the first sign another person has been here since we came down. Above my head is the outline of another hidden hatch.

"Here we are." George reaches over me to lift the cover and peeks through. After a tense moment, he hauls himself through. I pass up the bags and lift myself out.

We are in an empty, but clean space the size of a large closet. George swings a bag over his shoulder and eases the door open. I dust off my knees and step out after him into a corridor.

This building is modern with overhead lights and clean carpet, feeling out of place with the rest of the city. We don't meet anyone as we head to an elevator. George touches his finger tips to the panel on the wall and moments later, the doors slide open. The lift travels silently. The doors open to a view of a large wall-hung rainforest watercolour painting.

George walks confidently down the hallway. At the end is a window providing glimpses of harbour views as the first rays of sunrise creep over the city. I pause to commit the scene to memory, as George knocks on a door. He grabs me by the elbow and pulls me over to his side.

The door is opened by an elegantly dressed woman who ushers us into a luxury apartment. Once the door is closed behind us, she holds out her hand for my jacket and trousers, leaving me in the skin tight black garments. She shuts herself in a room off the hallway.

George keeps hold of my elbow until we enter a living room. I drop my bag at my feet. A middle aged man, dressed as elegantly as the greeter, leans against a bookshelf. A slightly younger athletic woman stands with her hand on the back of a dining room chair. A girl my age in black skin tight clothing is gagged and bound to the chair.

"We were beginning to think you wouldn't make it, George. There was an impressive bounty on the girl." The woman nods in my direction. The other girl glares at me.

"Who's that one?" George asks. The woman grabs the girl by the hair and yanks her head back.

"She's Trident's proposed Monitor. Care to offer us a better option?"

"This is Luce." George nudges me forward. I'm pretty sure I have the expression of a startled possum.

"What does she know?" the man asks. He swirls the dark contents in his crystal glass.

"She's been wiped. Her family probably didn't want any repercussions if she's caught," George says.

"It works both ways as I'm sure your daughter is aware," the woman says.

She jerks the girl's chair back suddenly and drags it backward as the occupant kicks and squirms. They disappear through a door and a moment later I hear a door slam. The woman returns.

"You, girl. Come here."

I stumble in her direction thanks to a shove in the back from George and stand before her nervously.

"You will be Monitor to a trainee Trident guard. Keep an eye on your target and gather intel. Don't be fooled into trusting him. He works for Trident and you need to convince Trident you also work for them," the woman says.

"You want me to act as a double agent in a war I know nothing about?" my voice comes out sounding slightly hysterical.

"Trident has locked up the Southern Hemisphere's water supplies and is eliminating anyone who opposes their rule," George says.

"LJ believed everyone should have access to the water produced by her husband's desalinators, but the politicians disagreed. She fought with the Cause until her death several months ago. Without her, none of us would be alive today," the elegant man explains.

"I don't know anything about being a Monitor," I say.

"Follow instructions, act dumb and don't speak," the woman says.

My eyes sweep the room looking for jumps in reality signifying a dream. There is nothing to indicate I'm not actually standing in a stranger's living room in the future discussing a rebellion. I'm finding it hard to breathe.

"Do I have a choice?"

"We only have one other Monitor on the inside. If the two of you fail to find the desalinator control codes, the entire population of the Southern Hemisphere, bar those loyal to Trident, will die," George states.

"Do you swear to honour the mission of our founder LJ and promise to do your utmost to deliver water to the people of this world?" the woman asks.

I stare at her. I'm all for people having water, but why should this involve me? On the other hand, I'm stuck here and it seems safer to be with these people than out on the street with the dead girl. I wish Will was here.

"Sure," I say.

The woman grabs my arm, people here seem to like doing that, and positions me in front of a portrait of Neptune holding a trident above his head. She reaches out and flicks what I thought was an oddly placed light switch.

"Say it to her face."

The image shifts, like my vision has blurred and then refocused, to a regal looking old lady with an expression halfway between controlled superiority and an amused smirk. She looks down on us with my 'witchy' eyes. The plaque beneath the image states: LJ Phillips Carter, 1999–2084. The same year I was born.

"No!"

I step back, away from the painting. My mind churns, repeating the words; seventy more years.

"Stop it! I don't want to play this game anymore!" I'm screaming, hysterical. Why am I not dead? It's some kind of trick. That picture isn't me. I only had three more days to get through.

"Shut her up before someone hears," the man says.

Something pricks my arm and my body goes limp. This is what I want. To go to sleep and never wake.

I'm calm when I come to a short time later. Nothing matters anymore. I'm an observer in my own body. Nothing can touch me. I'll find the codes for them because I have nothing better to do.

There's a knock at the door and a few minutes later, a man dressed also in black, only with elaborate pattern down the sides in blue, strolls into the room.

"Ryder will be your guard on the bullet." The woman nods to the new man who looks me up and down as though he expected something better.

"She's the one you've got monitoring Carter's boy?" Ryder says.

"We don't have any other options," the well-dressed man says.

"She hardly looks like she could talk a tap out of a bottle of water, let alone convince a trainee guard he's on the wrong side of the Water War," Ryder says.

"That's no longer the plan. She just needs to get the code. Someone else will take care of the rest." The adults talk as though I'm not present. I'm a pawn in my own mind.

"If that's the best you can do, we better get going," Ryder says. "Grab your bag, Monitor."

This is it. I try to focus on the mission I've been given. I want someone to hold me, tell me I'm important and that my life has just been a bad dream

219

I'm about to wake from. I bite my lip and follow Ryder out the door, my head bowed. I want this to be over.

Ryder and I emerge in a dimly lit subway tunnel and blend into the crowd of people. Our IDs allow us to pass through the gate then our bags are put through an airport type scanner. Ryder leads me to a platform already crowded with scruffily dressed people pretending no one else exists. There are no business suits and many look like it's been some time since they ate a proper meal.

"They're going to the farms," Ryder says. I nod as if I understand.

A streamline train whooshes into the station. People board and it leaves as quickly as it arrived. Ryder glances around us as we wait. Our train arrives a few minutes later. Ryder strides purposely aboard with me pushing through the crowd so I don't lose him.

The carriages consist of a large open space with hanging hand grips and small compartments at either end. Ryder uses his ID to open one of the doors and we slip inside the empty space. The door closes behind us and Ryder darkens the tint on the glass. Fatigue finally claims me. I curl up across the seats opposite Ryder and everything goes dark.

In my dream, I stand in a crowd of people calling my name, but they all ignore me, focused on the twisted body beside a truck. There are flashing lights everywhere like an outdoor disco. Orange hazard lights from the truck. Blue and red from the police and ambulance.

Tayla stands beside me. She reaches out and puts her hand in mine. It's warm and fits neatly in mine. We look across at Jennypha who is the same shade of white as the police car. La-a cries into her phone.

"Did you find what you were looking for at the shops?" Tayla asks.

For a moment, I'm confused. I have nothing with me. Why was I here? Then I remember, I was running from Frank. Before I can reply to Tayla, someone speaks directly into my ear.

"Lucy, squeeze my fingers."

I'm no longer standing next to Tayla. I'm on my back with ambulance officers leaning over me. I try to do as I'm told, but the pain is excruciating and I can't move. I'd scream, but I have no voice. The bullies stole it from me. I am broken beyond repair.

A computerised voice announcing our arrival in Melbourne, jerks me from sleep. Ryder doesn't make a move to get off. The train starts again and descends underground.

"Have you been this way before?" he asks.

When I shake my head, Ryder lifts the tint on the outer windows. I gasp in surprise and press my nose against the glass. The transparent tunnel our train travels through, lies across the ocean floor. I feel like I'm in a submarine and I hope the infrastructure is better cared for than the buildings in Sydney.

"Where are we going?" I ask.

"You're heading for Davistown, but I have business in Hobart. That's as far as the bullet line goes. A ship will take you the rest of the way."

I try to work out where Davistown is without looking ignorant or a fraud. The only thing south of Hobart is Antarctica. My head hurts. I stare out the window watching the ocean outside.

"Don't trust anyone you meet. LJ's grandson is not on the side of the rebellion. He doesn't know about her role in the Cause and it would risk the whole operation if he found out. Keep quiet and act dumb," Ryder says.

He dims the window as we approach land and we sit in silence until the bullet train pulls into the final station.

"Ready to serve the people, Monitor Luce?" Ryder asks. I nod because it is expected of me.

We take a shuttle to the dock where Ryder points out my vessel. He hands me a ticket printed on some form of plastic and leaves me at the base of the gangway. I hitch my bag over my shoulder and walk the last few metres on my own. At the top, I turn to take one last look around me. Ryder loiters in the shadow of the buildings on the wharf. Watching me.

"Do you have a ticket, Ma'am?" A crew member appears by my side. I hand over the thin piece of plastic. "This way, Monitor."

He leads me along the side of the vessel before heading inside. Ryder has disappeared. I reach my cabin, drop my bag on the floor, curl up on the narrow bed and try to sleep.

Second Chance

Antarctica 2084

When I wake, I'm still here, wherever here is. I eat in the vessel common room and retreat back to my cabin. In my bag, I find changes of identical black clothes, toiletries and a manual on what is required of a Monitor. It's short with lots of small words. My job is to watch and record. Thinking is discouraged. I could really do with a book on how not to think.

According to the manual, Davistown is the location of a military base that trains guards for the water desalinators, the people I've been tasked with defeating.

The Cause wants everyone to have water. Trident wants to control it for themselves. Is anyone telling me the truth? That portrait of LJ Phillips Carter has me rattled. When I close my eyes, the reflection of my aged face looks down on me.

We travel across the ocean much faster than I expect. When the motion stops, I pull my hair back into a ponytail and wash my face in the small bathroom with a damp cloth. Water is rationed even on a vessel with its own desalinator plant. I sling my bag over my shoulder and head out on deck. We are tied to a dock in a large bay and the air is cool, despite the sunshine. Low buildings stretch out before us with green hills behind.

"Welcome to Davistown, Antarctica," a crew member tells me.

"Where's the snow?" I ask. He laughs.

"It only snows in winter," he says.

I walk down the gangway slowly as if my next move will come to me if I allow it enough time. On the shore, I hover nervously, glancing around. There was nothing in the handbook about where to go. Workers on the dock ignore me as they go about their business.

"Are you the new Monitor?" A familiar voice by my side makes me jump.

I flinch when I look at the face of the girl wearing the same skin-tight outfit as me. Tayla wears a blank expression and her long auburn hair has been chopped short and jagged.

"I'm meant to meet the new Monitor," she states.

I open and close my mouth several times before any words form. I glance around, expecting the other girls to appear and tell me the last several days have been an elaborate joke. It doesn't happen.

I'm used to Will in these alternate lives and occasionally Elizabeth. I've never encountered

225

anyone I know from my real world. Without Will, I have no reference point.

"Monitor Luce." I remember to use my new name.

"I'm Monitor Tai." She holds her hand out for me to shake and leads me to a waiting vehicle with the words, 'Trident Water Corporation' marked on the side.

She slides into the driver's seat and waits for me to get in. I take one last look around the dock, but find no better option. I take the seat next to Tai. I don't look at her, instead staring at the green countryside as she directs the automated vehicle to her requested destination.

Antarctica should be covered in ice and snow all year round. My mind is unable to connect what I see with what it knows, so it shuts down, my expression as blank as Tai's.

We pull up at a gated facility where we present our IDs and the guards scan the vehicle. We're cleared to enter and Tai stops the vehicle by a building at the side of the complex.

She opens a door to a simple bunk room, the only wall space taken up with a painting of Neptune holding his trident. I leave my bag on the vacant bed, rake my fingers through my hair and re-tie my ponytail. Tai hands me a black wrist band that looks like a faceless watch, and a flat tablet computer.

"I know it's old fashioned, but it's all we get. The instructions are provided. Monitor your Trident Authority trainee and record the actions in the appropriate templates," Tai says. I nod.

Tai leads me through the compound pointing out the various buildings I need to know from the canteen to the training rooms, while maintaining an air of vacantness. Then she takes me to the recreation room to meet the trainee I need to shadow while I'm here.

I enter the room behind Tai and he looks up at the sound of our entrance. Will's brown eyes slide across us and return to his female sparring companion who has her back to us. I clamp my hand over my mouth to prevent any sound that may emerge. My hands shake.

"You are to monitor Trainee Willis." Tai points to Will, who continues to ignore us. "The girl, Genfa is my Trainee. We don't exist, never speak unless spoken to."

Genfa turns away from Will and this time I do gasp. I'm in a room with Tayla, Jennypha and Will. For a second, Genfa's gaze settles on me and her eyes open wide, before Willis topples her onto her behind. She glances up at him as he offers her a hand up. I hold my breath waiting for her to say something, but she doesn't look at me again.

Tai grabs my arm roughly to stop me staring. The Monitors in the room all have the same vacant expression. I attempt to adopt the same as Tai shows me to a seat and runs me through the assessment forms I need to fill out on Will, some already completed by the last girl.

The Will I know would never support the wrong side of a war. I look at Will and I know I'm not dead. I'm in one of my dreams, but is it him or me

227

working towards what is right? If I die here, I will wake up back where I started.

"Please wake up. Can you hear me, Lucy?"

In my dream I think it's odd Mum wants me to wake up. I've been awake, trying to complete the mission I've been given. Also there is nothing wrong with my hearing.

"If you wake I promise we'll do something special for your seventeenth birthday. I know it's still a few months away, but we'll invite all your friends and have a cake. Squeeze my hand if you're there."

Has she forgotten my eleventh birthday and every one since? I have no friends to invite. Will is here and Emma is dead. There is no one else. There won't be any cake, especially if she doesn't go to work.

I don't move my hand, instead shutting out the sounds of Mum weeping and an irritating beeping near my head. I think I hear Willis calling my name. My eyes snap open.

Tai stands over the bed repeating my name. The Antarctic dawn creeps through the window of the room I share with the other Monitors. I crawl out of bed and pull on my uniform. I have a mission to complete before I can fade into oblivion.

The morning starts in the gym. There are six in Willis' training group. I stand with Tai and four others by a wall and try to imitate Tai's blank

228

expression. As Willis does circuits of cardio and weights, I check his improvements over the six months he has been stationed at Davistown. Will is top of the group and yet the trainer pushes him and Genfa the hardest. I want to ask Tai why, but the look she shoots me as I'm about to speak, silences me.

The afternoon brings an exam. We sit quietly until they're finished. Tai pinches me whenever I start fidgeting or thinking too hard. The trainees have free time when they are done and Willis leaves with Genfa. Neither of them acknowledges our existence. My stomach twists as they leave the room.

I take Willis' paper and check the answers on my screen. I do it automatically, but part way through I start paying attention to the questions. The hairs on the back of my neck stand up. What Will is reciting contradicts what I've been told.

Willis is training to protect the desalinators from terrorist attacks, from the people who have recruited me to take control of the water. These answers portray the people as evil, yet I have seen them as desperate and thirsty. Someone is playing both sides off against each other.

"How did this happen?" Mum sobs into Frank's shoulder. I wish he would leave the room and take his cologne with him. I've never understood how Mum could stand so close to such an overpowering smell.

"I don't know," Frank lies.

229

He's cheating on you, I want to say. Don't trust him. But I have no voice.

"Is it my fault?" Mum asks.

"Of course not. Lucy brought this on herself..."

The band vibrating on my wrist snaps me awake. I'm still in my shared room in Davistown. Will is somewhere nearby.

"What's going on?" I ask Tai as the others leave the room.

"Our unit's been posted to McMurdo. A water tanker was hijacked on the Ross Sea and they want backup."

"You seem awfully happy about this," I say.

"We're going to the main desalinator grid. This is the best opportunity we've had yet to find those codes."

"What code?" I say. Tai rolls her eyes at me, so I try for a change of topic instead. "Where have the other Monitors gone?" I ask watching Tai shove her belongings into her bag.

"The trainees will be debriefed before leaving. We pack their bags."

Tai walks with me to the trainee quarters. Several doors are already open with Monitors inside collecting items. I pause awkwardly outside the room marked 'Willis Carter,' but Tai marches straight by me and flings open the cupboards, before throwing an empty bag on the bed.

"A list of required items has been uploaded to your tablet. I'll be across the hall in Genfa's room." Tai walks out leaving me alone.

230

The room is small and tidy, with everything packed away in cupboards. It could be anyone's room except for the fact it smells like Will. I close my eyes, breathe deeply and remember our previous lives together. A drawer slamming in an adjoining room snaps me back to the present.

I'm working my way through the list, pulling items from the cupboards and drawers when my fingers brush over a hard container concealed behind Willis' winter jacket. I glance over my shoulder, but I'm out of the line of sight of anyone passing the open door. I pull the non-descript box from its hiding place and pop the latch.

I force my eyes to focus on the words inside the lid, instead of the fact it's my handwriting.

To my Grandson Willis,

Once upon a time, two friends called Lucy and Will travelled through time together, collecting memories and learning why life is worth living even through the bad times. This box of lucky charms holds their memories and the key to the future.

Love Grandma LJ

I tip the contents onto the floor and pick up a folded page. When I spread it open, I find my art assignment where I tried to copy Wu and my handprints on the cave wall. My signature is scrawled in the bottom corner along with the date.

Tears roll down my face. Something of my life has survived seventy years. I sort through the other items finding a lump of volcanic rock and a small cat statue before finding the gold locket. My hands tremble as I open the catch.

The miniature is fading, but William's and my face still stare back at me. I use my fingernail to lift it out and check the reverse is as I remember. 'William and Lucy 1746' is still there. I put our picture back in its place and lay it gently in the box.

A second gold chain lies among the pile on the floor, a bullet hanging from this one. I roll it between my fingers reading the words, 'Hawaii 1941' engraved into it. I add it to the rest and pick up a thin black rectangle the size of a photograph. When I touch it with my fingers, an image appears. I fumble and nearly drop it.

Staring back at me is LJ Phillips Carter looking some years younger than she did in the portrait I saw in Sydney. She smiles as she sits on the grass under a tree, holding a young boy on her lap. He holds one arm bent to stop a silver bracelet from sliding off his small arm.

"Are you planning to report me for having non-military issued items?"

I jump at Willis' voice behind me. I keep my back to him so he can't see my tear strained face. I hurriedly pack the memories back into their box.

"I was packing your things." My voice catches slightly. I shove the box into his bag and continue packing without looking at him. He moves to stand directly behind me.

"I'm trying to work out if you've been planted to spy on me by Trident or the Rebellion," Willis says.

I think of George and the young boy begging for money to buy water. I recall the limp body of the girl who should be sitting in my place right now. Willis is committed to a cause he believes is right. He has probably never seen the poverty on the street that I saw. On top of that is the box of memories that have been and might have been.

"I don't understand. I'm just a Monitor. My QI is not as big as yours." He makes a noise behind me, struggling not to correct my deliberate slip.

"My last Monitor pretended to be not very bright. She disappeared after being suspected of working for the Rebellion. So are you her replacement or did the Trident get in first?"

When I don't answer, he grabs my arm and spins me around. The silver bracelet fits his wrist now. Willis loosens his grip and tilts my head up so I'm looking into his familiar brown eyes.

"Why are you crying?" he asks gently. My eyes fall to the bag where I placed the box.

"Why have you kept those items in the box?" I ask.

"They're just memories belonging to my Grandmother. She had a story for each one before she ended up at the Port Arthur Mental Hospital," Willis says.

"She couldn't have been. She was the leader of the Cause up until her death."

"You're spying for the Rebellion," Willis says.

"I don't know why I'm here. Why are you training to be a Trident guard?"

"Grandma LJ wanted me to take this job." He spins the silver bracelet on his wrist.

I'm about to voice my confusion when I catch sight of Tai standing in the doorway with a look of betrayal on her face. I take a step forward causing Willis to glance over his shoulder and Tai bolts. Willis grabs my arm before I can follow.

"The Monitors are required to have the bags packed and ready in the next ten minutes." He walks out of the room.

I dump the remainder of Willis' belongings on top of the hidden box. I close the bag and drag it to the Monitors' quarters to get my own things. Tai is not in the room and her bag is missing. I hurriedly pack my clothes and run out the door. I'm the last one ready.

The other Monitors and Trainees wait on the airstrip as I pass the bags over to be loaded. Tai is the only one not present. I really need to speak to her to let her know I haven't betrayed the Cause. At least I don't think I have.

"Has anyone seen Monitor Tai?" Genfa demands marching past our group as though expecting Tai to suddenly appear. I look straight ahead careful to maintain my blank expression. Willis doesn't speak either. "Well what are you waiting for? Go look for her," Genfa orders.

We stand there like dumb children until one of the girls realises Genfa means us. The rest of us follow meekly behind her. An officer chases after us to make sure we look in different directions. We follow his orders.

I'm doing a lap of the perimeter behind the sleeping quarters when I notice the hole cut in the bottom of the fence. I glance around me, but this location was chosen for its lack of traffic. A short piece of wire lies on the ground. I bend down and use it to pull the fence back into shape. When I'm done, no one would notice the gap unless they looked very closely. I continue my search knowing I won't find Tai anywhere on the grounds. We leave for McMurdo without her. I have to find the code on my own.

I can smell Frank's cologne. It makes me need to sneeze, but I can't move my body. There is an annoying beeping noise in the background. Frank places his hand over the machine as if willing the sound to stop.

We're alone in the room together and my body is frozen in place. I don't know how far he will go to keep his secret. Why is Mum not here to protect me? Frank leans in to whisper in my ear. My skin crawls like a thousand bugs are trying to make my useless body their home.

"Your mother and I are getting married. She doesn't love you. No one wants you. You're good for nothing. Do us all a favour; stop hanging around and just die."

He runs his fingers across my cheek. I panic, trying to force my eyes open and get away from him at the same time. My body jerks and I'm falling.

My eyes fly open as I hit the floor wrapped tightly in my blanket. I gasp for breath, covered in sweat in the chilly room. I lie still on the floor of the sleeping quarters at McMurdo, listening in case my panic attack woke anyone. The sound of even breathing continues. The Monitors have been placed in the same room as the Trainees. I glance over to the only empty bed in the room illuminated by the continual twilight of the Antarctic night.

I scrub my cheek against my shoulder. I'm too tense to go back to sleep so I pull my skins on and slide a small torch up my sleeve. I focus on the present to force Frank from my head.

I pad softly over to where Willis' clothes are draped over the end of his bed. His security tag is tucked into the top pocket. Someone moves in their sleep and I freeze in place barely breathing. I stand still for several slow minutes before I move to the door and slip into the corridor.

I avoid the areas I saw during the afternoon orientation, pausing when I reach a door marked 'authorised personnel only'. Glancing around, the corridor is silent. I swipe Will's security tag through the slot by the door. A small beep sounds and the door slides open. I step into the unknown.

The corridor is dimly lit with dull grey walls. I start walking. At the far end are three doors. The one directly in front of me is protected by a coded pad as well as the swipe card. The dull light on the touch pad illuminates four oily marks from people's finger tips.

I try to calculate how many different combinations it could be assuming each number is only used once. It's still a lot.

I try top to bottom and left to right. It doesn't work. Neither does right to left. I realise I haven't swiped the card. I try that and then the first combination. Still nothing. I swipe again and try the second combination. I jump when I hear a click. I push on the door and it swings inwards. I hadn't expected my reasoning to be valid.

It's dark inside and my footsteps echo making the space sound huge. I take a few cautious steps forward listening to the sound of each footfall. I tumble down a short flight of steps landing in a heap in the dark, with a twisted ankle and a banged elbow. I gasp in pain.

I lie still hoping no one is hiding in the shadows waiting to kill me. Silence envelops me. I pick myself up off the floor, feeling for the steps I fell down then I remember the torch up my sleeve. I retrieve it and switch it on.

I get to my feet and test my ankle. It's sore, but I can still walk. I shine the torch around the space. The beam of light reveals the hulking shape of a fighter plane. This is a military base, so I shouldn't be surprised, but it feels wrong, dangerous, evil and I don't know why.

The torch slips in my sweaty grip. I want to get out of there. I turn to leave when I remember how excited Tai was about coming to McMurdo.

"What's the worst that could happen? You've already tried to kill yourself," I mutter to myself.

I approach the fighter plane and flash the light around. There are more lurking behind the first one, but the darkness makes it difficult to make out numbers. I shine the torch up onto the grey monster. The word, 'Wellington' is painted across the belly. I creep over to the next one to find 'Canberra' scrawled there. My ears pick up a faint click in the silence. I flick the torch off and stand in the darkness.

"Have you found the girl yet?" a nasally woman's voice asks from over where I entered, the hangar amplifying the sound.

I forget to breathe. She's the woman I overheard where I first woke under the bed in Sydney. Light floods the entrance to the hangar and I throw myself behind the wheel of the fighter jet.

"She's disappeared into the inland settlements. My people are searching for her as we speak." I feel like I should know his voice, but I can't place it.

I peek around the landing gear to see the man speaking. He has his back to me as he leads the way to an office set back from the steps I fell down. The light comes on and the door stays open.

I strain to hear the conversation, but I only catch a handful of words, such as 'assault', 'planes' and 'desalinator'. I can't get any closer without giving myself away. I wait for them to hear my heart pounding from where they stand in the office.

My legs are cramping by the time the woman steps out of the room. I stay low, watching from the shadows, so I can see her face and recognise her in the future. The light flicks off and the man closes

238

the door to the office. He turns around and I see his face. I gasp.

"Ready to go?" Ryder asks.

"I've seen enough," the woman replies. She follows Ryder back out the door we all entered and the hanger is plunged into darkness once more.

I collapse into a ball on the cement floor, hugging my knees to my chest and whimpering. If there was any chance of finding the code, Ryder would have already done so. I can only assume he doesn't want it to be found.

It won't do me or Willis any good lying here. I pull myself together, shake my aching legs and flick on my torch, using my hand to dim the light so I have just enough to not trip. I'm glad Tai has disappeared already. There's no need for us both to die attempting to achieve the impossible.

I limp on my sore ankle towards the office and ease the door open. It gives under my hand and I close it behind me. I take my hand away from the beam of light and shine it around the room. A map of the world hangs on the wall, only the polar ice caps are almost non-existent and there is less land mass than I remember.

I search the room in case a scrap of paper with 'desalinator code' written on it, lies out in the open. I bump the screen sitting on the desk and it springs to life. 'Do you want to complete shut down?' is displayed across the screen. I hold my breath and I touch the cancel button.

The operating system is completely foreign to me, but after touching multiple icons I find what

I'm after. I don't have a camera, so I sit down and commit to memory the details of an attack on the main population centres around the world. In another file are mock-up media releases blaming the assault on the Rebellion, who I know as the Cause. When they are done, the only habitable location on the planet will be Antarctica.

I shut the computer down and creep from the room. The sound of the door shutting behind me makes me flinch. I bound up the steps and find the exit button by the door. I yank it open and run all the way back to my room. I dive under my blanket and lie still trying to calm my breathing.

"You dropped this." I pass the security tag quickly to Willis on the way to breakfast, but don't meet his eyes. "If you lose it again I will have to record it," I add. Willis looks like he is about to say something, but then he turns away and walks over to Genfa as if I don't exist.

"Monitor," a voice behind me says.

There are no other Monitors standing nearby. I turn around careful to maintain a vacant expression. I face Ryder as though I've never met him before.

"I need these taken to my office." Ryder thrusts a box of computer tablets into my arms.

I glance behind me to where Willis sits next to Genfa. I'm not meant to leave his side, but I've also been given an order. I follow meekly behind the traitor. He doesn't speak until he has closed the office door behind us.

"What have you done to your ankle?"

240

"I fell out of bed," I say.

"How is the mission progressing?" he asks. I hug the box to my chest while I consider how to answer.

"No leads yet," I say.

"What happened to Monitor Tai?"

"She disappeared. I figured you'd know." I look him in the eyes.

"The Carter boy, any progress with turning him to the Cause?"

"That wasn't the task I was given," I reply.

"Good, good. You can put the box down here." Ryder points to his desk.

"Is that all? I have to get back to my Trainee," I say.

"Keep me up to date with any leads." Ryder doesn't look at me as I walk out the door and go in search of Willis.

I lose track of my checklists throughout the day. I monitor Genfa as well until a replacement is found for Tai, but my mind isn't on the job. I sit at the back of the theatre with the other Monitors as the Trainees watch a film on desalinator security. I try to keep my eyes open and follow the talk about how William Carter created the current system, but the dim lighting and lack of sleep the night before eventually claim me.

"Come to finish the job?" Mum asks in a broken voice. "It was an accident," Tayla's mum insists.

"How dare you think you can come in here like you care about my daughter. You think Jennypha can get away with this because her father is a lawyer?"

"The girls have come to apologise for their part in this. I never said…"

"Shush!" A nurse arrives to see what the commotion is about. Mum storms out in tears.

Jennypha and Tayla shuffle forward and the scent of boronias waft through the room from the bunch of flowers Tayla holds. There's a house in my street that has boronias.

"Do you have a vase?" Tayla's mum asks the nurse. The woman hurries off to find something suitable. When she returns, she places the bunch gently in a lonely vase of water by my bed.

"Don't they smell nice," she says.

"They're Lucy's favourite," Tayla replies. I'm surprised she remembers.

The nurse leaves the room and Tayla's mum follows tactfully leaving the girls alone in the room with me.

Jennypha stands by my bed and recites her apology. I want to tell Jennypha it's too late to apologise, but I cannot speak. I never could tell her what I really thought. I wish someone had stood up for me when I couldn't find my voice. I wish I'd had the strength to do it myself.

"Luce."

I'm drifting somewhere between here and there. I don't know where I should be.

"Luce! Wake up." I move towards Will's voice.

I open my eyes to Willis standing over me. The lights are on and we are alone in the theatre. The movie has ended.

"Big night roaming the base with my security pass?" he asks.

"I was meaning to talk to you about that," I say.

"I have someone who wants to talk to you too."

"That doesn't sound good," I say.

"Don't worry. He's on our side."

"Which side is that?"

"The right one hopefully," Willis replies.

Willis strides from the room with me following after. We pass several people, but they don't question us. We don't see Ryder or the woman he was with last night.

Willis pauses at a non-descript door marked only with a number and raps on a panel twice. The light on the touch screen turns from red to green and he eases the door open. We step into a windowless meeting room.

One of the chairs is occupied by Jennypha's doppelganger, while a man stands with his back to us as he studies a map of the world hanging on the wall. He turns to face us as we enter. He wears a military uniform with a rank I don't recognise displayed across the shoulders, and holds a black tablet computer in his hand.

"Sit down," he instructs. I do as I'm told, keeping my distance from Genfa. Willis sits between us. "I'm Major Stevens. I believe you already know Trainees Willis and Genfa."

"Why am I here?" I ask.

243

"Genfa believes you can help us, although I'm not convinced yet," the man responds. He glances between the tablet screen and me, before raising an eyebrow at Genfa.

"What's going on?" Willis asks. "I thought we gathered to find out what Luce has discovered while she's been here."

"You haven't worked out who she is, have you?" Genfa asks.

"She's the Rebellion's Monitor," Willis says.

"Do you remember all those crazy stories Great Aunt Libby used to tell about LJ?"

"Of course I do. That is why everyone believed LJ was committed to the mental hospital when she disappeared." Willis frowns.

Genfa stands and points at me. "She is LJ."

All three of them look at me. Stevens has an expression of someone who has already heard this information, but is still sceptical, and Willis looks like he is waiting for the punchline of a joke.

"I don't know what you're talking about," I say somewhat unconvincingly. I am not the leader they are looking for. I just want to be gone. I don't have the strength to survive seventy more years of life.

"You're denying this is an image of you?" Stevens slides the tablet across the table. It comes to rest in front of me and Willis leans over to see the photo displayed on the screen. It's me, in school uniform, positioned between Jennypha and Tayla. We have our arms around each other and smiles on our faces.

"Jennypha and Tayla hate me," I say. I've never seen this photo, nor can I conceptualise a reason for us to be hugging.

"Hate you? Tayla McKenzie and LJ Phillips were my grandmother's only close friends. She had a hard time letting people close to her. She didn't like anyone knowing her mum was an alcoholic," Genfa says.

My mind sticks on the word alcoholic. Jennypha has a perfect life. She is popular and rich. She doesn't have problems like me. Thoughts crash through my head like waves across a shallow reef.

"Jennypha pushed me in front of a truck!"

"I never heard that story." Willis glances at Genfa, who shakes her head.

"So you're saying you are LJ?" Stevens asks.

"What if I am?"

"Tell us the code to control the desalinators," Stevens says.

"I don't know it!"

"If you are who you claim to be, the Rebellion is your idea. Why are you here if not to help us achieve your own goals?"

"I don't know! I tried to kill myself. I'm not even meant to be here!"

"Well, that's not good," Willis says.

"If LJ dies, there is no Rebellion. Trident will have already won," Genfa says.

"If she doesn't have the code, she won't be any help to us. We can't act without it." The Major frowns. He glances towards Willis who silences the buzzing coming from the band on his wrist next to his silver bracelet.

"I'm being summoned," Willis says. The Major waves him from the room.

"What if LJ is here to find the code and then plant it somewhere we can find it?" Genfa asks. I turn her suggestion over in my mind. It sounds complicated, especially considering I don't know the first place to begin finding the code.

"LJ died several months ago. If she had done something like that, we would know already. We've been here too long. I suggest we go about our business as usual and continue with our original plan. We can't act until we have the code," Stevens says.

Genfa stands, salutes Stevens and walks from the room. I follow after her, a Monitor trailing behind her Trainee. We walk through the base looking for Willis. When we don't find him in any of the common areas, Genfa heads towards the sleeping quarters.

I smell the burning paper as soon as we step into the room. I push past Genfa into the bathroom. Willis spins around at the sound of the door opening, dropping the piece of burning paper he held between his fingers. On the edge of the sink is a faded blue plastic folder like the students in my real life use to present their assignments. I can't afford that sort of thing. I normally borrow a stapler from the librarian.

Willis grabs several more pages from the plastic sleeves and uses the flame from the last piece to light it. I reach out to read the contents. Only the cover page remains and ash has already burned through the title. What remains is the subheading: 'A Story of the Future'. Underneath it says: by Jennypha A Grant and Lucy J Phillips.

In the depth of my consciousness, a memory of an assignment sheet I shoved into the bottom of my bag rises to the surface. I had no partner. Jennypha was probably paired with La-a like she was for every assignment.

"Where did you get this?" I ask.

"LJ left it to me in her will. It was delivered today." He looks up at Genfa standing in the doorway.

"Tell Major Stevens we're ready to act," Willis says.

"You have it?" she asks.

"I know where it is," Willis replies. She raises her eyebrow, but doesn't question him. She backs out the door.

"Why are you burning it?" I ask.

"I've read it."

"I never did the assignment," I say.

Willis drops the empty folder in the waste chute and wipes the remains of the ash out of the sink before looking at me.

"You really believe you're Lucy Phillips, you'll do it," he tells me.

"I die," I say with as much conviction as I can muster.

"What happens to me then?" Willis says. "If you don't live, I never have a chance to be born, to live, to make a difference. You're throwing my life away and I have no say in it."

"What if the world is a better place without me in it?"

"My grandmother made a huge difference to the lives of so many people. Now we need to go before we're discovered in here."

I see the woman as soon as I step from the room. She is flanked by two burly guards and heading straight for where I stand. Our cover has been blown before we can act. I frantically wave my hand behind my back hoping Willis will get the point and disappears from sight.

"Monitor, what are you doing in the hallway?" The nasally voice sends shivers down my spine. There is no doubt in my mind they have come for me.

"I was searching for Trainee Willis. I couldn't find him in the cafeteria so I went to look in his room, but he's not here either," I ramble on as they approach, hoping they won't smell the burnt paper.

"Don't worry about Willis. I have men searching for him as we speak. You need to come with us," the woman says.

I sprint away from the room as fast as I can, grateful for the grip on my Monitor issue boots. I make it several metres down the hall before something hits me in the back. I drop to the floor twitching in pain, reminding me of the time I accidently touched an electric fence, only so much worse. For a few moments I can't breathe and then a tingling feeling spreads through my body.

The two men grab my arms, haul me upright and drag me down the hallway in the opposite direction to which I ran. As my head lolls to one side, Willis sneaks from the room and disappears unnoticed down the hall. I hope I've given him enough time to put his plan into action.

I come to in a sparsely furnished room. My hands are cuffed behind the chair I'm slumped in and my vision is blurred. The woman leans over and slaps me hard across the face, making me uncomfortably aware feeling has returned to my body. I think she suspects I'm a spy. The thought makes me swing between the urge to laugh hysterically and cry.

"Who is your commander?" the woman asks.

I remain silent, staring at her without seeing. I'm good at that, retreating into myself. I've had a lot of practice in life, learning how not to react. One of the guys behind me kicks out at the chair and I topple backwards, crushing my arms beneath me and smacking my head on the cement floor. Pricks of light spark across my vision. The woman looms over me.

"Who on this base works for the Rebellion?"

My head rolls to one side and I focus on a tiny bug scuttling across the dusty floor. If I try a little harder, I can tune the whole world out. The man's hand moves at the edge of my vision pressing something cold to my neck. The bolt of electricity is worse than what I felt in the corridor. My body cramps and I stop breathing. When I regain consciousness, I'm upright in my chair and have blood in my mouth. I spit on the floor.

"This will go much smoother if you answer my questions," she tells me.

"I'm not afraid to die."

"You're not going to die." She laughs. "We have ways of keeping people alive until they – cooperate." I swallow back bile.

"Where did Monitor Tai go?" the woman asks.

My mind goes blank as I try to recall the thought pattern I'd been on moments ago. Something about bugs running across the floor, closing my eyes, dying – the code. I still don't have it. Just like I failed Bill, I've failed Willis.

The woman clicks her fingers and the second man steps in front of me. He flicks what looks like a small glass oil bottle at me. Several drops fall on the front of my uniform. I scream as the liquid burns into my skin.

"Where is the Monitor?" Tai. The girl who looks like Tayla.

"I don't know," I gasp. They haven't found her. Perhaps she is gathering her people to join Willis in the fight against Trident.

The woman holds up her finger and the man steps forward again.

"I don't know. She ran away. She thought I was working for Trident. She never told me anything." Suddenly I'm laughing hysterically, in large gasping breaths that won't cease. She slaps me hard across the face making my ears ring.

"Did you really think you could fool us? The last girl they sent was more subtle than you and we still killed her."

"Considering Ryder escorted me here, I figured you already knew."

Her eyes flash and she glances at someone by the door out of my line of vision. I think they exit, but I could be imagining it. I'm losing my grip on reality. I shake my head. What reality? I'm in the future.

I should probably be scared, but instead I'm dizzy. My head spins and I have difficultly focusing. The room is dimly lit, but I'm getting flashes of bright lights in my eyes that have little to do with being slapped. Both men stand several paces from me, but I hear whispers in my ears as though someone is leaning over me.

"Lucy, Lu-cy. That is your name isn't it," Will's voice whispers.

"How many Monitors are part of your organisation?" the woman demands. I want to end this.

"They all are." I give her a crazy look like the ones Emma was so good at.

"You're lying."

"Of course I am. I'm the best they have. They didn't need to send anyone else." I'm in a dreamlike state. The acid falls on me again and the haze of pain swallows me.

"I know you, I walked with you once upon a dream. I know you – hello?"

251

The girl's voice stops singing. The darkness is so complete I can almost hear her listening for a response. Greyness swirls around me, lightening the space until I can see her face. It lights up in a beautiful smile.

"Lucy, I was wondering if you would join me here," Will's sister says. She is older than I've seen her before, around my own age although she is thin and fragile.

"You know me?"

"Of course. It's me, Libby. Have you not been living the dreams also?"

"Where are we?" I ask.

"A waiting room. We stay here until our bodies are ready for us to come back."

"What's wrong with yours?" I ask.

"I'm having a transplant. When I wake up, I'm going to dance, sing, run, and do all the things I haven't been able to do for so long." Libby laughs and twirls in a circle with her arms above her head.

"What if I don't wake up?"

"I don't think we get another chance. If you die here, you'll be gone forever."

"Wake up," Will says.

Icy water cascades over me, stinging my skin and jerking me back into the room and away from Will's voice. The cold clings to my body making my tied arms ache.

"We can revive you every time. Why do you insist on throwing your life away for this one little code?" The woman tugs a small coil out of her

252

necklace pendant and places the unrolled rectangle of plastic in front of me. The black lettering stares back at me.

A6λ#2g5JσdT48α-9.

This is what I have been searching for. I focus on the code, committing it to memory as quickly as I can. My lips move as I concentrate. Capital A, six, lambda, hash symbol, two...

An idea flashes through my mind of grabbing the strip of plastic and running for the exit. The door is locked and guarded. I wouldn't make it out of the room, let alone get the code to anyone who could use it. Small g, five, capital J, sigma. My shoulders slump as I realise I have no way of getting it to Willis.

"What's your real name?" The woman smacks the table making me jump.

"LJ Phillips," I say.

Before I can flinch, one of the men steps forward and holds the cold device against my neck again. I scream as the electric current flows through my body making me jerk like a fish. Lights flash in my head as I try to hold on. Small d, capital T, four.

"Are you there, Lucy? If you don't wake up, the machines will get turned off." There is a pause. "Open your eyes." Will's voice is pulling me into the darkness.

I have to focus. I shake my head to clear the words. Eight, alpha, hyphen, nine. I repeat the code from the start to force it into my memory where it can't be taken from me.

"You're a bit young to be LJ," the woman sneers.

"I'm a time traveller. Actually I'm crazy. You shouldn't believe anything I say. I'm killing time, keeping you occupied while the Rebellion takes control with the code you've just given me. I'll probably disappear soon." My laughter turns into hysterically gasping, cut short by a blood curling scream as the acid lands on my chest again.

"Look for the bare necessities, the simple bare necessities. Forget about your worries and your strife," Libby sings. We're back in the grey waiting room.

"The thing is, I don't think I can leave a dream without dying," I say.

"Of course you can. You have to wake up," Libby says.

"Why haven't you left?"

"It's not my time yet," Libby says.

"I just wanted to be normal," I say.

"Why try to fit in when you were born to stand out?"

"I'm nothing special. I'm drowning," I whisper.

"Then kick out. Put one arm in front of the other. That's all there is to swimming."

"Wherever you are, it's not real. Wake up, Lucy," Will whispers.

As I open my eyes to the woman grinning evilly over me, there's only one way out of this room with the code. I have to wake up, go back so I can leave the code for Willis to find. If I wake, he has a chance.

"What do you know about the desalinators?"

"Everything," I say. I focus on the code. It is a mantra against the pain. Repeat. Remember. I have to tell Willis.

An explosion outside shakes the foundations of the room. The woman clutches the table between us as though it will offer her protection. One of the men darts out of the room to investigate. Tentacles of smoke drift into the room.

"We're under attack," somebody yells from down the corridor, his voice drowned out by the roar of jets flying low over the compound. The woman pulls a knife from her waistband and holds it to my neck.

"What do you know of this?" she yells.

"WAKE UP!" Willis shouts in my ear, but he is not in this room. I follow the sound of his voice. I've never tried to go back before, to wake up.

Remember. Capital A, six, lambda, hash symbol, two, small g, five, capital J, sigma, small d, capital T, four, eight, alpha, hyphen, nine.

My world turns black.

Life

Willis speaks my name again, his tone implying he's been trying to gain my attention for a while. I snap my eyes open and am blinded by whiteness. I squeeze them shut again. My head spins and the world tilts sideways.

"I need a pen." I focus on the task. My voice is quiet and raspy from lack of use, or screaming in pain. I don't remember now.

A chair scrapes across the floor. I repeat the code over and over in my head as I lie still. It is like a dream trying to fade away into my subconsciousness, but I can't let it. I have to record it before it's lost.

My body aches as though I have been lying motionless for a long period of time. I wriggle my toes, sending pins and needles shooting through my legs.

"Here you are," Willis says. I fumble and drop the pen. My fingers won't obey my instructions.

"I can write for you," Willis offers. His voice is comforting.

I start to speak, but no sound comes out. I clear my throat and try again.

"Capital A, six, Greek letter lambda, hash symbol, two…" I rattle off the code. It's done. I can sleep now. Willis slips a piece of paper into my hand as I slide back into the darkness.

I stand by the hospital bed in the clothes Mum brought in for me. The medication the nurse gave me earlier muddles my thoughts and makes me dizzy if I'm upright. I reach out a hand to steady myself against the bed.

I've lost track of time since I first opened my eyes, if what I remember is the first time. I can't trust my mind anymore. The line between dream and reality has blurred. There was a truck, and a lack of water, and Tayla and Jennypha were with me. Or was it Tai and Genfa?

I'm awake, but I'm teetering on the edge of a fine line between here and gone. Something holds me here for the moment. If only I could remember what it is.

"Hurry up, Lucy," Mum exclaims for what may not be the first time.

I stare at my belongings laid out before me, trying to work out what is missing. There is little more than tattered clothes and a thin wallet devoid of money. I was sure I had been wearing a black uniform. Something else is missing.

"Where's the piece of paper I had?" I ask out loud.

A noise by the door makes me look up to find Mum frowning as though she has no idea what I'm talking about. For a moment I'm surprised to see her in the room. Shouldn't she be at work? I close my eyes and try to separate the two realities in my mind. I couldn't have dreamed up the code, not something so important.

"The random numbers and letters?"

"That's the one." My eyes snap open. I'm not crazy. There is a code. Willis wrote it down for me because my fingers wouldn't function.

I reach a hand up to my head to squeeze out the throbbing. Willis hasn't been born yet. He couldn't have been here.

"I threw it out. It didn't look important," Mum says.

My stomach twists as I dive for the small bin in the room, but it's empty. I sink to my knees beside it, thrusting the waste basket to one side in the hopes the paper fell behind it. Besides a small accumulation of dust, the floor is clean.

"They emptied that days ago, Lucy. Come on. Frank's waiting for us with the car."

Capital A, six, some Greek letter. Another number. Blank.

I don't remember the code. My arms fall limply beside my body and the bin rolls onto its side. It was all for nothing. Suddenly I'm scared. Scared of Frank, scared of staying in this life, scared my existence has been for nothing.

"Get off the floor, Lucy!" Mum rarely raises her voice.

Besides the faint trembling of my body, I can't move. My eyes fix on a scuff mark on the wall by the bed as my mind shuts down. Mum grabs my arm roughly, jerking me out of my trance.

"Frank is waiting."

I don't resist as she hauls me to my feet. I can't stay on the floor of the hospital room forever. I place one foot in front of the other. I am a walking, empty shell being led by a woman I call Mum. I want this to be the dream so I can wake from it.

"What took so long?" Frank meets us at reception. I don't know how we got here, but Frank's agitation triggers a faint memory inside me. I have something to tell Mum.

I don't speak.

There is no energy inside me to face the consequences. Frank throws a possessive arm over Mum's shoulders. I am cold inside.

Frank guides Mum through the room kicking out at a wheelchair partially blocking his path. I turn my head to catch the angry expression of the woman standing beside it, before she bends over to check on the elderly man seated in the chair.

The old man stares at me like I'm a ghost.

It wouldn't surprise me if I'd turned into one. I've lost my grasp on the present.

He struggles in his chair pulling at the opening of his shirt, but he is hampered by the oxygen tube draped across his face and chest. He utters a single sound, but it's lost in the noise of the busy hospital waiting room. My feet stop moving as I look into his old brown eyes.

"Come on!" Mum grabs my arm, dragging me away. I take several steps backwards still staring at the man. He has pulled his shirt to one side. There is a tattoo on his chest, but I'm not close enough to make it out.

"Lucy?" he says louder. The woman crouched beside him looks up at me.

There is a roaring in my ears. I'm in a dreamlike state, doped up on various medications. Reality and imagination have collided and tangled. Mum yanks my arm, spinning me away from the scene. I turn and my knees buckle.

"Stop messing around and get in the car." Frank's arm wraps around my waist, dragging me away. I take one last look behind me before the door closes behind us.

The old man in the wheelchair watches, his attention on the scene we make as we leave the hospital.

"Save me," I mouth silently as I'm dragged out the front door.

Frank half carries me across the car park as Mum jogs after us hitching her handbag up her shoulder and clutching my plastic bag of worthless belongings. She opens the back door of the car and Frank bundles me inside.

"No," I protest weakly. I want to run, but my legs won't move.

Mum takes the front seat where she can't see me gripping the door. I wind down the window so I can breathe, while I pretend Frank isn't watching me through the rear view mirror. My stomach churns. I think I might throw up.

The car pulls into our driveway and I nearly fall out of the car trying to get the door open. I need Frank to leave, but he turns off the ignition and puts his arm possessively around Mum's waist as they walk to the front door. I am the outsider in my own home.

I snatch my pathetic bag from the back seat and clutch it to my chest as I stand on the front lawn in the mismatched clothes Mum brought to the hospital.

"Lucy," Mum calls.

The curtains in the window of the neighbour's house twitch. I wonder how long I could just stand here, but my body wants to lie down. I force my feet to move towards the house.

They wait for me in the living room. Mum glances at the coffee table where my sketchbook sits. I move forward to grab it, but Frank puts his hand over it.

"Who's the boy, Lucy?" Mum asks. Frank flips open the book to a picture of William of England to emphasise who she is talking about.

"I'm not going to tell you in front of Frank." My words are quieter than I intend and I have to repeat myself to be heard.

"He's part of this family." Mum frowns at me. I sway on my feet. There is nothing left. If Frank is here, I'm no longer welcome.

"We'll be hanging onto this until you tell us what we want to know." Frank pulls my sketchbook towards him.

A burning fury sweeps through me. They have taken everything from me right down to my memories of Will. There is a bitter taste in my mouth. I won't go without a final fight.

"Is the girl you had your tongue down her throat, part of the family as well?" I ask clearly.

Frank leaps off the couch and smacks me hard across the face. I crash into the bookshelf with my ears ringing. A book falls onto my head. My cheek burns from his handprint.

"Liar!" he yells.

"Frank!" Mum exclaims.

From my position on the floor, I look up at Mum and see a weak woman. She doesn't have enough love for herself, let alone me. She does nothing, because she will not do or believe anything that will take Frank away from her.

I use the shelves to haul myself to my feet. A trickle of blood runs down my cheek, most likely from Frank's watch. The room spins. As Frank steps towards me, I turn and bolt from the room. Adrenaline fuels my limbs. I slam into the wall as I take a corner. Frank's footsteps sound purposely as he strides after me.

I fumble with the catch on the back door. I'm shaking so badly I can hardly open the door. I slam it shut behind me and throw myself down the steps somehow managing not to twist an ankle. My bike leans against the house where I left it last. I grab the handlebars and swing my leg over the seat. The pedals cut into my bare feet as I fly across the road without looking.

The chain is stiff from lack of use, the tyres a little soft, and I am weak from lying in the hospital for so long, but I am moving. My heart pounds and I have to remind myself to breathe. Sweat makes my shirt cling to my body.

I stick to walking tracks so I can't be followed in a car. With the last of the energy in my tortured body, I pedal my bike towards the lookout. I'll be safe there. Bill is the only one I ever told about my secret place.

The car park is blessedly empty. I have no idea what day of the week it is. I lean my bike against the safety railing. Someone will eventually find it sitting there if they come looking for me. Otherwise it will get stolen and I will be lost forever. It doesn't matter.

I pause as I climb over the barrier, thinking about all the times I've come this way with the intention to return. I don't rush the final climb down to my rock ledge. Lying on the sun-warmed surface, I try to force out all the tears for everything I have lost in my life. A single tear eventually slips down the side of my face.

Is it silly to feel sad for my lack of tears?

When there is nothing left inside of me, I climb to my feet, standing with my toes hanging over the edge of my rock. The wind swirls gently around me, bringing memories of all the times I sat here wishing I didn't exist. I wonder if this is how Emma felt. Did she have any regrets? Did she think of me before she died?

The person I think about is my eleven year old self standing at the window waiting for friends that didn't exist, to come to her party. Silly, isn't it? Of all the hurts I've suffered in my life, that's the one that cuts the deepest on my final day. The memory of the hope I held that I'd be accepted by someone.

Anyone.

For the final time I take in the view that has given me comfort over the years. The lookout is beautiful, but I've always liked the feeling that the view from this angle belongs solely to me and will remain untouched once I've gone. In those final moments, I am calm and clear-headed. It's over.

Crunching gravel announces a car pulling into the lookout, but I ignore it. No one can find me here. In my mind I hear Will calling my name. He hasn't crossed my mind since I left the hospital. As much as I hope there is nothing after death, if there is, I want him to be waiting for me.

"Lucy!"

My name on the wind sounds so real, but it can no longer touch me where I've gone. It only makes me hesitate for a moment. With my arms outstretched and eyes squeezed shut, I picture Will in each lifetime we have met. When I reach Bill's face, I take a final breath and step off my rock.

Something catches my hand as I fall. I scream and twist my body, slamming into the rocky cliff face. Hanging onto life by the perilous grip of one hand, I stare up into the eyes of an angel.

Many years ago, Tayla came to school the day after her birthday with a new necklace. Hanging from the chain was a silver guardian angel clutching her birth month gemstone. It was the first possession of a classmate of which I was truly jealous. If I had an angel of my own, my life would be better. All I needed was a little guy out there somewhere looking out for me. I begged Mum for one, but it never came. I was on my own.

This angel is paler than I expected him to be. There is fear in his brown eyes as he lies precariously across my rock, grasping my hand. My left flails in the air. I'm not sure how he managed to stop himself going over the edge after me.

"Give me your other hand," Will gasps, reaching out to me.

Am I dead already? I didn't feel the fall. I stare at the hand grasping my own as I dangle in the air. It feels real, but Will isn't. It's all in my head, isn't it?

A bead of sweat rolls down Will's nose and falls onto my cheek.

I glance at the drop beneath me. I haven't fallen to my death yet. If I stay here I'm likely to take the boy who looks like my Will with me.

I swing myself upwards reaching for his free hand with mine. Our fingers brush for an electrifying moment, before the touch is lost.

"Again," Will commands. My hand slips in his grasp.

I swing again. This time my momentum carries me a fraction higher. Will's fingernails bite into the skin of my wrist, slipping until our fingers lock together.

My feet kick in empty air before they connect with a solid surface. For several tense moments, we struggle as Will tries to drag me to safety. The rock scrapes my chest as my upper body reaches the top of the ledge. My feet kick air as Will gives one final pull. I fall on top of him.

My whole body trembles. The unknown is terrifying, but Will's body is warm and real against mine. I close my eyes and imagine we're back in the Pompeian amphitheatre before the world ended.

"Are you okay?" Will asks, slightly breathless.

"I haven't been okay for a long time." I didn't know I'd give an honest answer until the words are out of my mouth.

"Oh," he says. "Do you think we can have this conversation on the other side of the barrier? I'm actually scared of heights." His complexion is still pale.

I roll off him and take the hand he offers to pull me to my feet. I feel its loss as soon as he lets go, but as much as he looks like the boy from my dreams, I don't know him and he doesn't know me. Will stays between me and the edge until we are over the barrier.

The car park is empty except for one vehicle which I assume belongs to Will, so we walk to the seat at the lookout. I sit down, hug my knees to my chest and stare out at the valley.

"You're not going to jump again are you?" Will stands in front of me. I think about it before answering. The rock isn't going anywhere.

"Not at the moment."

Will scuffs the dirt with the toe of his shoe. Dust settles on the hems of his faded blue jeans. It's odd to see him wearing normal clothes. It makes him feel distant. He doesn't know me. I'm not a spirit or a messenger of God. I'm not unique in any way. I'm just a girl who tried to kill herself.

"Do you want to talk about it?"

"Not really," I say. Will is quiet for some time.

"Do you have somewhere to go?"

His words echo those Bill once asked me and my throat tightens with the memory.

"Well this is awkward. You probably don't remember meeting me before today." Will laughs self-consciously.

My head snaps up so fast I'm surprised I don't pull a muscle.

"You know who I am?"

"Libby, my twin sister, has been waiting for a transplant at the hospital. I sat with you sometimes when your mum wasn't there. I thought you might want the company."

I stare at Will.

"You called my name," I say. He shrugs.

"It's meant to help, talking to people in a coma," he says. I stare out over the valley processing his words.

"I heard you."

"Really?"

267

"Why are you here?" I ask.

Will cheeks turn a pinkish colour. He grinds the toe of one shoe into the dirt again.

"Pop said you'd be here."

"How did he know?" My mouth is dry.

"That's a funny story. He's actually Mum's pop, so he's pretty old now. He always says he's hanging around to keep a promise to a girl who saved his life during the war. He thinks you're that girl." Will sounds apologetic.

There is a roaring in my ears. I lean forward and put my elbows on my knees.

"Are you alright?" Will places a hand lightly on my shoulder.

"It's not real," I whisper.

"Pop doesn't have much time left. It would mean the world to him if you came to the hospital and pretended you were the girl. It wouldn't be hard. Her name was Lucy, as well. You don't have any other plans for today, do you?" There's a hint of a smile in his voice. I sit up so suddenly my head spins and my vision starts to black out. I'm having difficulty breathing. He was dying beneath my hands.

"We better get going," I say. I glance out at the view one final time. It will still be waiting for me later if need be.

Will looks at me uncertainly as I stand by his car waiting for him to unlock it. He takes several moments to fold down the back seats and wrestle my bike into the car. I slide into the passenger seat.

When we are both seated he turns to me and holds out his hand.

"I'm William James Carter. My friends call me Will," he says.

"I'm Lucy Janette Phillips," I reply.

"Nice to meet you, LJ," he says. Warmth flows through my body. I have a nickname.

Will is quiet for the drive to the hospital although I catch him glancing at me several times. My head is a mess of thoughts. I lean my head back and close my eyes.

I wake when we pull into the car park. For a moment I am confused to see Will sitting beside me. I'd been dreaming of the past, or maybe the future.

"Are you sure you're up for this?" Will asks as he locks the car.

I nod, letting Will lead the way to his pop's room. I hesitate when we reach the doorway. Am I about to shatter an illusion that has kept me going all these years? Will takes me by the elbow and steers me into the room.

"He asked to see you," he reminds me.

The room is empty bar one bed and a person appearing to be asleep. I walk quietly to the side of the bed. Will stops at the foot, giving me space to pretend to be someone he thinks is only in Pop's head. I stare down at the man I saw sitting in the wheelchair in the hospital reception earlier today. His eyes snap open.

"Lucy," he says.

"Bill."

He reaches out and I take hold of his hand. I hook my foot around the nearby chair leg and drag it over to the bed. His free hand reaches out to brush the cut on my cheek from Frank's watch, before dropping back onto the bed.

"You look terrible," Bill says.

"You don't look so hot yourself." I smile weakly.

"I'm old." He motions me closer and I lean towards him. "Don't tell the boy, he thinks I'm going to live forever, but I'll be gone soon," Bill whispers.

"I thought you died." My voice catches in my throat.

Bill uses his free hand to pull the hospital gown away from his chest. A tattooed hand print above his heart surrounds a circular scar from a bullet. Underneath, the name Lucy is scrawled.

I place my hand where it pressed so many years ago, before tracing the scar with my fingertips. It was an open wound last time I saw him. Blood coated my hands.

"You saved my life." Bill looks into my eyes and I see him as he was that day, lying on his back telling me he wasn't going anywhere.

"Hello there." I glance up to see a woman standing in the doorway with her handbag slung over one shoulder and an aged yellow envelope in the other. She glances between Will, Bill and I.

"Mum, this is Lucy," Will says.

"You're not playing that game too, now are you, Will?" she asks. I move to stand, but Bill won't release my hand.

"Don't just stand there, Cherie, hand over the envelope." Bill waves the woman over.

Cherie crosses the room to stand by the bed next to me. She gets a good look at me as she passes the bulky envelope to Bill. Her face changes as she takes in my appearance.

"Who hit you, sweetheart?" she asks. I reach up to touch the mark on my face.

"Mum's boyfriend," I whisper, hoping I don't start crying.

"Do you have anywhere to stay?' she asks walking around to my side of the bed.

I shake my head, focusing on my hand in Bill's old wrinkled one. Cherie gathers me up in a hug as though she has known me all her life.

"We'll work something out. There's no need to play along with Pop's idiosyncrasies. Is your name even Lucy?" Cherie asks, still holding me.

"I am Lucy," I say.

"Don't patronise me, Granddaughter. If you let go of Lucy for a moment, she can see what I had you fetch for her," Bill interrupts.

Cherie lets me go as we look at the envelope in Bill's hand. He holds out the old yellow paper with my name scrawled across the front. My hand trembles as I take it.

"Open it up, Lucy. I'm not getting any younger," Bill reminds me.

I smile at him before carefully peeling the end of the sealed envelope open. I tip it upside down, pouring the contents out. Gold chain pools into my palm followed by an old familiar locket. Will has crept closer to see what I have. I trace my fingers over it.

"Are you going to open it?" Will asks. I hold the locket up and flick it open to show Will and Cherie the miniature portrait I know it holds.

"That's us," Will exclaims.

"Actually it's my several times great-Grandfather from Scotland and Lucy," Bill says.

"How is that possible?" Cherie stares at the image.

I turn my attention to the chain remaining in my hand. As I untangle it, I see the engraved bullet hanging from it. I hold it up in front of me feeling strangely dizzy.

"I've seen this before," I say. Bill frowns.

"I made it from the bullet left behind after you disappeared," Bill says. In the future, it sits in a box of memories belonging to Willis.

"There you go dear. Looks like the whole family is here." We all turn at the nurse's voice.

A slender brunette girl around Will's age, with brown eyes like his, sits in a wheelchair pushed by a nurse. She has grown up since I first met her as young Lee in Africa. Her eyes open wide when she sees me.

"Lucy?" she says wheeling herself up to the bed and reaching out to hug me. The nurse leaves us alone as everyone in the room turns to look at me.

272

"Libby," I say. I feel lightheaded, like pieces of my life are beginning to fit together.

"You two know each other?" Will asks.

"We've met several times, once upon a dream." Libby grins.

I look at the people in this room and wonder if I have made a difference with my life. Everything I've done has made its mark somewhere, even into the future.

"I wrote you a letter, Lucy." Bill squeezes my hand. He is growing weaker, his voice barely audible. I look down at the envelope and pull the folded pages from inside. I look at Bill as I hold them in my hand.

"Are you scared?" I ask. He shakes his head.

"No. Life is beautiful, Lucy. It has so many ups and downs, but lying here knowing my time is up, it's the good times I remember. Read the letter."

As his family gather around him, I unfold the pages and look down at the words in front of me.

My dearest Lucy,

I am alive today because you saved my life and I want you to let me return the favour. In 1941 I was too young to be able to give you the reasons for why life is worth living. Now I am older and I have seen what life has to offer. It is not full of happiness every single day. There are many bleak days, but these are what allow us to grow strong and appreciate the good.

Surround yourself with family and treasure your time together. Family aren't always blood. They're the people in your life who want you in theirs; the ones that accept you for who you are. The ones who would do anything to see you smile and who love you no matter what.

Be kind to others. Sometimes a smile is all that is needed to change a person's day. The more happiness you put out into the world, the more will find its way back to you.

Actions speak louder than words. Be a good person. Do the right thing by yourself and others, even if it terrifies you. Doing nothing is much worse. Value yourself and your knowledge.

You, as much as anyone else in the entire world, deserve your love and affection. No one is perfect no matter how hard they pretend they are, so don't compare yourself to them. There will always be people greater and lesser than yourself.

Stand up for yourself and others. Don't let bullies succeed, but also know when it is best to run away and fight another day. Be brave. When you're going through hell, keep going. Don't stop. Don't give up. You have to be strong and extremely brave and then one day you will look back on that pain and it will be a memory. It will hurt like hell and feel like it will never end, but it does. Eventually.

Speak up. Tell your family, friends, doctor or a counsellor how you feel. You started with me, now keep going. It's easier to continue when you have support.

Everyone has a good and bad side. Give people a second chance if they deserve it. Don't judge others. You don't know what their journey is about.

Life has many ups and downs, but it is a beautiful thing. Hold onto it with both hands. No one saves us but ourselves, no one can and no one may. We ourselves must walk the path. Today is a new day, a new beginning.

Sometimes it's ok if the only thing you did today was remember to breathe. Just breathe. Just start, anywhere, and then start again. Small steps.

So you see, you don't need me to save you. Everything you need is already inside of you. Everything will be ok in the end, so if it's not ok, it's not the end.

Always in your memory,

Bill.

Tears blur the words, dampening the pages before me. My whole life I wanted to feel special and valued. Bill has given this to me. He kept his promise.

Bill's hand slips from mine. He leaves the world surrounded by family, with a long and mostly happy life laid out behind him. I was a part of that.

Dreamless

Monday. I stand nervously in the school car park smoothing down my new uniform. I take a deep breath and try to calm down. I'm killing time again, waiting. There's one more thing I have to finalise before I make the decision to stay or go.

I ignore the stares of the passing students as Libby clutches my arm in excitement. She's missed so much school due to illness, she wants to be here. The driver's side door of the car clicks shut as Will joins us.

"Lead the way, LJ." Will gestures grandly towards the buildings.

I breathe again and take a step forward, one foot in front of the other. I open the glass door and let the twins through first. I hover behind them as they approach the reception for their joining instructions.

"Lucy! You're back. It's good to see you." I turn around to see my history teacher smiling at me.

"Hello, Ms Miller," I reply. She walks over and wraps her arms around me in a big hug.

"I've been so worried about you." She steps back and rubs her eye, smearing mascara. "I'll make sure we get you notes on the classes you've missed. We'll have you caught up in no time. I'll see you in class," she says.

"Okay." I smile at my favourite teacher. She heads off to prepare for her day's classes.

Will comes over to me with the timetables. Both are on the way to my classroom. I lead the way down the corridor feeling like I've slipped into a parallel universe. Everything looks identical, but at the same time, completely different.

We have nearly made it to class when I see Bianca and Tayla arguing by the lockers. I slow, wondering if we can backtrack or sneak by without them noticing. Bianca looks up, frowning when she sees us.

"Willie. You never told me you were enrolling at our school. What are you doing with *her?*" She glances at me.

"You know each other?" Will asks.

"Everybody knows Loser Lucy." Bianca frowns. Will throws his arms over Libby's and my shoulders. Bianca's jaw drops in surprise. Tayla smirks.

"Sorry, can't stay and chat. My girls and I are on our way to class," Will says.

"Hi, Lucy," Tayla says. I look at her suspiciously as we walk away.

I leave my friends reluctantly at their classrooms and I go to English. The front seat is still vacant so I sit were I have always sat. I run my fingers over the desk and wonder why nothing has changed.

Mrs Carmichael calls the roll, smiling at me when I answer. She doesn't read out La-a's name. I glance behind me to check. She's not here and Bianca sits across the room from Jennypha and Tayla.

The student closest to me passes over a stack of papers from the teacher, his dark hair falling over his glasses. I've never seen him before. He smiles at me as I take the handout.

The smile slips from his face, making me realise I haven't responded. I return the gesture, but he has already turned away, staring at his desk, his shoulders slumped.

"Lucy? Can I have a word with you outside?" the teacher asks. I stand hesitantly, wipe my palms on my skirt and step out into the corridor. The teacher closes the door behind us. I shift my weight from my left foot to my right as I wait for her to speak.

"Lucy, did you do the story writing assignment?"

I stare at her blankly until an image of an old blue plastic folder and Willis burning the pages enters my mind. The scrunched up assignment paper is probably still at the bottom of my old school bag. I have a new bag now that matches Will's and Libby's.

"No," I reply. Does it matter, considering I failed to remember the code?

"Who was your partner?"

"I didn't have one."

"The competition I was entering the stories in has ended, but I'd still like you to complete the assignment. Two of the students were asked to re-do their work, but as one of them has left the school, the other girl has no partner. I understand you've had some issues with the girls in the past, so I'm asking if you would be willing to pair up with Jennypha for the assignment?"

La-a left the school. Was it because of me? It takes me several moments to realise I've been asked a question. I've been offered a choice whether to work with Jennypha or not. I open my mouth to refuse.

"Okay," I say.

"Are you sure? It's entirely up to you."

"Yes." Somewhere in the future is a photo of me smiling with Jennypha and Tayla.

"I'll let her know."

At lunch time, I go looking for Libby. Will kicks a football around with a bunch of other students, looking like he is already friends with everyone.

Libby sits on a bench at the edge of the oval with Tayla. I pause and consider walking away, but Libby waves me over.

"LJ, this is Tayla." She turns to Tayla. "LJ's my foster sister. She lives with us now," Libby says. I eye Tayla warily.

As Tayla looks at me as though she has never really seen me before, I realise I have become a different person. I'm LJ now.

"We're having a party on Saturday. You should come along," Libby invites Tayla.

"Sure. That would be great," Tayla replies before excusing herself to meet up with Jennypha.

"Poor thing," Libby says. "Her cousin has cystic fibrosis and is waiting for a transplant. Tayla wanted to know what the operation was like." I stare after Tayla. I've known her for years, yet I know nothing about her.

Tuesday. I tap the brass knocker timidly against the grand white door. Footsteps pound towards me from the other side before the door is yanked open. Jennypha has changed into jeans and a tank top with matching pink socks.

"You took your time," she says holding the door open. I have an odd thought that I did leap off the cliff and ended up in an alternate reality where everyone looks the same, but they're not really.

I step into the foyer, hoping my shoes don't dirty the plush carpets. The door clicks shut behind me and Jennypha bounds past into the dining room. I follow more slowly taking in the display home feel of the house.

Jennypha has already taken a seat at the oversized timber table, where she has set up a laptop and two perspiring glasses of Coke. Her school bag leans against her chair. I walk over to the seat beside her and let my bag slide to the floor. My fingers trace the suede chair back.

"You really should talk more. No one can tell what you're thinking behind your witchy eyes," Jennypha says.

It hadn't occurred to me to speak. I've gone so long without anyone listening, I stopped bothering. Will is often telling me to speak. Jennypha rolls her eyes at my silence and leans over to pull out a plastic assignment binder from her bag. She places it on the table between us.

The plastic cover of the binder is a bright, new blue. I grab it and flick open the cover. All the plastic pockets are empty waiting for the typed pages to be placed inside.

"Where did you get this?" I ask.

"I use these for all my assignments. I had a spare in my locker. I did pay for it if that's what you're worried about. I'm not like La-a." Jennypha frowns at me.

I shake the image of the faded blue folder in Willis' hand and sit down beside Jennypha. My eyes don't leave the cover. Jennypha gives up waiting for me to say something.

"I'm open to suggestions on where to start. Mrs Carmichael wasn't impressed with what La-a and I came up with, but you're good at stories and I'm great at typing, and spelling and stuff. How do you imagine the future?" Her fingers hover over the keyboard. I open my mouth and tell her a story.

"It's completely dark. I shut my eyes and open them again, but it makes no difference. I turn my head, but the vision of nothing doesn't change. I'm lying on my back against a cool, smooth surface. I

282

try to sit up, but smack my head on a low flat object.

"I hear the faint sound of something going whoosh followed by what sounds like two sets of footsteps. With the sounds come a hint of greyness in my dark world. One set of footsteps stops near my feet while the other set shuffles nervously by my head. Someone speaks."

"Jenny-babe, get your mother the painkillers would you." We both jump at the voice behind us. A woman leans against the doorframe, wearing dark glasses with a hand pressed to her temple. Jennypha shoots me a horrified look.

"What are you doing home?" Jennypha asks.

"Oh you know how it is. The young can't party as hard as they used to." Jennypha's mum waves her hand vaguely as she teeters on her heels through to the living room. Jennypha disappears while I sit in my chair trying to look inconspicuous. Jennypha comes back looking worried.

"Perhaps we should take this to my room," she whispers.

I nod and pick up our bags while she packs up the laptop. I follow her upstairs. Her room is huge with a double bed, built-in robe and desk. She drags a second chair over and sets the laptop down.

"You're not going to say anything?" Jennypha doesn't look at me.

"About what?" I say. Jennypha turns a relieved smile in my direction.

"So where were we?" She sits down and her fingers wait for me to continue my story.

Wednesday. Jennypha and I are in the library. I've never seen her in the library before. She sits in Emma's spot, her laptop in front of her as she types. I relay the information I found on Ryder's computer about the planned attacks, stopping the story in the interrogation room with the code sitting in front of me and the bombs falling. Jennypha looks up when I stop speaking.

"So what happens?" she asks.

"I don't know," I say.

"How can you not know? It's your story," she demands.

"I woke up," I admit.

"Well make something up! Willis needs that code," Jennypha says.

"I can't make it up. It won't be true."

"Okay, Willis and Genfa burst into the room, save Luce and steal the code."

"Wouldn't work," I say.

"Genfa takes Ryder hostage and forces him to tell them the code," Jennypha raises her voice and is shushed by the librarian. The bell rings for class.

"Ryder would never give up the code even if he knew it," I say as we walk to our lockers.

"If you don't come up with an ending, I'm going to ask Tayla how it ends. She's already passed this assignment." I roll my eyes at Jennypha as I open my locker. I don't let on how much the lack of ending bothers me.

I glance up at the sound of a yelp and books hitting the floor. The sound is familiar to me. I've picked my books off the floor many times. The victim is the spitting image of the new boy from my class, the one I forgot to smile at, only younger.

He is surrounded by three taller boys around the same age. One of the bullies grabs the boy's glasses and tosses them away. They clatter against the far wall. Students give them a wide berth.

I freeze in place overwhelmed by my own memories and thoughts. I search the empty corridor for my missing bag. I clean the white powder from my locker. I stand by Emma's grave all alone. Bill lies on his back bleeding from a bullet wound. I imagine the young boy standing on my rock preparing himself for the leap into death.

I slam my locker door shut and stride over to where the boy's glasses lie on the floor. I pick them up and approach the group. I smack my hand against the lockers, making as much noise as possible. They all jump and look at me. I stand up straight to appear taller than them. There are three of them, and only me and a scrawny little boy without his glasses opposing them.

"Who the hell are you?" the fatter of the three demands.

I hold onto the strength Bill believed I possess and press the glasses into the young victim's hand. He hurriedly puts them back on his face.

"We don't accept bullying at this school," I say.

The kid has the nerve to laugh at me. He glances at his mates to check they are still backing him up. The young brother of my classmate searches around to see if he can escape and leave me as a sacrifice.

285

"You plan on doin' somethink about it?" the fat kid sneers. The three of them step closer to me. My heart pounds in my chest. I remind myself I have faced the Battle of Culloden and the Japanese attack on Pearl Harbor.

Something brushes my elbow. I flinch. Tayla stands beside me. She doesn't say anything, just glares at the three boys with her arms by her sides. One of them swallows nervously.

"Don't let us catch you picking on anyone else," I growl.

"Or what?" There are three of them to two of us.

"We'll smash your pimply little face in." Jennypha appears beside us. She punches one fist into the palm of her other hand to emphasise her point.

I glare at her. Although I appreciate her support, I don't want people to see me as a bully.

"Or we could tell the principal," Jennypha amends.

"Crazy bitches," Fatty mutters as he and his friends back off. I turn to the kid.

"I'm LJ," I say. "Your brother, Steven is in my English class." The kid stares at me as though wondering why I'm speaking to him. "My friends, Will and Libby are having a party on Saturday. The two of you should come along," I offer. "I'll give your brother the details."

"Sure, like that's going to happen," he mutters as he scurries away.

"What about my invite?" Jennypha demands. I glance at her standing beside me with her hands on her hips. Bill told me I would find friends in strange places and Willis was friends with Genfa.

"Okay," I say. I walk off down the corridor.

"Okay, I can come?" Jennypha calls after me.

Friday. I've agreed to meet Jennypha at the café near school when I finish class. She skipped her last class so she is waiting for me when I arrive. Wooden blocks displaying today's date sit on the counter. I glance at it as I pass, stopping to stare at it until a customer clears her throat and I move out of the way. It's my seventeenth birthday tomorrow and I hadn't even realised.

Tayla sits next to Jennypha, reading the pages in the plastic sleeves of the blue folder. I slide into the empty seat at the table and study the two girls. Tayla gets to the final page and lays the assignment on the table.

"Well?" Jennypha demands.

"It's good," Tayla says.

"But it doesn't end!" Jennypha cries.

"Oh, I thought you were trying to be poetic with the whole 'we don't get to know what the future holds'," Tayla says.

"What about the code? Luce never got it to Willis," Jennypha says. Tayla looks at the two of us.

"It's engraved on the inside of his silver bracelet from his grandmother," Tayla says. "Why are you looking at me like that? You wrote the story." I close my mouth and Jennypha throws her arms around Tayla.

"You're the best," Jennypha tells her. There is one final thing bothering me.

"How does his grandmother get the code to put on the bracelet?" I ask.

"She's got years to work that out. Maybe her husband who designed the desalinators tells her," Tayla says. "How are you getting home anyway?"

"Will's picking me up. He had some errands to run before tomorrow night," I say.

Saturday. I stand by the front window as the party draws near. There are no balloons on the fence to mark the house. That's for children's parties. A small red car pulls up in front of the house. I hold my breath as the door opens. Tayla and Jennypha step out in their party dresses and heels. They get halfway up the path before Tayla turns around.

"Bye, Mum," she calls out.

"Thanks, Mrs McKenzie," Jennypha adds.

I stay at the window until I hear the knock on the door. I skip into the hallway and pull it open, smiling at the girls from school. I step aside to let them in.

"Where's the music? Let's get this party started." Jennypha waltzes into the Carters' house to find the stereo.

"Love your dress," Tayla says as she follows behind.

"Thanks," I say looking down at my simple green dress. It's new. Libby helped me choose it at the shops this morning.

People continue to arrive. I am greeted like a friend by people who have never uttered a word to me in the past. A timid tap has me back at the door. I open it to find Steven and his young brother standing nervously on the doorstep.

"Come in." I beam at them. They glance at each other before the younger one steps inside. Steven turns to wave to their mother still in the car. Satisfied, she drives off.

I hover at the edge of the room watching the people having fun. I'm still an outsider, the one who doesn't quite fit in, but today it doesn't bother me. Will wanders over to the food table next to me, with Steven in tow. He smiles when he sees me. I grab a cup to pour a drink.

"That's really cool," he continues his conversation with Steven. "When I finish school I'm going to study Mechanical Engineering."

"What are you going to do with that?" Steven asks.

"I read an article recently about how scarce water will be in the future. I was thinking about designing water desalination plants that use renewable energy."

My drink sloshes out of my cup.

"Careful there, LJ. Maybe it's time to cut back on the lemonade," Will jokes.

"It's our party, I can do what I want," I reply, trying to sound calm and collected as I use napkins to mop up the mess.

"That reminds me." Will pulls a neatly wrapped box from his back pocket. "Happy birthday."

He hands me the present. I cradle it in my hands waiting to see if it is real, or something I've imagined that will vanish if I unwrap it.

"How did you know?" I ask.

"I saw your birth date on your chart when you were in hospital. You don't mind the party being on the same day do you?"

"No." I shake my head.

I tug on the ribbon and lift the lid gently. The box contains a silver bracelet. My knees buckle and I sink into the nearest chair set around the edge of the room.

"Oh my God," I whisper. My hands shake as I trace a finger over the gift, afraid to look inside.

"Is it your birthday?" Tayla bounds over to our group followed by Jennypha.

"Hey, that's the bracelet," Jennypha exclaims.

Her hand swoops down and snatches it from its velvet cradle. I reach out to stop her, but it's too late. Jennypha holds my gift up searching for the engraving. She shows it to Tayla.

"How did you know?" Tayla asks Will, passing the bracelet back to me. Inside, the combination 'A6λ#2g5JσdT48α-9' is engraved.

"LJ asked me to write it down when she woke from the coma. It seemed important to her, so I kept a copy. Seeing as her mum threw hers out, I figured she wouldn't lose it this way." I throw myself at Will, wrapping my arms around him and crying tears of happiness into his shirt.

There may be a future for me after all and one day, I may live long enough to give this bracelet to my grandson. Willis knew he had the code as soon as he read the assignment in the blue folder. It's in his hands now. As Tayla said, it's the future, we don't get to know how it ends.

Sunday. Someone jumps on the bed, snapping me out of sleep. My first thought is that it was my birthday yesterday, so where and when am I? I open my eyes to see Will grinning down at me.

"Morning beautiful," Will says.

"Go away." Libby throws her pillow at him, but he ducks, undeterred by her lack of enthusiasm.

"Are you girls planning on getting up anytime today?" he asks.

I sit up to find myself wedged between Libby and Tayla on Libby's queen bed. Jennypha is sprawled across the far end of the bed with her head hanging off the edge. I glance down at the silver bracelet around my wrist.

I'm still here.

Author's Note

For a long time suicide has been something no one talked about. I started writing this story after noticing a change in the media around the topic. It is now being discussed in an attempt to destigmatize mental health issues. Depression is a health issue. A person doesn't develop it through any fault of their own. On average, 1 in 6 people will suffer depression during their lifetime. We need to talk about this to prevent people from feeling like suicide is the only way out, because it's not.

People who have been lucky enough not to experience depression often struggle to comprehend its grasp on a person. They may think it's like being sad and a person should just 'snap out of it'. Unfortunately, that is about as effective as asking an asthmatic why they can't breathe when there is plenty of air.

I wanted to end this story on a hopeful note. Depression is a long, hard journey, but it is possible to come out the other side. If you or someone you know is struggling with depression, it's important to reach out. You don't have to keep feeling like this. There are various helplines available and even a doctor or counsellor can help get you started on your journey to recovery. Telling the first person is the hardest. It gets easier after that.

It's important to remember that suicide doesn't end the pain, it transfers it to someone else.

To everyone: be aware of your actions. You never know if that careless insult may be the final straw for someone. On the other hand, a kind gesture may be the action that gives a person enough strength to hang on for another day.

Remember the importance of asking people if they are okay and be interested in their response. They may not want to talk at that time, but knowing someone cares, even a stranger, is important.

Below are some of the services available in Australia:

Lifeline - 13 11 1

4 Kids Help Line - 1800 55 1800

Suicide Call Back Service – 1300 659 467

Beyondblue - www.beyondblue.org.au

Headspace - headspace.org.au

In the UK:

www.depressionuk.org/national_links.shtml

In the US:

https://suicidepreventionlifeline.org/

About the Author

Nikki Moyes writes YA fiction and her first book, 'If I Wake' was published in 2016. She was born in Victoria and has moved around Australia amassing an eclectic range of occupations including tall- ship watch leader, apiarist, rose farm hand, and sandwich artist. In her spare time she learns tissu, static trapeze, and aerial hoop (she couldn't decide on one) in case she needs to run off and join the circus.

You can find her here:

[f] www.facebook.com/moyes.nikki/

[t] @NikkiNovelist

[g] www.goodreads.com/author/show/15606198.Nikki_Moyes

[ig] @nikkimoyesauthor

Other books by Nikki Moyes

Risha is the first successful child to be born with her father's memories. To avoid an alliance with a brutal warlord, she enters the virtual-reality game to seek help from the first warlord who resides at Castle One.

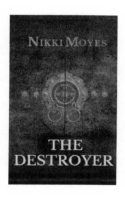

(coming soon)

In a world ruled by opposing Warlords, the mysterious Temple Keeper warns that the universe must be united under one rule before the end of the world.

In an act of defiance, Risha Suri shuns the expectation she encourage an alliance with Warlord Kllrarn, setting into effect a chain of events that will earn her the nickname The Destroyer.

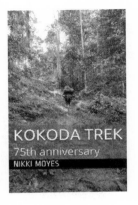

On the 75th anniversary of the campaign between Australian and Japanese troops, author Nikki Moyes trekked the 96km of track where her grandfather acted as a translator. This is what it is like to hike the Kokoda Track.

Made in the USA
Middletown, DE
25 July 2019